5-

THE MAN WHO LOOKED LIKE HOWARD COSELL

THE MAN WHO LOOKED LIKE HOWARD COSELL

John Bartholomew Tucker

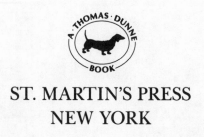

ST. MARTIN'S PRESS
NEW YORK

Design by Glen M. Edelstein

Library of Congress Cataloging-in-Publication Data

Tucker, John Bartholomew.
    The man who looked like Howard Cosell.

    "A Thomas Dunne Book."
        I. Title.
PS3570.U33M36   1988   813'.54   88-11668
ISBN 0-312-02248-4

First Edition

10 9 8 7 6 5 4 3 2 1

For Evi, Maud, Hilary, and Andrew,
four of *The Five Flying Tuckers*

CHAPTER

1

IT WAS the autumn of 1983, and we were sitting in the Oak Room Bar at the Plaza Hotel, having a drink.

Alice was wearing her usual-diaphanous blouse. She was also wearing that smile of hers that silently says, I-know-*exactly*-what-you-are-and-I-find-it-all-*amusing-stimu-lating*-and-*exciting*.

The smile was an affectation, but it was always effective.

Her eyes drifted away from mine for a moment and then quickly the smile changed to a stare.

"My God, look over at the bar. The resemblance is uncanny."

I turned to glance. She was right.

"And he's even wearing an ABC sports jacket."

"Maybe it *is* him," I said.

"But it's not, is it?"

"No, I don't know what the difference is—but that's not Howard. He looks *exactly* like him, but yet he doesn't."

She started to laugh and put her hand to her mouth to cover it.

"What—?"

Alice swallowed. "Can you imagine what that man thinks every morning when he sees himself in the mirror? My God, to look *exactly* like Howard Cosell—"

"As the English say—it's a daunting thought."

"That's David Niven."

"Excuse me—?"

"—Who said that. *Daunting*. That's a David Niven word."

"Well, *he* was English."

"No. Scotch."

"*Anyway*—that guy at the bar looks almost exactly like Howard Cosell."

"It is Cosell," Alice said. "And we've had too much wine."

"For the hell of it, I'm going to walk over."

"What'll you say?"

"I'll say, 'Hello.'"

"But then if it's not—?"

"I'll only say hello. Howard knows me. He'll either recognize me or he won't. *If* it's Howard."

"That's good."

"Thanks for the rehearsal."

I got up and started for the Cosell-Clone at the bar.

"Good luck," Alice said.

The second I stood up, his eyes met mine, and I knew that he'd been watching us.

It was his eyes that were different. That's what made him look so eerie. Howard has friendly eyes. This man's eyes were hard.

"Hello," I said. "Nice afternoon, isn't it?"

He stood up quickly, as if I were some prep school headmaster who had just entered the classroom.

"For a minute I thought I recognized you," he said. Even the voice was the same.

"As a matter of fact, I thought I knew you, too," I said. "It seems we both made a mistake."

Even though he smiled, he didn't smile. "That happens a lot to me. Sometimes I even give out his autograph."

"Must be fun."

"Yes, sometimes. Sometimes it's a bother."

I've never been interested in looking deeply into a ferret's eyes, but I had the feeling that if I ever did, its eyes would look like his. "Yes," he said again, "sometimes it's a bother."

I told Alice when I got back to the table.

"Well, if it's such a bother, why doesn't he just throw away that ABC jacket? That would be a start."

"I thought of asking him that, but since he's just as tall and just as big as Howard, I decided against it."

"Was Howard ever your client?"

"No. He told me once at breakfast that he doesn't need an attorney, or an agent. He has a law degree, you know. He acts as his own lawyer."

"There's an old saying that if a man is his own lawyer, then he has a fool for a client."

"That's what I told Howard."

"What'd he say?"

"He laughed. Howard has a good sense of humor."

"What about this fellow at the bar?"

"None."

Alice fussed with the collar of her usual-diaphanous blouse, another affectation acquired over the years, but as equally effective as all the rest of her poses. "But just what does this man do all day? Sit around bars and sign Howard Cosell autographs?"

"Who knows."

Alice pretended not to notice that she had accidentally unbuttoned another button on her blouse.

"Why don't you go over to the bar," I said, "and do your—'Aw, that button has a habit of always coming off' act and ask him."

Alice frowned. "You've been looking."

"What did you expect?"

"I didn't even realize it. That button has a habit of always coming—"

I laughed.

Alice smiled and rubbed the inside of my leg. "I think I'll just stay here. Let's order another bottle of wine. And I'll try not to talk. Murray, my Shrink, says I should practice that every day."

We sat for another half hour, watching the Tuesday afternoon crowds walk past. It was October and many people were strolling into the park. The only thing nicer than New York in October is Los Angeles when you're leaving it.

Howard Cosell-Clone left his place at the bar, only briefly, apparently to buy a cigar, which he was now savoring, along with a second drink.

"Have you noticed something?" Alice said.

"Yeah—he's still here."

"No, about me. And you."

"What?"

"1983 is almost over and we haven't been in bed together once this year."

"Of course I've noticed. I assumed that some of your boys were in town."

"That was a lousy thing to say."

"I didn't mean it to be."

"It was still lousy."

"Sorry."

"As a matter of fact, Roger"—she pronounced it Ro-*jeh*—"flew in from Paris on Tuesday. But that was still a lousy thing to say."

"Who's Roger?"

"It's pronounced Ro-*jeh*."

"Anyway, who is he?"

"He's the one I met in Guadeloupe two years ago. I must have told you about him. Blond, tall. Terrible temper. And jealous. He wanted to kill Herbie when he found out I had a husband."

"He sounds fascinating. What caused your heart to thump when you met him?"

"His looks of course. And he could hardly speak English. Only simple words. You know, like a child. He was

so cute. And then his jealous streak. He wanted to kill the
fellow I'd flown to Guadeloupe with."

"Sort of makes a woman feel wanted."

"Well . . . yes. You're teasing, but yes. Murray, my
Shrink, says that may account for a lot of things I do—a
need to feel wanted, I mean."

"Makes sense."

"Take Ro-*jeh*, for instance."

"The one with the blond hair and the jealous temper?"

"You *were* listening."

"The one who's standing over at the door looking at
me and frowning?"

Alice turned around quickly. "That's Ro-*jeh*, all right.
Wearing his killer grimace." She covered her mouth with
her hand. "I told him I couldn't see him this afternoon
because I was having drinks with a friend."

"I've never seen you before in my life."

"No, play it out. We're just friends. But don't be *too*
friendly. We're business friends. Is he coming over?"

"Striding-angrily-across-the-room would be more accurate."

Roger Ro-*jeh* didn't ask. He simply pulled a third chair
up to our table and sat down.

Alice did all the talking, mostly fast, and mostly highly
creative. It seemed that she had recently developed an
interest in crocheting (it was the first I had heard of it)
and was about to begin writing a book on it (it was the
first I had heard that she could write), and I was going to
represent her to the various publishers who were, of
course, clamoring for the barely begun manuscript.

Ro-*jeh* seemed to buy it all. He even smiled at me. I
wouldn't call it a warm smile, nor could I describe it as a
truly spontaneous smile, but the pit of my stomach accepted it with gratitude.

"More drinks?" he asked. Actually, it was more of a de-
mand.

We both said, "Of course," very quickly and smiled
back at him.

I motioned to the waiter and ordered another bottle of wine.

"I pay," Ro-*jeh* said.

"No, no, I won't hear of it," I said quite grandly.

His eyes became intense. "I pay." He reached across the table and shoved an envelope filled with hundred-franc notes into my jacket pocket. That seemed to settle the matter.

Alice started to talk again. It seemed that after she finished her crocheting book, she was going to write one about the wines of North America. Her baby talk was so basic that it bored me and was, apparently, too difficult for Ro-*jeh* to follow.

"Where room for men?" he asked me abruptly.

Gestures always seem to help at times like this.

"*À la porte—à gauche*—one *étage* down."

He looked at me and, for the first time, his eyes wrinkled into what came close to being the beginnings of a genuine smile. "Thank you."

After he excused himself, Alice let out a stage sigh. "My God, you just let me talk and talk. You weren't any help at all."

"You seemed to be doing so well. I didn't want to butt in and ruin it," I said.

"When he comes back—butt in, will you?"

"I'll try." I nodded my head toward the bar. "There goes the Cosell-Clone. Maybe they'll run into each other in the hallway and fall in love."

"That was a lousy thing to say," Alice said. "That's the second one today."

"Now what?"

"Why did you say they might meet and fall in love?"

"I don't know why. I just said it, that's all."

"Murray, my Shrink, says that the fact that I don't like women's company very much, and prefer to be with men, might be because I'm a latent homosexual."

"Murray, your Shrink, is a fag."

"I know, but do you think he's right?"

"No."

Alice sighed. "That's the first nice thing you've said to-day."

"Thanks."

Alice smiled. "Oh, what the hell, Harry. You're okay."

A party of eight was seating itself on our right. The cocktail hour was approaching, and the Oak Room Bar was beginning to fill.

Howard Cosell-Clone came back to the bar and headed for our table. He smiled as he got near us. Again, the eyes betrayed him.

"Excuse me," he said, "but your friend—the Frenchman—wants to make a phone call, and he's having some difficulty. He asked if you'd help."

"He should have come up and asked himself," Alice said. She glanced up at Cosell-Clone. "Sorry."

He made his ferret's smile again and raised his hands heavenward. "It's no trouble at all."

I got up. "Excuse me, Alice."

As we made our way to the door, Cosell-Clone said, "I tried to help him myself. But he kept saying, 'No trouble you—No trouble you.'"

"That was thoughtful of him."

"Well, it does seem to go part and parcel with that propensity for penultimate perspicacity as manifested by all Frenchmen—eventuating into the well-known Gallic charm."

I stopped and turned.

He smiled. "Sometimes I just like to fool around."

Going down the stairs, I said, "Don't put yourself out any more. You've done enough already."

"No trouble at all." He chuckled.

"I beg your pardon?"

"Nothing. I just thought of a joke someone told me this morning."

We walked past the entrance to Trader Vic's and headed for the bank of telephones on the wall. The only phone in use was the one Roger Ro-*jeh* was at, standing with his back to us. As we got closer, he turned. Both hands were in his pockets, his jacket was open, and blood was oozing out of his shirt near the belt line.

I had never seen a dying man's face before, but I realized very quickly that I was looking at my first.

His voice was low, almost calm. "You're just not—not at all . . ."

He was speaking with an American accent.

"We'll get a doctor," I said. I turned. Cosell-Clone had vanished.

The calm voice continued. "No—it's just . . ."

I moved to help him.

"No—it's—just not worth it. . . ."

He died first. Then he slumped to the floor. His eyes stayed open.

A man in a dark suit, wearing a hat, appeared quickly, wrapped a thick arm around my chest, pinned my arms to my sides, and extracted the franc-filled envelope from my jacket.

His accent was southwestern. "Thanks. You'll be hearin' from me."

He tripped me over one of his thick legs, and I landed on my side, looking into the dead man's face and wishing his eyes would close. By the time I got to my feet, the man with the hat had disappeared.

CHAPTER

2

I T WAS obvious that the men's room attendants had been around. They took charge of the situation with calm dispatch. Two of them dragged Roger Ro-*jeh*'s body into the lavatory, while the third—a squat Irishman—locked the door to keep out any possible fainting types, and went for the police.

He was back in a matter of seconds. "We're in luck," he said. "I ran into two friends from before retirement."

They were both big, given to extra weight, but friendly looking.

"You okay?" The first one asked.

"I'm fine," I lied.

The second man was bending over the body of Roger Ro-*jeh*. "Dead as a doornail," he pronounced.

"You detectives?" I asked.

"FBI. We just happened to be passing through when we ran into Billy here."

"What do we do now?"

"First, let's check you out. What you've just seen isn't much fun. Sit down and I'll get you a glass of water."

"Thanks."

I've seen it a million times: James Coburn, Sylvester Stallone, Robert Mitchum, Clint Eastwood, even James Garner—taking on five men at once and winning. But I'm somewhat of a realist about situations like that, so what I did was to grab for the door, pull it open, and run like hell for daylight.

I never had more than a fifteen-foot lead the whole way, but it was enough to get me into the Oak Room Bar again—twentieth-century sanctuary.

"Everyone is looking at you," Alice said. "My God, this isn't the Sheraton. This is the Plaza. You can't run through the Plaza like that."

"I can if I'm scared to death," I said.

"And look at you, you're sweating—"

"Alice—" I held both her hands very tightly. "Listen to me. We're not just two people bantering at a bar now— I'm serious." I glanced over her shoulder. The two FBI men were just outside the door to the hallway.

I told her what had happened. She didn't cry or raise her voice, but silent tears rolled down her cheeks.

"He wasn't *that* cute, Harry. But, my God, what a way to go."

"Why would anyone want to kill him?"

"I don't know."

"How well do you know him? Really?"

"I told you—just that time two years ago in Guadeloupe."

"That's all?"

"Well, since Tuesday—" Her left hand played with the collar of her blouse—"Since Tuesday I've known him maybe six or seven times. You see, Herbie had to go out of town on Wednesday, so—" She smiled—"He was French, but he was a lot like that bullfighter I met in Spain last year. I mean—"

"*Alice*—we're talking about a man who was just killed."

"I'm sorry. What's your plan?"

"*I* don't know."

"Well, you've got to have a plan. People always have a plan at a time like this."

"Alice, this isn't *The Hardy Boys Have Fun at the Plaza*—this is just me. I don't walk around with fifty-five plans in my head: Plan thirty-seven: What-to-do-when-someone-is-murdered-while-you're-having-a-drink-at-the-Plaza—"

"Don't raise your voice, Harry, you'll get us arrested."

"Maybe that's my plan."

"What?"

"I think you've just given me the beginnings of a plan."

"Well, *somebody* had to do something," Alice said.

I called over the waiter and told him about the body in the men's room. He hurried away and returned with the maître d'hôtel from the Oak Room itself. Both were trying to smile.

"You say he is dead?" asked the maître d'hôtel.

"I'm not quite sure. You'd better send for an ambulance as well as the police."

"You should have informed me immediately."

"There were several of us in there. Each of us probably thought that the others had reported it."

"And he's just lying there?"

"That's right."

"Thank you." The maître d'hôtel turned quickly and left us. The waiter simply backed away.

"What's going to happen now?" Alice asked.

"I don't know. But something will, and anything is better than sitting here with our two friends guarding the door."

"But what if you get arrested, Harry?"

"Then the two of us will be given a nice, guarded exit by the police."

"Is that what you're hoping for?"

"Exactly."

Alice let out a sigh. "Thank God, I had a plan."

"In the nick of time," I said.

"Harry—"

"Yes?"

"I just had a terrible thought. Are you *sure* those two

men are phony FBI agents? Maybe you shouldn't have run away."

"I'm not sure of anything, and I'm not Sherlock Holmes," I said. "But it crossed my mind that I'd never seen *three* attendants in a men's room before. That's hardly a giant observation, I know. But I've also *never* seen an FBI agent sans hat, overweight, wearing a plaid suit, with a diamond pinkie ring, and manicured nails."

"You sound like Matt Dixon."

"Who's Matt Dixon?"

"That guy I met in Puerto Vallarta last Thanksgiving. He was a divorce detective."

"For God's sake, Alice."

"Don't raise your voice, Harry."

■ ■ ■

Two patrol cars and an ambulance arrived at about the same time, parking just outside the Oak Room Bar on Central Park South.

But nothing happened. Five minutes that seemed like twenty went by and nobody came in to arrest me.

"You've got a helluva plan, Harry," Alice said.

"I thought it was your plan."

"Don't be silly. It was your idea."

A sergeant and a plain clothesman entered the Oak Room. The maître d'hôtel politely pointed out our table. They strode toward us. The sergeant had an odd smile on his face.

I stood up.

"You know, you wasted a lot of the taxpayers' money with this wild goose chase," he said.

"But this wasn't a—"

"Aw, come on, buddy. You had your laugh, now call it quits. We're all in a good mood today, so why don't you just apologize to the man who runs this room and we'll be on our way."

"You mean you're not going to arrest me?"

"For what? You're gonna pay a nice fine for your little

joke, but I'm not going to arrest you. Now, I need some identification. . . ."

Behind him I saw my two pinkie-ringed friends moving into the Oak Room Bar. I hauled off and hit the sergeant on his shoulder.

As they were taking me out, Alice hollered, "You're leaving me all alone, Harry."

"Hit someone," I shouted.

Alice jumped on the sergeant's back.

■   ■   ■

Mort Lewis, my attorney, bailed us out. He seemed ill at ease during the whole procedure.

"That's the first time I've ever seen you look unsure of yourself," I told him.

He chuckled. "You know something, you're the first person I've ever bailed out in my life. Contracts are my forte—and nitpicking."

"What law school did you go to?" Alice asked him.

"Harvard," Mort said.

"Don't they have a course in bailing out people at Harvard? I mean, Harvard of all places."

Mort looked at me. "I suppose they do. I must have missed it somehow."

We had a cup of coffee at Wolf's Deli, and Mort told us both to forget the whole thing.

"Look, in the year of our Lord 1983, you had a couple of bottles of wine—you thought some guy looked like Howard Cosell—"

"He did. Exactly. Almost exactly."

"*Almost* exactly," Mort said. "And one of Alice's old friends plays a joke on you—the body disappears—two men you *think* are phony FBI agents . . . Go home and get some sleep."

"It's too early for sleep," Alice said. She looked at Mort. "My husband's away on business—would you mind escorting me—?

"Alice," I said. "Mort's a happily married man."

Mort gave me a dirty look.

Alice took a cab home. Mort and I walked down to my office at Fifty-second and Madison, where we shook hands and parted.

"Harry—?"

I turned. Mort had an indecipherable expression on his face.

He tried to smile. "Would you do me a favor?"

"Name it."

"Please don't comment on my state of marital bliss ever again. Okay?"

"You've got it, Mort."

"Even with that promise"—now he did smile—"I seriously doubt that you have even a slight chance of redemption."

He continued on toward Park Avenue.

CHAPTER
3

M Y OFFICE door says *Baker,
Baker and Baker,* but there is really only me. It's a big office.
An agent has to have a good-looking place.

I always hire a young actress to be the receptionist.
They're almost always cheerful and efficient. And they
play the role well. This month her name was Susan. Actually, this was Susan's third time with me. The wreckage of
two plays that had closed out of town explained her two
exits and two returns to the fold.

She started to laugh as I came through the door. "Well,
well—you certainly had a nice *long* lunch. And it shows."

"I was also arrested," I said.

"For what?"

"Assaulting a police officer."

"People are into strange things nowadays. I suppose
conventional thrills get boring after a while."

"Very. Where's Jane?"

"In the conference room."

I have a big conference room, even though I don't

really need it. All the furniture in it deliberately looks very expensive. It's just there for show. It's something my mentor, Murray Baker (that's when there were two of us for the three names on the door) drummed into me: "We're in show business. So we gotta play the game," he always said. It's not very profound, but that's what he said, and, over the years, I learned that he was right.

Practically his last words to me in the hospital were, "Lease some new furniture for the waiting room."

That's exactly what I did on the afternoon of his funeral. To this day, if I've had a couple of drinks, I still get tears in my eyes when I see furniture ads in *The New Yorker*.

Anyway, there's just Susan, my secretary Jane, another office subleased by a literary agent, a direct mail fellow who rents Murray's old spot, and an accountant, along with the conference room and my office—but it looks as if it all belongs to *Baker, Baker and Baker*—and it's pretty impressive.

Jane came out of the conference room, a steno pad in one hand. "Hello, Harry," she said. "You look awful."

"Hello, Jane. Thanks."

"Do you realize that it's nearly seven o'clock? I just made some tea, and let me be the first to say, you could use some."

"Let me be the *second* to say I could use some. But let's hear the calls first."

"I'll lead with one bit of good news. Phil Persky called and wants to know when you'd like to get together about Tom Haskins' new contract."

"What'd you tell him?"

"I told him I didn't think you were in any hurry."

"Good."

"Then he tried to get out of me if we've heard from anyone else. I let it *slip* that both CBS and NBC had already called."

"Did you set a time?"

"I told him maybe tomorrow—*if* you have a moment."

"*Very* good."

Jane consulted her pad, flipping through several pages.

"There are a lot of calls you can return in the morning—
Dan asked you to dinner at Sardi's after Friday night's
news—Mike and Morley called to tell you a joke—and
then comes the bad news."

"I can guess," I said. "At least one call from Jessica and
two calls from Blanfield."

"Paul Blanfield called four times. He says he's sick to
death of the morning show and wants to quit—and this
time, he says, he means it. Wife number three has found
out about his simultaneous affairs and wants to leave
him—and both affairs have found out about each other.
Just another day in the life of *The Dean of American Morning News*."

"I'll see him for breakfast after tomorrow's show.
Would you call him?" Jane nodded. "And what about
Jessica?"

"What's Jessica *always* about? Someone upset her again.
This time, it seems the new stage manager made a pass at
her."

"In her opinion—has Jessica Rumbough *ever* met a
man who didn't make a pass at her—?"

"Truman Capote—"

"I forgot about him."

"Steve Schwartz said yesterday that Jessica Rumbough's
definition of rape is—are you ready—?"

"Go—"

"Rape, for Jessica, is any time she has sexual inter-
course with a man and it *doesn't* advance her career." Jane
grinned, Susan giggled, and I laughed.

"Send Barbara a copy of that—and remind me tomorrow to send a note to Steve. Anything else?"

"That's it."

"Good. Type up the B list for callbacks in the morning.
I'll call Mike and Morley then, too—tell Dan dinner
sounds fine—I'll pick him up at the Broadcast Center."

Susan stood up from behind the reception desk. "I almost forgot—I have something for you, too."

"Not another definition of Jessica. Steve's can't be
topped."

Susan shook her head. "No, it's this big package on my

desk. It came about an hour ago. Of all people, Howard Cosell brought it in. If he's going to be a client, you've got to buy us an unabridged dictionary and—"

I'd first seen Alan Ladd do it in 1949. A year later I saw Humphrey Bogart do it. Then Robert Young, Robert Mitchum, Robert Stack, and Robert Redford.

So I knew exactly what to do.

I shoved Susan into the conference room, crowded Jane ahead with my body, pulled us all to the floor, and fell on top of the two of them.

All those other guys always did it just in the nick of time, a split second before the explosion. But on my first try, my timing was off. Nothing happened. We just lay there in the middle of the conference room.

"Really, Harry," Jane said, "you make me feel like a Letter-to-the-Editor in *Playboy*."

Susan playfully squeezed my arm. "You know, Mr. Baker, that long lunch certainly changed your manner of showing affection—"

Just about then it exploded.

Susan and Jane gasped—something fell on my head— and I went out.

CHAPTER

4

"I BELIEVE you, of course," Mort was saying, "but as I told you this afternoon, my strong point is finding crafty sentences in contracts—like your divorce. I'm not a criminal lawyer."

We were sitting in the Friars Club, in a corner on the second floor, under the portrait of Will Rogers.

"At least no one was hurt," Mort said.

"Except my nerves."

"A lot of men are cowards," Mort said. "Don't worry about it."

I looked at him. "You didn't have to say that." Mort grinned.

An imposing figure came up the stairs.

"My God, there he is again."

"Who?"

"The Mad Bomber. I'm going to call the police."

Mort turned to look. "That's Howard."

"Are you sure?"

"Of course."

The man who was *apparently* Howard Cosell smiled at us.

"Well—?" Mort asked.

"That's Howard," I said. "The eyes are Howard's."

Howard came across the room. "Hello, Harry—Hello, Mort," he said. "I see by your presence that the rumor that the Friars Club had finally come to its senses and banished your names from the membership rolls was *unfortunately* not based upon truth, but was, in fact, merely a daydream devoutly to be wished, and—" he smiled—"alas, one apparently never to be realized."

"That's Howard, all right," I said to Mort. "Have a drink, Howard?"

"No, thanks. I'm on my way to Twenty-One—dinner with the family."

"Howard, were you at the Oak Room Bar today," I asked. "Mid-afternoon—?"

"I prefer the hospitality of the Brothers Kriendler or the warming presence of Mr. Alberto—*if* I'm not enjoying *Prae Omnia Fraternitas.*"

"What's that mean?" Mort asked.

"I usually go to Twenty-One or the Dorset Grill for lunch," Howard said. "Sometimes here at the Friars."

Mort tried to sound very serious. "Howard, are you aware that someone is running around town doing an impression of you?"

The Coach chuckled. "There've been a few ahead of him."

"Not just the voice," I said. "The whole way. The guy looks exactly like you."

"Interesting—" Howard had that look in his eyes that people get when someone is continuing on a dull course of conversation and won't quit. Smiling as pleasantly as possible, he started to back out of the bar. "If you see him again, have him contact Roone. Tell him I plan to cut back on my work by 1986. Maybe he can do a few of my assignments then." He smiled again and headed down the stairs.

"I wonder."

"Wonder what?" Mort asked.

"If that was *really* Howard."

"Oh, for God's sake, Harry—of course it was."

We sat for a while in silence.

"I don't know," Mort finally said.

"What's that mean?"

"It means—I just can't get an angle. Can't figure out what the game is. It's . . . and—" Mort laughed. "And I'm not making sense."

"Nothing is making sense," I said. Why did this Roger Ro-*jeh* have an American accent when he died?"

Mort smiled. "Ah—and why did he *die*, Harry?"

"Go ahead and laugh at me."

"I wasn't *laughing* at you. I was *smiling* at you."

"There's very little difference," I said acidly. "Okay, why was he killed? And the envelope with the francs . . . and the man who grabbed the envelope . . . the phony FBI agents. And where is the body?"

Mort shook his head.

My name was paged. I picked up the house phone beside the fireplace.

It was Lucille at the switchboard. "A man called and left a quick message for you and then hung up, Mr. Baker."

"Thanks, Lucille. What's the message?"

"Just—*Call Alice*."

I gave her Alice's number to dial, let it ring a dozen times, recalled it, and let it ring another dozen times.

"What's up?" Mort asked.

"One more unanswered question. I'll call you tomorrow—"

I loped over to Park and Fifty-fifth and caught a cab for Alice's place.

■　■　■

Soft disco music was playing, the lights were dim—everything looked fine. Except that the door was ajar. And—except that Alice was tied to the bed, splayed out, arms tied to each corner of the headboard, and legs the same way at the bottom.

I untied the handkerchief and pulled the gag out of her mouth.

"Oh, my God, Harry, it was awful. I just kept gagging and thinking I'd choke. Oh, my God—"

"You're okay now," I said. "You're okay."

When I had loosened the last of the knots, she pulled up her knees and lay in a kind of ball. "Let's get under the blankets," I said.

"Please, Harry. Just let me lie here for a while."

"A drink?"

"Please. A brandy."

■ ■ ■

Two men had done it. They had worn stockings over their faces and those glasses with the big nose. They had given her a shot of something, and she had gone out almost immediately.

The talking helped. By her second brandy, Alice was up and walking around, checking the condition of the apartment. "I don't understand it. They didn't take anything. And they left the place looking as if the maid had just been here."

Her voice was full again, and she seemed to be in control. Out of the blue, she said, "Sexy, wasn't it?"

"What?"

"I mean me, my beautiful body absolutely stark naked, drenched with sweat."

"I didn't notice. I was too concerned about you."

"Aw—" She sounded petulant.

"Well—I might have noticed a little bit."

"Thanks."

"You're welcome."

Alice had a half-smile on her face. "Harry—I can either get dressed now or just stay naked the way I am, my magnificent body filling the room with incredible sensuality, driving you mad. What d'you think?"

"Alice, let's just have another drink together. And let's talk."

Her eyes were suddenly wet, her lower lip quivered, and very quickly her arms were around me.

"I'm glad you're here, Harry." She tried to smile. "Because I'm scared."

■ ■ ■

It was after midnight when I got back to my apartment. I wasn't even surprised when I opened the door and saw the wreckage. Somebody had either been very messy, or had really wanted me to know that they had been there. My instincts told me it was the latter.

I nosed around to make sure no one had tarried, locked the door—it hadn't helped before, but what the hell—then showered and got into bed.

It had been one hell of a long day.

CHAPTER
5

THE CLOCK said seven-thirty when the alarm went off. The apartment looked even worse in the light.

The first thing I did was call Alice. She sounded fine. "I just needed some sleep, you cute thing. And thanks for getting Roberta to stay with me last night." She made a kissing sound. "Have a good day."

As soon as I hung up, the phone rang. It was Jane. "Good morning. If you notice, I'm using my sickeningly cheerful voice to confirm your morning schedule because you've got a corker today."

"Shoot—" I grabbed a pen and my date book. "By the way"—I tried to sound casual—"somebody wrecked my apartment last night. It's the latest craze."

"Were you hurt?"

"It happened before I got home."

The cheerfulness left Jane's voice. "Harry, may I ask you something?"

"Sure. But when you say 'Harry' in that tone of voice, it's usually serious."

She hesitated. "Harry—after what happened yesterday—and now this—what's going on?"

I answered her truthfully. "I don't know."

"I mean—obviously *something* is. Well—we've known each other a long time now—over a year—can I help?"

"No—but thanks."

"You're sure—?"

"For now. I'll remember what you said, though."

Her business voice returned. "Okay, Mr. Baker—here's what the morning looks like. In forty-five minutes you leave for the Morning News and a postprogram breakfast with Paul Blanfield, *The Dean of American Morning News.* A reminder: He wants out—*again.* And his third wife—the charming Elaine—has just found out about his simultaneous affairs."

I chuckled. "Other than *that*—he's in great shape."

"When you finish with the great Blanfield, call me. Phil Persky is keeping ten through noon free to talk with you about the new Haskins contract."

"Call him around ten and say I'm sorry but I can't make it. Tell him *maybe* next week."

"Yes, Maestro."

"What else?"

"Friday's dinner with Dan at Sardi's—did you call Dan?"

"No—but I will. Keep pestering me about it."

"And Mike and Morley. They told me the joke. It's hilarious."

"After Paul, I'll come straight back to the office and make all the calls. Now—let me ask you an awful question. Where should I take the lovely Jessica Rumbough for lunch?"

"You mean someplace where her subtle and sensitive mind will know that you appreciate her intellect, her talent, her beauty—and where, if she makes a scene, you can get the hell out of in a hurry?"

"Exactly. So a lot of my favorite places are out."

"How about Goodale's?"

"Perfect. Percy is the most understanding man I know. He'd let me back into his place if she pulls one of her big ones. Maybe."

■ ■ ■

It took an order of corned beef hash, two poached eggs, three pots of tea, and an hour and a half of my time—but most of all, a tremendous amount of concentration in order to appear to be listening to him—to get *The Dean of American Morning News* calmed down. But I've always liked the guy—and that helped a lot.

"How long have we been together, Harry?" The Dean asked as we left the restaurant.

"Let's see—since 1971. About twelve years."

"When you signed me I was just Paul Blanfield, WKYM, Syracuse. And within five years the two of us turned it into"—his voice broadened with emotion—*"Paul Blanfield, The Dean of American—"*

"I know," I said quickly.

"A lot of damned hard work," said The Dean.

"A lot." I gave him a solid, confidence-inspiring whack on the back. "I'm going to leave you here on the corner and head back to the office. You're okay now? You'd rather talk to Hank yourself?"

"I think I should."

"Good. So do I."

"And about the other thing—you'll do what you can?"

"I'll try. But three wives and two simultaneous chippies is a problem."

"I know—I know," said The Dean mournfully. Then he grinned and gave a thumbs up sign. "Thanks for breakfast, Harry—and your time."

Walking back across town, I began to whistle. For some reason, I liked my job.

■ ■ ■

Back at the office, I made all my calls, held a bomb drill—in which Jane, Susan, and I yelled, "Bomb.", fell to the floor, and groped each other—voted to hold a bomb drill a day, and headed for Goodale's and Jessica Rumbough.

Goodale's was crowded as always. Percy himself met me at the bar, wearing his traditional Bermuda shorts.

"You have the choice," Percy said. "A table here at the front—so that if she makes a scene you can get out—or a table all the way in the back—so that if she makes a scene nobody will know who made it—and you can walk out fast."

"The envelope, please—and the suggestion is—?"

"Table at the back," Percy said.

"Thanks. I'll take it."

"Would you like a drink at the bar, or the table?"

"The table. And thanks again, Percy."

Percy laughed. "We go back a long way."

I drank two glasses of club soda, read *Variety*, wrote two notes to clients, and called the office twice. Jessica arrived right after my second trip to the phone. As usual she was half an hour late, and, as usual, she didn't apologize.

"That fucking stage manager has got to go," were her first delightful words.

"Why?" I asked.

"What the fuck do you mean—why?"

"What's wrong with him?"

"It's not *him*—it's *her*."

"That's something new," I said.

"What do you mean by that crack?" Jessica had the unpleasant habit of spitting, just slightly, as she talked, and she always assumed that everyone *meant* something.

"I mean, you're usually getting a hard time from men."

"I only have trouble with incompetence."

"Is the stage manager incompetent?"

"Totally. On top of that, she made a pass at me."

"How?" I was trying to look interested and sympathetic. I had heard this same story, with variations only in the details, about a dozen times.

"With her eyes."

"Her what?"

"Her eyes."

"I'm sorry," I said, "but I'm not in the same conversation. She does *what* with her eyes?"

"Talking to you is like talking to a wall," Jessica said. "You asked me how she made a pass at me, and I told you—with her eyes."

"How the hell do you do that?"

"When someone does it, you know."

"Maybe she thinks you're doing it to her with *your* eyes," I said.

"Son of a bitch," Jessica said.

"Excuse me—?"

"I'm talking seriously, and you're making jokes."

"Yes, I am. But I'm also listening—as eagerly as I. F. Stone."

"Who the fuck is I. F. Stone?" Jessica asked in her lilting manner.

"A journalist."

"What the fuck do you think I am?"

I didn't tell her.

"I want a fucking drink, and maybe I ought to have another fucking agent."

"What would you like to drink?"

"You know—"

"I'm afraid I don't."

"You *should* know. What kind of a fucking agent are you, anyway?"

"A pretty good one. What would you like to drink?"

"Vodka and tonic with lime."

"And who would you like as an agent?"

I didn't say it in anger. It had been on my mind for weeks. I had learned from my mentor to represent only clients I liked. I represent only newsmen and newswomen. They are all intelligent, interesting, and—excepting Paul Blanfield, *The Dean of American Morning News*—they all have a sense of humor. I like them very much.

Until Jessica Rumbough. As I watched her drinking her vodka, complaining all the while, the decision was made. Very pleasantly—without emotion—I decided to nudge her out.

"Have you thought about Harding Associates?" I asked, squeezing through a crack in her diatribe.

"What—?"

"You mentioned a moment ago that you were thinking of another agent. And it's been bothering me for weeks—maybe I'm not doing the job for you that I should—"

That's how it began.

It ended with Jessica saying, "Don't make a pass at *me*, Harry."

Good-bye, Jessica.

I felt ten years younger and five pounds lighter.

■   ■   ■

Back at the office, Susan gave me her southern-southern voice. "Mr. Baker, Mr. Baker—Mercy, Mr. Baker, we've been looking all over for you."

"Whenever I don't call in, something happens. I just left Goodale's ten minutes ago."

Her voice came back to normal. "I know. Percy said I'd missed you by two minutes."

"A Mr. Wendell Crittenden called. He's with a Washington law firm—Reed, Selby, Ash and Crittenden. He says they have a client who'll pay more for the services of Tom Haskins than any of the networks." She smiled, fully appreciative of what she had said.

"Nobody would pay more."

"That's what he said."

"Did he say for his services as a *broadcaster*?"

She frowned. "I'm not sure."

"Maybe it's a flak job. Where can I reach Mr. Crittenden?"

"He's at the Sherry-Netherland. He'd like to see you for cocktails and dinner."

"Call Mr. Crittenden and tell him cocktails but no dinner. Where's Jane?"

"At Sid's. Something about city taxes."

"Thanks for handling the phones. If this works out, I'll get us all something nice."

"Just get me another show," Susan said.

I spent the afternoon at NBC and Westinghouse, walked back to the office at four, and by five had returned all of my phone calls.

I shaved, changed my shirt, dictated three or four letters to Jane, and called it quits for the day.

"I'll be in Wendell Crittenden's suite at the Sherry-Netherland if anyone calls—but only if it's important."

"Walter said he might call later—"

"If Walter wants *anything*—it's important."

CHAPTER

6

I WALKED over to the Sherry-Netherland. It was a lovely afternoon. I whistled all the way.

"Harry, what are *you* doing here?" It was Alice. She was coming out of the bar as I walked into the lobby.

"I'm about to have cocktails with someone. And you?"

She rolled her eyes skyward and fumbled at the top button of yet another diaphanous blouse.

"It's that hockey player I met in Montreal. He's in town. He might be playing for the Rangers this year. What am I going to do?"

I rejected two or three bad puns and said, "What do you *want* to do, my child?"

"That's just it, I know what I want to do, but not with him. I mean not for an entire hockey season."

"You could tell him just that—and come with me for cocktails."

Alice's face suddenly reddened. "Oh, Harry—"

"What?"

"How I hurt you."

"I repeat—what?"

"You must love me very much to put up with the *myriad*"—it was a new word for her—"ways I hurt you."

"I love you for all the reasons everyone else loves you—the same reason the Canadian hockey player loves you, the—" (No, the truth is not always kind.) I stopped. "I love you, Alice," I said. "Come to the cocktail party."

"I'll tell him the—no, I can't. The truth is not always kind, Harry."

"Yes—I know."

"I'll tell him my uncle is dying of gonorrhea."

"And he'll believe that?"

"You don't know Canadian hockey players, Harry."

By the time I had checked with the desk on Wendell Crittenden and called up to his suite, Alice was back. She had tears in her eyes.

"I'm sorry it was so painful," I said.

"It wasn't."

"But you've been crying."

"Oh, Harry, I thought you knew."

"Knew what?"

"That I can cry at the drop of a hat." She came close and looked me in the eyes. "Say anything. I'll cry."

I put both hands on her shoulders. "Alice—I had orange marmalade on my toast this morning."

Tears rolled down her cheeks.

"See—it's a God-given gift. I thought you knew."

"Alice—I really *do* love you—or something."

"Me, too, Harry."

"Let's go. His name is Wendell Crittenden, and I don't know him. It's business and it could be good."

"This is your big week, Harry. What should I do?"

"Just be your usual pleasant self—and don't cry."

Alice looked at me and tears ran down her cheeks.

I gave it my Jack Benny voice. "Now *cut that out.*"

Wendell Crittenden, of Reed, Selby, Ash and Crittenden, was short, had a high-pitched voice, never seemed to smile, and fingered, but did not smoke, a pipe.

He didn't seem to be the sort of man to stand with at a bar and enjoy a glass of beer.

"Hello, Harry," he put out his hand. "It's good to see you again."

We shook hands.

"Forgive me," I said. "But I'm afraid that you have the advantage—"

"Sorry, that was boorish of me. 1963. Twenty years younger—twenty pounds lighter—no glasses—U.S. Army—Jefferson Hall Station—Corporal Crittenden—?"

We both laughed and really shook hands.

We had never been friends, but I had known Wendell Crittenden in the army. After basic training I'd been sent—God knows why—the army didn't—to Jefferson Hall Station, a small intelligence post just outside Washington, on the Virginia side of the Potomac.

I was as fit to be in Intelligence as I was to be Chief of Staff, but there I was. On the other hand, Wendell Crittenden, with his encyclopedic mind, belonged. Nevertheless, we shared the same MOS and walked around with the same large, red, plastic-covered security-clearance cards on our uniforms.

But those were almost the only things we shared. Wendell was intelligent and was in Intelligence. I was kept on because the major I worked for liked the idea that his unit, through my efforts, always passed the Post Commander's weekly inspection.

After shaking hands, Wendell and I did the obligatory couple of minutes of "What ever happened to So-and-So?" and "Remember the time the Colonel—?" and "I'd forgotten all about—" before our voices were normal again.

Wendell introduced me to the four men with him.

"It looks as if you brought the whole law firm," I said.

"Just four junior partners, eager to see New York."

I introduced Alice.

A kind of steward came in and took our drink orders, and another junior partner brought out hors d'oeuvres.

Wendell either had a lot of money on his side of the table, or he was putting up a good show.

We talked for half an hour and nothing happened. It's the negotiating game. He wants to make a deal, and you want to make a deal. Yet you can sit through a whole lunch at Twenty-One, pretending you're just there for the food and each other's company, before one of you breaks the ice in the last ten minutes.

Once I even finished an entire meal, shook hands, and was walking down Fifty-Second Street before Cy Michaels said, "How about seven years at four hundred thousand, Harry?" It ended up six years at six hundred thousand.

But this time, with all three networks bidding, I had the courage of a Swifty Lazar.

I decided that half an hour was enough time. "Thanks for the drinks and canapes. I'm taking Alice to dinner, so we'd better be on our way. What did you have in mind for Tom Haskins?"

That's when Alice fell over.

Before I could reach her, three of the junior partners were picking her up and carrying her toward the bedroom.

"What the hell is this?"

Wendell shrugged and made a conciliatory gesture. "I'm sorry, Harry. I'm afraid I just assumed you'd be coming alone. She'll be fine. Let her sleep a bit."

I started toward the bedroom.

"Isn't this a nice weapon, Harry? Didn't have this sort of thing when we were back at Jefferson Hall Station. It's a Browning. Nine millimeter. Thirteen rounds in the clip and one in the chamber. And it has all the wallop of the old Colt .45." Wendell laughed. "Only with this one you *can* hit the broad side of a barn—"

I tried to sound bored. "What do you want, Wendell?"

"Just a talk."

"About Tom Haskins?"

He smiled. "What an agent you are, Harry—Yes, in a way, yes."

"Then let's talk."

"Outside, Harry. It's easy to see that you've forgotten

everything we learned at Jefferson Hall Station. But that's unfair of me, isn't it. It's been twenty years for you. I, on the other hand, stayed in the business." Wendell smiled. "From Military Intelligence to Civilian Intelligence."

The Browning Nine has a four-inch barrel. He motioned it slightly toward the door. I moved.

Outside, the October sun was low in the sky, the fountain was leaping in Pulitzer Square, autumn was in the air—and I had to be taking a stroll with Wendell Crittenden.

It seemed that when Wendell walked, everybody walked. We were surrounded, front and back, and across Fifth Avenue, by junior partners trailing at a discreet distance.

It was Wendell who broke the silence. "By the way, I think you'll be pleased to know that your reputation as a broadcast agent is of the first water."

"Who told you that?"

"The people I work for."

"Who's that?"

"Oh, *come on*, Harry—"

We walked all the way to Sixty-Sixth Street before Wendell spoke again. He was looking straight ahead. "We need your help, Harry."

"Since I'm supposed to know who you're working for— am I also supposed to know what kind of help you need?"

Wendell looked at me and smiled. "You never had a temper twenty years ago."

"You never pointed guns at me and drugged my dates twenty years ago."

"Touché."

"If that's your idea of sounding sophisticated, forget it, Wendell, it doesn't become you."

"You're getting touchy, Harry. That doesn't go well with that incipient temper of yours."

I stopped walking. "What do you want, Wendell?"

"I just told you—I want *you. Uncle Sam* wants you."

"You're serious—?"

"Harry—to paraphrase your dramatic speech of just moments ago—would I be drugging your girlfriend and pointing guns at you if I *weren't* serious?"

"And what about this regiment of *junior partners* that's surrounding us?"

"I suppose that's to show you that I'm *very* serious."

I sat down on a bench. "I'm listening. What's it all about?"

Wendell sat beside me and started to run his hands on the underside of the bench.

"Aw, cut it out, Wendell."

"You never know about electronic gear—maybe you set up the bench in advance." He had a slightly excited expression on his face.

"I didn't even know we were going to *be* out here, for God's sake."

"How do I know that?"

"I don't know, Wendell. Go ahead—search."

He searched the park bench with all the pent-up passion of an amorous lover on his wedding night. He found nothing. He seemed almost disappointed.

"Okay, Wendell. All's clear. Let's hear it."

Wendell pulled a pack of mints from his pocket. "Would you like one, Harry?"

"No, thanks. They might be drugged."

Wendell smiled. "That's the spirit. On guard—always."

"Just *tell* me, Wendell."

He leaned back and watched a pigeon as he spoke. "We were both drafted for two years, right?"

"That's right."

"And then it was six long years in the inactive reserve—"

"I had champagne the day my discharge finally came."

"That's just what I'm getting to. Even though you got an honorable discharge—once you've been in Intelligence—you're never *really* out."

I stood up. "What the hell are you saying?"

"I'm saying that you were cleared for Top Secret at Jefferson Hall Station. And whether you were discharged or not, if they want you back for a job, they'll get you back."

He dropped another mint into his mouth. "And, Harry, they want you back."

"Oh, no—"

"Yes, Harry—"

"Maybe I was cleared for Top Secret, but my job at Jefferson Hall Station consisted of keeping the office ready for inspection and typing letters for the major."

"You're modest, Harry."

"Maybe my MOS said Intelligence, but I was never really *in* Intelligence—I mean, the *intelligent* part of Intelligence."

"You were in S-2 and G-2—yes or no?"

"Yes—but that doesn't—"

"S-2 and G-2 are Intelligence, Harry. And that's where you were. And that's where we stop talking, because it's just a waste of time. Because they want you back for a job, Harry, and that's where you're going. Back."

We sat on the bench staring at each other for a moment like two fighters waiting for the bell to ring.

I finally said, "Wendell, it's as simple as this. I'm forty-five years old—I served my time—I have an honorable discharge—I may have been technically in Intelligence, but I don't know a goddamned thing about it—and to hell with whoever you work for."

Wendell said nothing.

Finally he smiled. "Orders are orders, Harry. You know that."

"Who cut the orders? Let's see them."

He frowned and shook his head. "You don't think I walk around with orders out of the CIC that read: 'Former Sergeant Harold Baker will attempt to steal the entire Bulgarian gold reserve,' do you?"

"What the hell kind of crazy—"

"Just an *example,* Harry. Just an example."

"Well, then, show me an *example* of orders cut with my name on them," I said.

"I can't."

"Why not?"

He sighed. "I just told you—you don't walk around with Top Secret orders in your hip pocket."

"Then you're out of luck, Wendell."

Wendell stood up. "Let's walk some more, Harry."

We started on down toward Fifty-Ninth and Fifth again.

The timbre in Wendell's voice changed. Not urgent. Just patient and positive. "Just relax, Harry. Accept it. It's no big deal. Just come to Washington with me, listen to what they have to say, then take it or leave it. If you take it, they tell me it won't use much of your time at all. You might even have a little fun, a little adventure, and then—what the hell—you can come back to your job and say to yourself, 'Okay, I just did something for my country.' That is, unless you think that that's too silly a thing to do."

"You mean I'm volunteering?" I asked.

"Well, in a way, you are, Harry." Wendell smiled. "I mean, if you come along because you want to—then we can say that you're volunteering—and we'll all be happy. And if you don't want to come along—then you're *not* volunteering."

We walked some more. "But one way or another— you're coming. That's for sure, Harry."

Wendell squinted at me. "That's for damn sure."

CHAPTER
7

WE WERE making our way through the mazelike passages that lead passengers from the trains to the taxis at Washington's Union Station. Two of the junior partners were carrying our bags and two were trailing us.

"The best way to Washington is on the Metroliner," Wendell said.

"The best way out of Manchester is a bottle of gin," I said.

"What—?" Wendell frowned.

"A non sequitur."

"It doesn't make sense," Wendell said.

"No—"

I was impatient. It was nearly midnight, and I was tired.

"We're booked at the Jefferson," Wendell said. "It's a civilized hotel. The English stay there." He signaled for a cab.

Washington is a most beautiful city. I tried to concentrate on it and to remember the happy times on weekend passes when I was at Jefferson Hall Station.

"Wait a minute, Wendell. Why the Jefferson Hotel? Any significance? I mean—Jefferson Hall Station—"

"Nothing at all. It just happens to be a fine hotel. My God, and everybody tries to say that *we're* paranoid."

Sir John Gielgud was marching towards us as we entered the lobby.

"Good evening, Sir John," I said.

"Good evening. Just going for a turn."

"I'm impressed," Wendell said.

"Never seen him before—just seemed the thing to do." We finally got to my room.

"Just remember, Harry, it's six stories up—and there'll be two men in the hallway." After midnight Wendell looked even more unpleasant than usual.

The first thing I tried was the telephone.

"This isn't the desk, sir. And sorry, no outgoing calls."

■ ■ ■

I couldn't sleep, and I ended up thinking about my wife. Ex-wife. It was nearly six months since she walked out. "The kids are all in college and I need some excitement," was her cogent explanation.

She left me for some golf pro—the sort of guy you always envy when you're young because he has great teeth and knows how to squint his eyes into the sun. All the girls adore him. When you grow up, you realize that most women don't care for that type. Too shallow.

That was the kind of guy she ran off with. But we still speak on the phone every once in a while. I had a desire to call her now and give her a good laugh by telling her what was happening to me.

But, at least what was happening to me was a break from the past six months of work, work, and more work.

A little change was probably just what I needed. . . . I heard myself chuckle out loud. My God, listen to me. Talking to myself and laughing at the answers. This whole thing was turning me into a candidate for *Looney Tunes.*

I finally fell asleep.

■　■　■

We had breakfast in the Jefferson dining room. It was cozy and pleasant, and, under different circumstances, I would have enjoyed it.

"I don't like this idea of not even being able to make a simple phone call, Wendell."

"Umm? Of course. Good sausage."

"I wanted to call my ex-wife and give her a good laugh."

Wendell looked up. "Honest to God, Harry. You take the cake. You really do. Now enjoy this great breakfast, and we'll drive to Georgetown and see what they want."

"We're not going over to Virginia? To Langley?"

"That's for the big guys and all the bureaucrats. Our operation is run by—despite what you're thinking—some pretty sharp people. We try to be good, and we try to be efficient. And to be efficient in this town—you stay the hell away from any of those big buildings—the Pentagon, State, Langley—they're all the same. We stay away. That's why we're efficient."

I ate my breakfast. The sausage *was* good. So was the Irish marmalade.

Wendell was reading *The Washington Post.*

"By the way, Harry." He looked over the top of his paper. "My people apparently know about your little run-in at the Plaza."

"Run-in?"

"You know—the fellow in the men's room. The—" Wendell made a face—"the dead man? They know all about it. Just in case it comes up."

"What do they know? And how do *you* know it?"

"They told me. All they know so far—and I'm guessing—maybe they know more—is that some fellow was

killed in the men's room at the Plaza—you were there—
he gave you something, and you gave it to someone else."

"That's pretty accurate," I said. "Except that I didn't
really give anything away—somebody took the envelope
that the Frenchman had given me."

"Who was he?"

"Who was the dead man?" Wendell nodded. "I don't
know," I said.

"What about the fellow you gave it to?"

"I didn't *give*. And I don't know him either."

Wendell smiled. "Come on—you give a man something, and you don't even know who he is?"

"I just told you—I didn't give it. It was taken. And by the
way—who the hell is this *they* you keep talking about?"

He laughed and finished off a piece of toast. "Let's pay
the bill and head for Georgetown," he said.

It was a Mercedes limousine. There was a driver, someone sitting in front with him, and someone sitting in the
back with Wendell and me. We headed directly down K
Street towards Georgetown.

As we passed Dupont Circle, Wendell said, "I feel silly
saying this, Harry, but we're going to have to blindfold
you. I'm sorry."

His friend was less apologetic. Without a word, he
pasted two pieces of thick adhesive over my eyes, then
Wendell adjusted the blindfold.

"It must look strange to someone on the street," I said,
in my cheerful let's-have-a-drink voice.

"Tinted windows. No one can see inside," Wendell said.

"One thing, Wendell—"

"Yes—?"

"Did *they*"—I tried to chuckle as I said it—"did *they* re-
move the body? Because there was no body when the police arrived at the Plaza."

"I don't know," he said.

"Or—did *they* set up the whole thing?"

"That's preposterous, Harry."

"*They* know a helluva lot of details."

"Of course they do," Wendell said.

The limousine made a lot of stops and starts, before

finally turning into what I supposed was a driveway. I heard an iron gate open, we went through it, and the gate closed.

When I got out, my feet hit the gravel and then we were on what I guessed was a flagstone walk. It is interesting how, even through shoe leather, your feet can tell what you're walking on. It is also interesting what idiotic thoughts go through your mind when you're nervous.

"It's silly, isn't it?" Wendell said. "I mean, this blindfold business and all. I'm really very sorry, Harry." He squeezed my arm in an attempt at manly camaraderie. "But, believe me, it *is* necessary."

We went up a few steps, rang a bell, the door was opened, and we went in.

"Okay, Harry, we'll take it off now."

I felt the blindfold being untied, and then suddenly the adhesive tape was ripped off.

"Christ Almighty," I hollered, "you just took off half my right eyebrow!"

The young man who had done it was standing directly in front of me, a piece of tape in each hand, a weak smile on his face. "I'm sorry," he said.

"Get some witch hazel," Wendell said. And to me— "That wasn't necessary. I apologize."

Five minutes later we were climbing the broad stairs up to the second floor. It was an extremely large house, enormous by Georgetown standards, if that, indeed, was where we were. Thick draperies were drawn on all the windows.

There was a uniformed Marine posted in the main hall. Everything was quiet. I heard only a typewriter in one of the rooms.

The second floor hallway was very wide, and long hallways ran off on either side to other areas of the mansion.

We stopped in front of a huge oaken door.

"This is M's office," Wendell said.

"M—?" I laughed. "*M.* Come *on,* Wendell."

Wendell smiled, "Actually, of course, he isn't officially called M—it's just our little joke." Wendell's eyes looked a bit defiant. "We have a damned good sense of humor here." He gave his version of a hearty chuckle to show that he, for certain, had a keen sense of humor. "Actually, though, he rather likes being called M. He wouldn't admit it—but he does."

■   ■   ■

M looked as if he *should* be called M. Tall, gray hair, gray double-breasted suit, a striped Ivy League tie, horn-rimmed glasses. Half John Foster Dulles, half James Angleton. I was impressed.

"Sit down, Mr. Baker," he said. He indicated a chair in front of his desk.

He waited very formally until I was seated before he sat himself.

"I'll get right down to business." His voice was that of a patrician banker who had to deal with you because you were making a large deposit. "We need your help. It's as simple as that. And as a former Intelligence man, I'm sure you'll come to our aid."

"I'm not really a former Intelligence man," I said.

"Nonsense. Your files show that you were at Jefferson Hall Station with Crittenden here."

He sounded like something out of a Graham Greene novel, so I said, "Yes, but the closest I got to any real Intelligence was reading Graham Greene novels."

He laughed. That is to say, he pretended to laugh.

"Would you like a drink?" he asked. "You've had rather a bad time of it."

"No thanks. It's pretty early in the day for me."

"Yes, of course." He stood up and strode around the room. Wendell and the other two men remained seated. So did I—not moving a muscle—the way I sit in a dentist's chair.

"As I was saying, Mr. Baker, I like to keep things as simple as possible. We need your participation in an operation, and we need some information from you. First of all, just to bring you up to date, the man you killed at the Plaza was—"

"Just a moment," I said. "I didn't kill anybody at the Plaza."

M—or whoever the hell he was—chuckled. "Yes, you and I know that, but the police wouldn't believe it if they were to find some evidence to the contrary." He smiled stiffly. "But let's hope it doesn't come to that."

He sat behind his desk again. "Now here's what we would like from you: We would like to know the name of the man to whom you gave that envelope, and we would like to know how you came to know Jean-Pierre DuBois."

When I said nothing, he smiled and said, "Perhaps I've made this whole thing sound too much like a police interrogation. I didn't mean to." His voice softened. "It's just idle interest on my part about DuBois—frankly, you don't seem the sort who'd consort with an international—ah—troublemaker."

He poured himself a glass of water. "Oh, I'm sorry—would you like some?"

"No thanks," I said.

He sounded sincere now, like a life insurance salesman who's only concerned about your loved ones and not at all about his commission. "But the other information would help us a great deal."

"I'd tell you if I knew," I said. "But I have no idea."

"Really?"

"I was sitting in the Plaza having a few drinks when this Jean-Pierre what's-his-name came over and insisted on buying my friend and me a drink. Then he shoved an envelope into my pocket. The next thing I knew he was dead."

"And you'd never met him before?"

"No."

"Well, good." The man who secretly liked to be called M smiled. "As I said, you most certainly don't seem the type to be friendly with . . . a man like that. But what about your friend—Alice?"

"She met him on vacation. She meets a lot of men that way."

"Ah—I see—and what about the man to whom you gave the envelope?"

"As I was telling Wendell at breakfast, I didn't exactly give it to anybody. He grabbed me, took the envelope, said 'Thanks—you'll be hearing from me,' and disappeared.

M seemed interested. "You think you remember exactly what he said?"

"I believe so—'Thanks, you'll be hearing from me.' That's it."

"But you haven't so far? Heard from him, I mean."

"Nothing."

M looked genuinely serious. "If he makes contact with you again, let us hear from you immediately."

M stood up. "I believe that's all for now. You'll be on your own until—oh, let's say around six-thirty this evening. We'll have cocktails—and I'll lay out the operation for you and show you your part in it. If you agree to help us—and I hope you will—it will only take a week or two of your time. It would be a mild adventure for you, and it would mean a great deal to us."

I thought of my ex-wife and the golf pro. "I'll try to think positively," I said.

He smiled. "Good. Mr. Crittenden will take you back to the hotel. If you need to make any phone calls, you'll have a line now." He glanced at Wendell. "A bit of over-zealousness on our part, I'm afraid. Oh—man to man—" (I didn't go to Choate or Harvard, but I've always imagined that that's how they speak there)—"man to man, I should warn you: Be discreet. The phone will be tapped."

"Thanks," I said, and added, "old sport."

We shook hands. "See you at six-thirty—"

The ride back was the same, blindfolded and all. Only this time, Wendell himself took it off.

"I'm glad you're going to consider it, Harry," he said. "What the hell—you'll probably have some fun."

When I got back to my room, I sat in front of the phone and tried to decide whom to call—and when I called, what to say.

Being an agent, I did the predictable thing and called the office.

Jane answered. "Where the hell have you been?"

"Any crises?"

"Just you. You're the only crisis we have. Are you all right?"

"I'm fine."

"Are you sure?"

"Really—I'm fine. Any problems today?"

"Nothing. All quiet on the Western Front."

"What about the Eastern? Have you heard from Jessica?"

"Not a word."

"When she does call—tell her, yes, I meant it—she's no longer with the office."

"Got it," Jane said. "Harry, are you sure you're—"

"I'm in Washington—a possible new client. Sorry for not calling earlier. I'll tell you all about it when I get back." I debated about letting her know the name of the hotel and decided not to.

"Anything else?"

"That's it. I've got to run—" I hung up as she was saying, "Harry—"

I sat there for five minutes, wondering what the call had proved. I suppose it proved, if anything, that an agent is an agent is an agent.

With dull thoughts like that lying limpid in my brain, a walk seemed in order to clear it. And, like London and Paris, Washington is a natural town to walk in.

■ ■ ■

It was up around Dupont Circle that I noticed the man who was strolling too close beside me. That I even noticed him at all made me realize how uneasy I had become.

The man was bald and wore thick glasses. "Hello," was the extent of his eloquence.

His partner, on my other side, was Chinese, and one of the most beautiful women I had ever seen in my life. She was also about six and a half feet tall.

She smiled, and if she hadn't said what she said, I might have fallen in love.

"I have a gun pointing at your ribs," she said.

"How fascinating." Not brilliant, not Noel Coward, but the best that I could manage under the circumstances. I kept on walking.

CHAPTER

8

UNTIL THE Cosell-Clone at the Plaza, I had gone through forty-five years of life on this planet without anyone even pretending to point a gun at my ribs. Now this was the second time in two days.

And the second limousine in *one* day.

There was another Chinese woman in the back seat. She wore the same type of hacking jacket and the same kind of tight riding breeches as my Amazon walking partner, but she was short, and she wasn't pretty.

And she didn't smile. "I have gun," was all she said.

"You two should chip in and take a Berlitz course," I said. "You really need work on vocabulary."

It was meant to sound breezy. But even a deaf man would have heard the nervousness in my voice.

"Get in," the man said. He opened the back door. I got in, and the beautiful Amazon got in after me. After years of the good life, here I was in Washington, D.C., sitting between two armed Chinese women in the back seat of a car, without the foggiest idea of what was going on. My guidance teacher had obviously been wrong: An extra year of Latin hadn't helped at all.

The tall one looked at me and smiled. "I am afraid that we are going to blindfold you."

"Just be careful with my eyebrows," I said.

"I beg your pardon."

"Just don't tape my eyebrows and then rip them out," I said.

"Oh—you have had this done before?"

"Second time today."

She gave me a tentative smile. "I shall be careful."

She was. We drove for about twenty minutes. I had no idea where.

"I am going to carry you into a house," the tall one said. "Please do not try to struggle."

I felt pretty damned silly, wearing a blindfold, being picked up like a baby by a Chinese Amazon, and allowing myself to be carried in her arms.

A door opened. She eased me to the floor, and I was led down what seemed to be a long corridor and then into a carpeted room.

"Stand still, please," the tall one said. "I shall try to be very careful in removing the blindfold."

My eyebrows stayed in place.

"Thanks," I said. I was now a veteran at being blindfolded, and I appreciated a masterly touch.

She looked down at me. I'm six even and she looked *way* down at me.

"You seem to be an extremely nice man," she said, "and I am very sorry to do this." She smiled at me. I smiled at her. "Take off your clothes, please," she said.

The unattractive one pointed her gun at the center of my chest. Her voice was leaden. "Take clothes off."

I took off my clothes, very slowly. She made several disparaging remarks about my physical appearance. All untrue, of course.

The tall one had her back to me when she spoke again. "I am very sorry," she said. "We will question you soon." The ugly one snapped on handcuffs. They immediately left, and I was alone.

It was a large room, but with no furniture and no windows. I started to walk in large circles to relieve the tension. Usually I'm a fairly easygoing fellow: I like people, I like conversation, and I like small parties. Pretty simple. But in two days, while enjoying myself at the Plaza, and the next day accepting an invitation for cocktails, I had become involved in a murder, a spy caper, and a kidnaping. My own.

Damn. I vowed to ask my travel agent about monasteries.

The door opened and someone was pushed in. It was Alice, handcuffed and naked. The ugly one came in behind her, surveyed the two of us for a moment, and left, pulling the door shut and locking it again.

When she had gone, Alice made a good attempt at a smile. "Harry, what's going on? I mean, I like adventure, but this—My God, one minute I was shopping in Gristede's for a dozen eggs and some bacon, and the next minute I was blindfolded and in a car. We drove for hours. Where are we, Harry?"

"Someplace in Washington."

"D.C.—?"

"D.C."

"It's weird, isn't it?" I could sense the shift in Alice's mind. "You know me pretty well, Harry—but honest to God, I've never been alone in a room with a man with *both* of us handcuffed. I mean, there was that time in Switzerland with the Italian ski instructor—but that's really not the same thing."

I had to smile.

"So—what do you say—?"

"What—?"

"Shall we?"

"*Alice*—"

"What the hell, Harry." She made a funny face. "Who knows what tomorrow brings—"

"Alice—I love you, but you're crazy."

"Am I? Here we are—naked, handcuffed—I want some warmth, and you don't. Who's crazy? You or me?"

"Me," I said.

She grinned. "In the end, you were always smart, Harry." She let out a war whoop. "Hugh Hefner—here's your next editorial."

Afterwards, as we lay together, Alice said, "You know something, Harry? You're not exactly the best at anything, but you're more fun than anybody I know."

I kissed her cheek. "And with that remark I'll probably be impotent for at least six weeks."

"You know what I meant." She raised up on one elbow. "Does it bother you when I talk about other men?"

"If I say *yes*—it'll make you feel bad. And if I say *no*—it'll make you feel bad."

Alice smiled. "You know me, all right."

We lay there together for a long time without talking.

■ ■ ■

"What do you suppose they're going to do, Harry?"

"I don't know."

"Do you think it has anything to do with the Plaza? The murder?"

"Yes—Everybody seems to think that you and I know something that's important to them."

■ ■ ■

We sat quietly, the first madness of making love, the first feeling of almost collegiate gaiety now completely gone.

Within minutes, they came for us—two men in strange-looking suits.

"Here we go, Harry," Alice said. "Good luck to both of us."

CHAPTER

9

I T WAS another large room. Nobody new was there—just the men who had brought us, the driver of the car, and the two Chinese.

The ugly one spoke, and if she hadn't been so obviously Chinese, her accent would have sounded false. "As if not look foolish now, we have television tape of detention room. Would like see?"

Alice tried to smile. "Hey—there's a new kick."

The ugly one glared at Alice and made a threatening gesture.

Heroically, I didn't make a move.

The ugly one turned to me. "We want answers to questions. Any problem—torture *her*." She nodded and one of the two men who had brought us from the detention room twisted Alice's arm up behind her back. The other man half-carried her to the wall and began to strap her to it.

The ugly one spoke again. "There is old saying: 'Naked

is vulnerable.' If that is true, then 'Naked on wall is very vulnerable.'" She sounded like an evil fortune cookie.

Alice shouted. "Tell them anything, Harry. Tell them anything—just don't let them hurt me."

The ugly one tied me to the chair while the tall one strapped what I guessed were lie-detector electrodes to my wrists and ankles. They turned the chair so that I was facing away from Alice.

"Sometimes imagination makes worst torture even worse," the ugly one said.

It was the beautiful one who started the questioning. She read a list of every single one of my clients. "Do you represent these people?"

"You obviously know that I do."

"But I am asking *you*—do you?"

"Yes."

"And do they work in television and radio?"

"Yes."

"In what capacity do they work?"

"Well—on-camera mostly. News. Then I have three writers and four producers." I was beginning to relax just a bit. "I have a total of seventeen clients in all."

"And they all work for the networks?"

"All three television networks, cable news, and four radio networks."

"You represent some very powerful people."

"In a way—yes."

"Do you work for the CIA?"

"No, of course not. I just told you what I do."

"It is a very clever front which you have. But a front is only as good as its backing."

"Oh, God—you're both fortune cookies," I said.

She frowned and raised her voice. "I am sorry. You must understand that we are asking you serious questions. We expect serious answers." She glanced back at Alice.

I nodded.

Since the moment I had walked into Wendell Crittenden's suite at the Sherry-Netherland—when?—yester-day?—things had gone to hell for me.

On the whole, I would rather have been in Philadelphia, or even back in the men's room at the Plaza again. Almost anything seemed better than being tied to a chair with Alice spread-eagled on a wall.

"I'll tell you everything I know," I said.

"Good. That is good." The tall one was smiling pleasantly now. "So now—I'll ask you again: Do you work for the CIA?"

"I'll give you a straight answer," I said, knowing that she wanted me to answer affirmatively, and knowing that I was going to give her something of what she wanted. "I was in Army Intelligence for two years. That was twenty years ago. I was just contacted yesterday by a man by the name of Wendell Crittenden. I knew him in the army. He still works for some intelligence agency, but I'm not sure which one. His agency wants me for a job, but I don't know what it is. That's all I know."

Her eyes had been on the machine. She looked up and smiled again. "The truth. Good. But only my intuition tells me that you told the truth, not the machine." She gestured to the two men. "Take it away. It is useless."

"Now that you are in a more cooperative mood, so am I," the tall one said. "Let me try to get this over with as quickly as possible. Where were you taken in Washington?"

"Other than the Jefferson Hotel, I honestly don't know. I was blindfolded."

"The name of your old G.E. buddy's boss?" Her attempt to be idiomatic would have been funny in other circumstances.

"I don't know." I told her about the meeting. I eventually told her every detail I could think of. If he had witnessed my behavior, William F. Buckley would have developed a migraine headache.

She was smiling. "I thank you, sir. I thank you for telling the truth. It makes everything so much easier for all of us." Her eyes fell to my body. "If I had known that you were going to be so cooperative, none of this would have been necessary."

She rubbed her hands together. "Now—what about the day at the Plaza Hotel?"

I described it all in great detail, adding things that had never occurred, just to please her and to amuse myself.

When I finished, she asked, "And you have no idea who the man was who sat at your table?"

"No idea."

"But, my dear sir, you met him—you were introduced to him."

"I spoke to him for barely three minutes."

"Did not Alice," I saw her eyes dart up to the wall behind me, "tell you about him?"

"Only that she'd met him on vacation. She hardly knew him herself."

There was a long pause.

"I do not believe you," she finally said. Her eyes darted up to the wall again; she made a slight gesture with her right hand and, seconds later, I heard Alice scream.

"But I'm telling you the truth—everything I know."

Behind me Alice was groaning.

"What was in the envelope he gave you? I want to know."

"Nothing. Some French francs. That's all."

"And where is it now?"

"It disappeared. Somebody took it from me."

"Who?"

"I don't know."

"How?"

"He just grabbed me—a big guy—can't you cut her down?"

"No—"

"Cut her down—"

"Answer my question, and you can cut her down yourself."

"I've answered everything."

"I mean answer with the truth."

"I *have* answered with the truth."

She didn't speak for a moment—then, "Did you meet a man in the hotel who resembled the American broadcast journalist Howard Cosell?"

"Yes."

"Did you become friendly with that man?"

"Not really."

"I want the truth."

"That is the truth. I talked with him for maybe two minutes at the table and at the bar."

"You never saw him again?"

"Never."

"You are sure?"

"Yes."

"He gave you no message?"

"Nothing."

She raised her right hand slightly again, and again Alice screamed. "But he *did* give you something, did he not?"

"The *Frenchman* gave me something. Money."

"You are sure—?"

"I'm sure."

The tall one paused and took a deep breath. "Once again—I would like to have answers to the following questions: How well do you know the man who looks like Howard Cosell, how well did you know the dead Frenchman—*and* what message the Frenchman passed to you, and to whom did you give it when you found him dying?"

She glanced at her watch. "I shall give you ten seconds." She smiled. "No, that is too trite. I shall give you fifteen seconds."

I started to repeat everything I had told her. She interrupted. "Are you going to answer my questions?"

"I'm trying to—"

"Very well. I shall accept that as your negative response." She turned toward the wall behind me and raised her hand for a third time.

I heard Alice shout, *"Please, Harry—"* Then her screams and more screams and more screams.

■ ■ ■

Afterwards they let me cut her down. She was conscious and almost catatonic with hysteria. There was blood all over her body. I had nothing to wipe it with, so I tried to use my hands. They stopped me and took her away.

In her office, the tall Chinese was sitting behind her desk. "Would you like to have your clothes to put on?"

"Where is she?"

"She will be fine. And you are a very lucky man. There has been a change in plans."

I didn't answer.

She smiled. "You will be allowed to dress, and we will return you to the area near your hotel."

"What about her?"

"She will be well. Just consider yourself very fortunate that we are not tying *you* to that wall as we had planned."

CHAPTER

10

THE CAR was still moving, going up Connecticut Avenue, when they took off the blindfold.

The tall one finally spoke to me. "It would be wise for you to remember that—although there has been an orderly change of plans—we have not lessened our interest in you." She smiled in such an innocent way. "And you should keep in mind that we always have the body of your dead friend—" again the smile—"*on ice*. If he were to be found in your apartment, you would be in a great deal of trouble."

No one spoke again until the driver pulled up to the curb a block away from the Jefferson Hotel.

"Until we meet again," the tall one said. She actually pursed her lips and blew me a kiss.

Back in my room, I had just fallen into bed and pulled up the blankets when I heard a key in the door.

It was Wendell Crittenden. "Rise and shine, my good man. What are you doing in bed? It's five-fifteen in the afternoon. We'll be late for our meeting with M." He glanced into the mirror and began to comb his hair. "Where'd you have lunch? Oh—I should have made a suggestion. Sorry."

"I didn't have lunch."

"Not feeling well?" He didn't wait for an answer. He pointed his comb at me. "Hey, you'd better get the lead out. We can't keep the Old Man waiting. He even offered drinks, which isn't his usual invitation."

I told Wendell the whole story, starting from the moment the tall Chinese poked a gun into my ribs to the moment she blew me a kiss good-bye.

Wendell only interrupted once—when I got to the torturing of Alice. "Are you okay? Should I call our doctor?"

"I'm fine."

"Let me call M and tell him we'll be a bit late. Go on—"

I finished the story.

Wendell smiled. "So you'd just gotten under the covers when I walked in." He chuckled. "You need a drink and a good night's sleep."

"Yeah—but I'm more worried about Alice than myself."

On cue, the phone rang. It was Alice. "They said I could call you, Harry."

"Those bastards—"

"They're all listening, Harry."

Wonderful, I thought. I'm acting the role of macho hero, hurling long-distance insults, while Alice has to take the consequences.

"Sorry," I said. "How are you feeling? Really?"

She tried to laugh. "I wouldn't want to run into that sculptor from Stockholm just now, but—I'll be okay."

Crittenden was mouthing the word "Alice?" to me. I nodded yes. "Keep the conversation going," he murmured. He ran out of the room.

"You're brave," I said to Alice.

"Not really. It's just the shock—my body feels fine. I've had a shower, and now they're giving me food, and pretty soon they say I'll be on a plane for New York. I don't understand it."

"Alice, is there any way for me to speak to—"

Someone had hung up the phone.

Crittenden returned. "You sure as hell didn't keep her talking very long."

"I did the best I could," I said.

"Well your best wasn't very good."

"They hung up on me."

"Goddamnit. I was hoping to get a trace on the call." Crittenden sat down and eyed me. "You gonna be okay to come out to Georgetown?" He really didn't care about the answer; he was just saying, "Let's get a move on."

■   ■   ■

In the car I said, "You know something, Wendell? I'm getting worried about myself."

Wendell was adjusting my blindfold and didn't answer for a moment or two. "About what, Harry?"

"These blindfolds. I'd never been blindfolded in my life until this morning. Now I've had it done so many times that I'm worried that maybe I'll start to like it."

No reaction from Wendell. So I didn't try conversation again until we pulled into the yard at Georgetown head-quarters.

By now, I was expert at walking while blindfolded. Step high. Always. Then you'll never trip. I stepped high, smiled with satisfaction, continued stepping high—and ran into the edge of the door someone had opened for me.

"Sorry," Wendell said. "I should have warned you."

"That's okay, Wendell. But just don't let the young zealot who ripped off the tape this morning try it again."

"I'll do it myself," Wendell said.

"On second thought—"

"Now, now—" Wendell was *very* careful.

This time, the uniformed Marine came to *present arms* with his rifle as I passed him.

"What was that for?" I asked Wendell.

"He probably thinks you're somebody important."
Wendell chuckled. "And, actually, you *are*, Harry."

M was wearing the same double-breasted gray suit. I
had the feeling that he probably owned several, all exactly alike, which he wore like a uniform.

"Well, well—" His voice was friendly, almost jovial.
"From my conversation with Crittenden, I gather that
you could use a drink. What would you like—scotch, a
martini—I have Irish whiskey, very good—Bloody
Mary—I'm going to have a glass of sherry myself." He
gestured toward a white-jacketed steward who stood behind a portable bar.

Wendell toadied for a sherry with his boss. I asked for
a beer, and when I saw M's expression, changed my mind
and asked for a sherry. M smiled at that.

We finished our drinks in a kind of men's club corner
of the office over polite conversation and some very mea-
ger canapes, and M asked me if I'd like another drink. I
wanted one, but I said no.

M made a circular motion with his left index finger and
ordered another round anyway.

We talked baseball—it seemed that M most admired
Ted Williams and Willie Mays—until the second round
arrived, and business began.

M hunched forward in his leather chair, holding his
drink with both hands. "Tell me about it," he said, "from
the very beginning to the very end."

I did the best I could. I'd just finished doing the same
thing with Wendell, so by now I was beginning to feel like
a stand-up comedian doing his fifth show of the night.

I got down to the part about the dead Frenchman's
body and M said, "You mean that they indicated that they
actually have the body on *ice*?"

"I don't know that she meant that literally. She has a
good command of the language, but sometimes she gets
tripped up by idioms. And by the way, I thought *you* had
the body."

M's brow was furrowed. "No—no, we don't," he said.

"Crittenden—make a note." He turned to me again. "Go on."

I ended the story for M the same way as I had for Wendell. Only this time I had the tall Chinese blowing me two kisses. It seemed a bit snappier that way.

M sat back in his leather chair, still sipping his drink. "I would rather imagine that by now you appreciate that we are dealing with something very serious," he said.

I put my drink down on the coffee table. "*You* are," I said. "Not *we*."

"Oh, come now, surely you must realize that someone involved you in *something* long before we arrived on the scene."

"I hadn't really thought about it."

He gave me his spurious smile. "Well, think about it then."

I did. M was right. The Cosell-Clone, the bomb, Alice's ransacked apartment—all before Crittenden had contacted me.

"But when Wendell set me up at the Sherry-Netherland Hotel, he knew about almost everything."

"Of course he did," M said. "We'd had you under surveillance for several weeks. You were our hand-picked man for the job we're asking you to do." M leaned forward again. "And we are *asking* you, Mr. Baker. If you accept—we'll find out who these people are, what they want of you—and we'll protect you." M smiled again, a genuine smile. "Frankly, we would do that anyway, whether you accept or not. But we are *asking* you to accept."

He got up and strode about the room with great nervous energy. "Yes—we are asking you to help your country. Perhaps that's now passé—I'd like to think not—I hope that you feel as I do. Because—" he melodramatically gripped my shoulder—"believe me when I tell you, Mr. Baker, you are the only man for the job."

"And what if I don't accept?" I asked.

"Please—"

I heard myself sigh. "Well, at least tell me what the job's about," I said.

"We can't do that, especially before we know if you're going to come in on the show or not. You were in G-2 yourself once. You should know that."

"I was only a—aw, to hell with it—yeah, I was in G-2." I looked at my shoes for a bit, and then up into M's eyes. "What happened this afternoon was no fun. Is it dangerous?"

"All operations have a modicum of danger involved."

"Yeah, but does this one have just a bit more than a modicum?"

"I shouldn't think so—"

"But you don't know."

M shook his head. "One never *knows* anything."

Crittenden stood up suddenly and quickly moved to a position in front of me. "For God's sake, Harry. What the hell is the matter with you? We didn't know each other very well back at Jefferson Hall Station—but I thought I knew one thing about you then—I thought you were an *American*—"

"Hey, Wendell," I said, "please don't start—"

"Don't start sounding simpleminded? To you, maybe. To you—*now*. For Christ's sake, Harry, has all this—" he drooled out the words—"*charming, sophisticated, distingué* New York life changed you that much? I said the word *American* a moment ago and you almost cringed—"

"That's about enough, Wendell—"

He glared at me for another moment. "We're *asking* you, Harry. We're asking you to take on this one job—a couple of weeks—no guns, no knives, no *plastique*. Just a simple operation. We're asking you because we need you. It's that simple. We need you. No one else—*no one else*— can do it." Wendell went back to his chair and sat down. "Please?"

They were both staring at me now, their eyes imploring.

"May I have some coffee?" I finally said.

"Of course." M snapped his fingers. The steward moved quickly.

They waited with impatient patience until I'd had a sip of coffee.

"How much time do you think my part of the operation would take?" I finally asked.

M smiled and I could hear Wendell exhaling. "About two weeks," M said. "Perhaps a few days longer, perhaps a few days shorter—but two weeks is a fairly good approximation."

"Where would I be sent?"

M waggled his lips and made his mustache do a little dance. "You haven't told us yes, yet. But I suppose I can tell you this—it won't be behind the Iron Curtain, and it won't be Southeast Asia."

Something told me that if Jane had been there, she would have slapped my wrist as I said it, but I said it anyway. "Okay, I'll have a shot at it," I said.

"Splendid." M pounded me on the shoulder.

"And Wendell," I pointed my finger at Crittenden, "I didn't like that remark about my feelings for my country—"

"I was desperate, Harry."

"Just the same—"

"Harry, I didn't mean it. Really. I was just trying to goad you." He laughed. "And it worked. You gotta admit it, Harry. It worked."

"Splendid, splendid—" M was pacing the room. "Go into the bathroom, please"—he motioned me toward a door—"and turn on the shower."

"With my clothes on?"

M sighed. "Please, Mr. Baker. . . ." He followed me in, turned on the shower himself, wetting the cuff of his shirt. As he tried to dry it with a towel, he eyed me as if it had all been my fault.

When he spoke again, it was in a whisper. "This is all a very hush-hush business—"

I said, "I can't hear you."

He sighed a second time. "This—is—all—very—hush—hush," he articulated, some suppressed asperity in his voice.

"Ah—"

"Now that you're aboard, you should know this. So far, 1983 has been an extraordinarily good year for us. We're in contact with *The Office*. The one shaped like this." He did his best to form an oval with his hands.

"You mean you're speaking directly with *Him*?" The wonder in my voice instantly deified the President.

"Shhh. With someone who has direct daily contact with—*The Office*."

"Then you're under orders from the—" I corrected myself—"from the—ah—Office itself."

"Exactly." M's smile was slight, but proud.

He clapped me firmly on the back and his voice was encouraging and hearty. "So there we *are*—"

As we came back into the office proper, M was brisk and ebullient all over again. "Another sherry all 'round, Caldwell."

"No—" I stood.

"You mustn't change your mind. You simply mustn't."

"I'm not going to. But if I'm going to do a job for you," I said, "at least I ought to be able to have a glass of beer."

M's shoulders relaxed. "Why, of course. You should have said so in the first place. What would you like? Heineken's, Beck's, Molson, Rolling Rock—I believe I stock just about everything."

I picked Rolling Rock. "You surprise me," I told him. "Most people have never heard of Rolling Rock."

M smiled. "I suppose that that's my job actually—to hear of things." He raised his glass of sherry in a toast: "To constant surprise. And to knowing—*almost* everything."

Crittenden and M chuckled.

I chuckled along with them, just to be a good sport.

CHAPTER

11

I WAS TO go to London. And stay at Claridge's. Not bad. It sure as hell beat Bulgaria, Bangladesh, or Buffalo, New York.

"You'll find, when you get there, that it's the loveliest of hotels," M was saying. "Some prefer the Connaught, or even, I suppose, the Savoy, but I'll always pick Claridge's every time."

"Spencer Tracy used to say, 'When I die, don't send me to heaven—send me to Claridge's.'"

"He did?" M smiled. "Oh, that's a good one."

"I've never stayed there."

M was plainly pleased. "You're going to like it very much. You must call me straightaway and let me know what you think of it."

"Now there's a problem," I said.

"What is?"

I was relieved that it had finally come out. "I don't know what to call you."

"Um? Oh. Just call me—M." He chuckled, trying to throw it away. "Of course, my official designation is *X*."

I almost gagged, stifling a hoot of laughter.

"But call me M. It's a little affectation the boys have. But I let them have their fun." He leaned forward with forced intimacy. "It's good for morale, you know."

"And good morale is very important," Wendell said, "especially in a business like ours."

"Besides," M sighed, "*X* is such a silly sounding appellation, isn't it?" He leaned back and took a puff of his cigar. I could sense that I was finally going to be let in on something.

"There are several reasons for our need of you, Mr. Baker. Not the least of which is your reputation in New York as a representative of some of the country's—the world's—best-known broadcast journalists. So part of your role in this operation will be public, very public indeed. However, a very small, but extremely important portion will be clandestine.

"We're through being coy with you. So please don't think that when I say that we can't tell you the whole operation at once—its grand design, its goals—that we are playing games with you. It's just that the integrity of this operation, and your own safety, depends greatly upon your not *knowing* the big picture. In that way, you'll be able to say, just as you did this morning, that you know nothing."

M was pacing briskly again. "The first phase of the *public* portion of your part in the operation—and by the way, the operation has been titled Morris—"

"Morris—?"

"After the William Morris theatrical agency. It seems to fit right in, doesn't it?"

"Yes—yes, it does."

"Good." M resumed his pacing. "As I was saying, your first *public* act in *Operation Morris*—and we want to make it as public as possible—do you know a good press agent?"

"Quite a few."

"Get one of the best and have your activities well cov-

ered as you return to New York. Spend four or five days
doing your job—quite ostentatiously—calling on clients,
having lunches, meetings—ending with a large cocktail
party, where you'll announce that you are off to London
for just a bit of business—and a lovely holiday."

"Where are you from?" I asked him abruptly. "Origi-
nally?"

"Indiana. Greencastle, actually. Why?"

"I just wondered."

M frowned. "You *are* listening, aren't you?"

"Of course—"

Incidentally, all expenses will be borne by our agency,
naturally. And you'll receive your pay at a G-18 level. Is
that satisfactory?"

I had no idea what a G-18 level was. "Fine," I said.

"Good. Important: All bookings, such as Claridge's, air-
lines, et cetera, will be made by your office. We want to
stay entirely out of it. Will that be a problem? Will you
need an advance?"

"I'll be fine."

"Excellent. So—back to New York you go, plunge into
work, and let the world know about it. The big cocktail
party, your holiday announcement, and off to London."

"I've got it."

"And once again, it's *Operation Morris*. The passwords
are these: You say *William Morris;* I say *ten percent.*

I swallowed my laughter and choked.

"You okay?" Wendell asked.

"I'm speechless," I told him.

"What d'you mean?"

"I mean—you're kidding."

"About what?" Wendell asked.

"Yes, about what?" M asked tartly.

"I say *William Morris,* and you say *ten percent.*"

"Yes—or it could be the other way around."

"It could what?"

"You—or I—could say *ten percent* first. In that case, the
other person would say *William Morris.*"

I couldn't help myself. I started to laugh, knowing that
I was deeply hurting two people's feelings.

"I *must* say that I am *just* a bit annoyed," M said.

"Hey, Harry—" Wendell was motioning to me from behind M's back.

I tried to regain my composure and, thinking of Alice, attempted to segue from laughter into tears. Alas, I don't have that rare talent, but I did my best to assuage M's damaged feelings.

"I'm sorry," I moaned, muffling my voice with my hands, and doing my damnedest to imitate a teary voice. "I've been through a lot today."

M seemed instantly pleased. "Of course you have. And on top of that—no sleep. Don't be ashamed, Mr. Baker. We're used to this sort of thing."

Once recovered, I asked him about Alice, feeling pretty damned guilty that I hadn't talked about her before.

"We'll do our best," M said. "And our best is pretty bloody good."

"She's a good friend of mine—"

"A friend of yours—is a friend of ours," said M with the air of someone who had just gotten one off that equaled Oscar Wilde.

"Do you want to tell him about his contact in London?" Wendell asked.

M sized me up. "Not this evening." He addressed me: "You're exhausted. Go back to your hotel—I suggest room service for dinner—and get some sleep. And tomorrow morning, on your own, take the nine o'clock express Metroliner back to New York. Better make your reservation this evening. You'll be under surveillance, but it will be friendly."

"By the way, just out of interest, why always the Metroliner?"

M paused. "It's Petersen—"

"Petersen?"

"Yes, he's one of those who'll have you under surveillance."

"Yes, but—"

"Petersen is afraid of flying."

"Oh—"

"But a fine man."

"I'm sure," I said.

"Now," M rubbed his hands briskly together as if to restore his energy and rid his thoughts of Petersen, "it's back to the hotel for you, a good meal, a good night's sleep, and tomorrow New York. And remember—"

"—A press agent, ostentatious at my work, a big cocktail party, and off to London."

"Perfect." M beamed. "Crittenden was right—you *are* just perfect for this operation."

"See, Harry," Wendell said. "I *did* put in a good word for you."

"Thanks, Wendell—"

CHAPTER
12

MONDAY morning in New York. I had never loved the city more. The train ride had been delightful, the coffee fine, the breakfast delicious, the scenery brilliantly autumnal, my fellow passengers bonnie—and I was even met at Penn Station by a smiling Jane.

"Hey, boss, it's good to see you." She stuck out her hand. We shook and pretended to arm-wrestle, a gag we'd had for months, which pleased only us and seemed to annoy everyone else.

"I thought I told you on the phone last night not to meet me."

She grinned. "And I thought I told you on the phone last night that I was going to meet you anyway." She slapped me on the backside.

"Hey, I'm not just a sex object."

"You are to me, boss."

"Thanks."

We went up the escalator to find a taxi.

■   ■   ■

At the office, Susan was wearing tight gray slacks with a blouse that was unbuttoned nearly to the waist.

She greeted me with, "Welcome back, Mr. Baker, from wherever you were."

"Top secret," I said, laughing, and then realized that it really was.

"Beautiful morning, isn't it?"

"Beautiful. What's coming up today?" I asked, indicating the blouse. "An audition for *Oh! Calcutta!*?"

"Just a commercial. I'm going over to Petrak, Miller and Bedloes. You know what the guys are like over there."

"How we men are manipulated."

Susan grinned. "It's at three o'clock. Okay?"

"Sure, but you should be going up for a play, not a commercial."

"I know. Can't you do something? Here I am in the same office with one of the greatest agents in New York, sharing my secrets, baring myself—"

"Almost literally—"

"Almost literally—and he does nothing to further my career."

She was really serious, so I was too. "I wish I could, but I'm only in news. What about that luncheon I got you with Billy Friday?"

"He's *sent* me out exactly once and *asked* me out a dozen times. He says he's got to get to know me intimately before he can really do anything for me."

"I thought Billy would sound brighter than that."

"Is he a friend of yours?"

"No—"

"Good. Because he's a schmuck," Susan said.

"Noel Coward, *Private Lives*. Act Two—"

"Right—"

I poured myself coffee. "Give me half an hour to get myself straightened out, and then remind me to call Ed

Robbins over at William Morris—he's one of the best—
and a gentleman."

Susan blew me a soft, southern kiss, and then threw in
a bump and a grind. There are many things about my job
that are rewarding.

Jane was waiting in the office. "Are you sure you're all
right?"

"I'm fine."

"You sounded so strange on the phone yesterday."

"I was tense. It's something—that I really can't talk
about."

"Not even to me, old Aunt Jane?"

"Not even to you."

"Okay." She opened her notebook and started our
morning routine. "Let's get you started on your appointed rounds."

"Only what I absolutely must do today. I'll make my
appointed rounds tomorrow. How are the Big Three?"

"Dan, Morley, and Mike are fine. Paul Blanfield is back
with his wife, so *The Dean of American Morning News* just
needs a quick call of congratulations."

"Fine. Remind me right after we finish this."

Jane went through the rest of the clients, ending with
"—and you've got to call Jessica Rumbough—she's half
hysterical on the phone *every fifteen minutes*. She can't believe that she's out."

"If she calls again, tell her I'd like to take her to lunch
tomorrow. I'll have to tell her all over again."

"And another thing I don't know," Jane said. What
happened with Reed, Selby, Ash and Crittenden? Did
they make an offer that you and Tom Haskins can't re-
fuse?"

"Not really." I paused. "It was just an old army buddy.
His idea of a joke."

"Some joke."

"Yeah—"

"Is that how you ended up in Washington?"

"Sort of—"

"I'll bet there's a woman involved. Cherchez la femme,
I always say." Jane started to rub the back of my neck.

"But you'll never find anyone who can give back rubs the way I do."

"True—"

She kneaded away for a good minute before she broke the news. "I got one of those phone calls from the ex-Mrs. Baker yesterday."

"God, what's wrong now?"

"Late check again. By one day."

"Did you tell her to call Sid?"

"I suggested—"

"I should have known the minute I brought her home and introduced her to my family—and my mother said, 'Griselda?'" Jane chuckled. "I should have known then," I said. "Now I'm going to relish London."

"London—?"

"I'll be leaving in a week. Just decided yesterday. A little vacation."

Jane was pleased. "Just what you've needed for a long time."

I stood up. "Thanks. I'm ready for the world again. Who's the best public relations person we know? I need some first-rate personal PR for a week."

"That doesn't sound like you," Jane said. "And anyway, you don't need it."

"I do for a week. I can't explain, but there's a good reason."

"There you go again."

"I'll explain later."

"You're beginning to sound more and more like some character in an Evelyn Waugh novel," Jane said.

"I'll accept that as a compliment."

"One of his *lesser* characters." Jane gave me her cutest smile and crossed her eyes.

"Some day they're going to stick."

"Never. What about Hal Goodman or Mabel Hann?"

"Perfect. Give them a call and tell them I need a favor—but not a freebie."

"Right away. In the meantime, start making your calls, starting with Jessica Rumbough and *The Dean*."

"I'll call Paul and everybody else," I said. "But you call Jessica."

"What a way to start the day—calling Jessica Rumbough." Jane crossed her eyes again as she left the office.

It took about an hour to make my calls—one of them was to Phil Persky at ABC who said simply, "Let's get together on Tom Haskins this week."

"Okay, Phil," I said. "I've talked to everyone now. "Let's meet with our cards on the table."

"Good. How about lunch on Thursday? I'll make the reservation. Let's settle. Okay, Harry?"

"If you're ready to make a deal, Phil."

"I am. See you Thursday."

That sort of talk makes an agent smile. I almost forgot about Washington, and Wendell, and M.

Jane came into the office, and I told her about the Persky call. "The world is your oyster today," Jane said. "I just spoke to Hal Goodman and Mabel Hann. They both volunteered to pitch in. And they'll split the fee."

"But they're competitors."

"You can't help it if you're loved, Harry. They even offered a late lunch at Gallagher's, and you can let them know what you need."

"Tell them, thanks, and I'll meet them for coffee and dessert."

"And, Harry—"

"Oh-oh—"

"Yup. I talked to Jessica Rumbough. She's *demanding*— she used the word nine times—demanding to have dinner with you *tonight*. She can't wait till tomorrow. So I made an eight o'clock reservation at La Fenice."

"Hey, thanks."

"You can always cancel," Jane said.

"No, you're right—let's get it over with. Anything else?"

"Isn't that enough?"

"Yeah—that's enough. I'm off to Gallagher's then. Call them—tell them I'm on my way—and I'll be stopping by NBC on the way back—Catherine Ross."

On my way out, Susan yelled, "Hey, you were going to call William Morris for me."

"Later—"

"Did Helen Hayes have to go through this?"

"Worse. She did it the hard way. Talent."

"Harry—"

I'd hurt her feelings, and I hadn't meant to. I went back and squeezed her hands. "I didn't mean that *you* don't. You know how talented I think you are."

"Really?" Her eyes looked uncertain.

"Give me the goddamned phone. I'm gonna call William Morris."

"Aw—"

CHAPTER
13

GALLAGHER'S Restaurant is on the south side of Fifty-Second Street, right off Broadway. It has a great bar, magnificent steaks, and the best corned beef and cabbage in the world.

Hal Goodman and Mabel Hann were sitting at one of the tables to the right of the entrance, finishing off some of that corned beef and cabbage.

Hal always looks as if he eats three portions at every meal—which he usually does. Mabel, on the other hand, weighs about a hundred and ten stark naked, which, I always get the feeling, she has never been in her life.

"What're ya gonna have?" Hal asked before I even sat down.

"The corned beef and cabbage is terrific again today," Mabel said.

"Just coffee."

"Coffee—that's all?" Hal was aghast.

"Make it an Irish coffee and I'll have one with you," Mabel said.

The waiter came by. "Two Irish coffees," Mabel told him.

"—And I'll have some apple pie with ice cream," Hal said.

We talked about my PR needs for the next few days. Big. Splashy. Liz Smith in the *Daily News*, Page Six in the *Post*, any place in *The Times*—plugs on local radio and television—all aimed toward the big party on the coming Monday.

"It doesn't sound like you, Harry," Mabel said at one point.

"It sure as hell don't." Hal shook his head.

"That's the second time someone has said that to me today."

Hal chewed fast on his last forkful of apple pie. "Well, it's true."

"Harry, just one question." Mabel had a funny smile on her face. "Why?"

"I have a very good reason."

"Ah, *that* explains it," Mabel said. "Now I understand. At first I didn't, but *now* I do, now that you've explained it all so well."

"Where do I have the party on Monday?" I asked.

"The Friars Club," Mabel said. Hal nodded in agreement. "I'll set it up—Hal's got his hands full with the new Reynolds play that opens next week."

"I should've done this before." I shook Mabel's hand and then Hal's. "Thanks to both of you for helping me out. Even though you both think I'm crazy. And especially since you're in competition with each other."

"Any time," Hal said. "Our pleasure."

"And the competition isn't that keen," Mabel said. "We've been sleeping together pretty regularly for the past year."

She could have told me that they were doing anything else in the world together, and I wouldn't have been more surprised. "Oh—" I said, with amazing panache.

We had another cup of Irish coffee. I thanked both of them again, this time looking at them quite differently, and I left Gallagher's for NBC with the feeling that my public relations blitz was in good and affectionate hands.

■   ■   ■

Catherine Ross is the only person I allow to call me Baker. Catherine is a southerner, and it always seems appropriate when she addresses me by my last name.

She only does it when she is upset or angry, and now she was both. "I tell you, Baker, I've worked for this news organization for twenty-five years, and there isn't a finer one in the world, and I know that someone has got to do this job, and I appreciate that fact—" (Catherine is one of the finest writers I know, and a grammarian; and when she begins to speak in anything but incisive, declarative sentences, you know that she is really upset) "—we all do, in this business. One does many things that one does not especially like, but goddamnit" (and Catherine seldom swears) "why is this the fourth blasted *feminist* (she sandpapered the word with her voice) "documentary that I've had to write within the past five years? Why? Because I'm a woman? You've got to talk to Ned, Baker. I've talked until I'm blue in the face, and all I get from him is, 'Now, Catherine.' Will you talk to him, Baker?"

I did. Immediately. It always makes me proud when I say that I represent Catherine Ross, even in arguments. All I got from Ned was, "Now, Harry." But at least he agreed to think it over *seriously*. I told Catherine, but it didn't help much.

"How about a drink at around six?"

"No thanks," Catherine said.

"Come on—"

Catherine hesitated. "No—I've still got to find a piece of film for some cutaways on a Friedan speech."

"You've got a raincheck then."

"And I'll take it." Catherine's frown turned to a smile, her first. "Thanks for dropping by, Harry."

"It's my pleasure." And I meant it from the heart; I've got some of the best clients.

■　　■　　■

I had extra time so I doubled back to the office. Susan greeted me with a big smile. "I've got an appointment with Ed Robbins over at William Morris—for which I thank you—and you just walked in in time to take a phone call. It's a Mr. Crittenden."

Wendell's voice sounded studied, and his laughter was stilted. "In case we're being taped, Harry, let's keep this light." I got the message.

"I'm not taping, Wendell."

"Nor am I—" And I knew right away that he was.

"How's your public relations campaign coming along?"

"Just fine. As a matter of fact, I just came from a luncheon meeting, and I think we're on our way."

"We haven't seen a thing."

"My God, Wendell, give me a couple of days. You ought to be seeing something by Thursday."

"Not until then?"

"I've got two of the best outfits in New York. Don't worry."

Wendell gave his very bad impression of a hearty laugh. "I'm not worried, Harry. Just wanted to say hello."

"Then, hello—"

"What?"

"It's good to talk to you, Wendell," I said.

"Oh, same here. By the way, I plan to be up to see you off to London."

"That's nice."

"And—*my boss* will be up too."

"Oh, good."

"You don't seem pleased."

"Oh, I am, Wendell. I really am. That's very nice of—your boss."

"Yes, that was my reaction, too. Very considerate of him. Well, let's keep in touch. And, as the saying goes in your business—" Wendell chuckled—"don't call us, we'll call you. Good-bye, Harry."

"Good-bye, Wendell." I put down the phone and examined the back of my hand for several seconds. It's always strangely depressing to talk on the phone with someone like Wendell Crittenden.

The next hour or so was a pleasant one, however. My oldest client, a writer, dropped by. His visits were always accompanied by wonderful stories, and he had the rare technique of a true raconteur when it came to telling them.

It was nearly seven o'clock by the time he left, and I was in a good mood again. Susan came into my office pretending to be petulant: "We haven't had a bomb drill today—"

"*Bomb*—" I shouted.

Susan and I fell to the floor, wrapped in each other's arms.

"Wait for me—" Jane came hurtling through the door and fell on the top of the two of us. At the end of a long day, it's good therapy, and we laughed—therapeutically.

Jane began rubbing the back of my neck. "Keep laughing a little longer, Harry, while I remind you of your dinner engagement tonight. Remember?"

"*Hell*—"

"I had the feeling you'd forgotten."

"Do I have to?"

"You answer that," Jane said.

"Yes, I have to," was my answer.

"Then you have half an hour before your rendezvous with the lovely Jessica Rumbough."

Both Susan and Jane thrust out their hands and tried to be solemn.

"Good luck tonight with Jessica," Jane said.

"Our thoughts will be with you, Skipper," Susan said.

"Just in case," I told them, "I'm going to take along my cyanide pellet."

CHAPTER
14

Dr. JOEL HIGGINS, the philosopher, once told me that the only three places in the world where he felt completely civilized were the British Museum, anywhere in Paris, and the Ristorante La Fenice.

I agree with a passion.

La Fenice is my favorite restaurant in all of New York, and, until now, the thought of going there for dinner had always made me smile, and I would usually break into a whistle.

Not so this time. Forget the whistle, I told myself. Just go in, get it over with as quickly as possible, and get out.

It was seven forty-five. Tony Buonsante and Pino Castriota, the two proprietors, greeted me, thrust a kir into my hand, and gestured in the direction of my favorite table.

"Thanks, but I'll wait at the bar," I told them.

Pino poured himself a glass of San Pellegrino and sat

with me, while Tony supervised solo. We talked about golf, his good game and my bad.

After some twenty minutes, I glanced at my watch and ordered another kir.

Pino smiled. "She must be very beautiful for you to wait so long. It's not like you."

I smiled, too. "No, she's not beautiful. Inside, anyway. It's one of my clients. Jessica Rumbough."

"Oh—" Pino's face told me what he thought of Jessica. "Excuse me—" He moved to the other end of the bar to answer the phone. "*Buona sera. La Fenice. —*Oh, hello, *Professore.*"

She arrived at eight-forty, and I was glad that my friend, Dr. Higgins, who loves the civilizing atmosphere of La Fenice, wasn't present. "You didn't even notice, did you? That fucking cloakroom attendant gave me a hard time," were her first delicate words.

"I'll take care of her," I said. In my mind I was planning an apology and a big tip.

"Good. And I need a fucking drink. I'm horny today and it always calms me down." I've always had the feeling that Jessica had formed her impression of how men spoke from reading rubbings of truck-stop washroom walls.

"We're a bit late," I said. "Let's go to our table first."

"I got here *early* for me," Jessica said defiantly and without much logic.

"Fine. But let's sit down—"

She caught up with me at the table and hissed, "Some day I'm going to break your balls for things like this, Harry."

Tony took our cocktail order—nothing for me at the moment, and a vodka on the rocks for Jessica. We didn't speak until her drink arrived.

Jessica raised her glass. "This'll put hair on your chest," she said.

Yes, I thought, La Fenice is *usually* one of the most civilized places on earth.

I'd had only a few sips of my drink when Jessica said,

"I'd like another. And tell the son-of-a-bitch to put some vodka in it this time."

We pretended to make conversation until her second drink arrived. After she had quickly swallowed about a third of it, she said, "I don't need you, Harry. Not at all. I hope you know that."

"Of course—"

"I mean, I *don't fucking* need you—"

"Fine. You've made your point very nicely."

"I just wanted to establish that," she said.

"Nobody needs anybody, Jessica. But sometimes when we work together, we help each other."

She scrutinized me for a second. "What the hell is that—Commie talk?"

"I'm an Independent," I said.

"*Jokes.* My God, what a jerk you are, Harry. Do you know that? That's why I *don't fucking* need you."

"I got it the first time, Jessica. You don't need me. Fine."

Pino and Tony had inconspicuously moved closer to our table, and several diners around us had turned to look. Jessica had been recognized. And heard.

"Let's keep it down," I said. "I wouldn't want to be asked to leave. I like this place too much."

She lowered her voice to a venomous snarl. "Oh, excuse me, Mr.-fucking-joker."

"Jessica—" I wasn't angry, just annoyed and bored with her dullness, but I feigned anger. "Lower your voice and stop calling me names. Now, what do you want to talk about?"

"Me—I wanna talk about me."

"Really? That surprises me."

"And you—"

"I'm listening." I tried a medium smile.

"I want to keep you as my agent."

"I'm sorry, Jessica. But it just hasn't worked out. And, as you said, you don't need me."

"I've got a contract."

"No, not with me."

"I *know* I signed a contract."

"Impossible. None of my clients has a contract. It makes life easier—for everyone."

"Are you trying to screw me?"

"Not at all. We've been together for just over a year. You told me you're unhappy. Well, I'm unhappy, too."

"What have you got to be unhappy about with me?"

I paused—no, I wouldn't tell her.

"You've collected your ten percent every week, I noticed that."

"And now I won't. You'll be happier and so will I." (I was now taking the High Road, feeling very virtuous and good about myself.) "I think you ought to talk to someone over at Harding Associates. Maybe Jerry Benson." (Jerry Benson is one of the few people I dislike.) "You two would probably hit it off right away." (My brain was giddy from the rarefied atmosphere of the High Road. I tried for even higher.) "In fact, to tell you the truth— you're right. You don't need me. I think Jerry is your man."

She looked at me. "You mean you're gonna dump me?"

"I wouldn't put it like that."

"Yeah? How the fuck *would* you put it?"

I sighed. "Look, Jessica—" I tried to hold her hand in an avuncular way—"you've got a lot of talent—you're attractive—"

She snatched her hand away. "Don't try to make a pass at *me*, Harry."

"Jessica, I'm just trying to tell you—"

"And not only do I not need you as an agent, I don't *want* you as an agent."

"Good," I said.

"Good? I'm the one who says good, you bastard."

"Jessica—"

"You son-of-a-bitch."

"Jessica—"

"You no good, dirty, goddamned, lousy—"

It went on for another forty-five seconds or so before my exasperation welled over. A man can take the High Road for just so long.

"Jessica," I said, "to borrow from your charming way with the English language—fuck off."

She recoiled. "What did you say?"

"I'm sure you heard me."

"Yes, I heard you." Jessica is one of those people who is never happier than when she feels that she is justified in filling herself with righteous indignation. "I heard what you said—and—I'm shocked." Her voice rose. "Do you hear me—I'm *shocked.*"

She rose quickly and faced me across the table, a stern expression of horror on her face. Jessica's voice has always been just a bit too loud, but it now rose to a volume that would have filled an amphitheatre, much less La Fenice. Everyone was looking at us.

"All you men want to do," she bellowed, "is fuck, fuck *FUCK.*"

She turned dramatically and strode to the door, all eyes on her. (At least, all those that weren't on me.) At the door she turned and looked back. Then it came. The coup de grace.

She gazed at me for just the right amount of time, and then, with all the precision of a great actress, she shouted for all to hear: "And *you,* Harry—*you're not even GOOD at it.*"

Only then did she make her exit.

It took what seemed to be about two decades from that moment until any kind of conversational hum returned to the restaurant. I spent the time staring at my glass.

A hand appeared within the periphery of my vision. The hand held a check marked Paid.

It was Pino. *"Coraggio, signore,"* he murmured. *"Coraggio."*

Farewell, Jessica. Farewell, La Fenice.

It was at least seventeen miles from the table—to the cloakroom—to the door.

CHAPTER

15

NEXT MORNING at the office, Jane and Susan were both solicitous. Susan made tea and even went out to Shelley's to get us all pastry.

"More tea, boss?"

"Yes, please."

"And how about another Danish?"

"Just a half." Their thoughtful fawning helped. As the three of us sipped tea and munched on the pastries, my poor, crumpled ego was slowly returning to normal.

The phone rang once, a wrong number. Eventually, without meaning to, I sighed.

"If only I'd picked some other restaurant. Why La Fenice—?"

"Harry—" Jane squeezed my arm.

"Now, now—" Susan murmured.

The phone rang again. This time it was Wendell Crittenden. "Nice going," were his first words.

"For what—?"

"I take my hat off to you. That was one helluva way to begin a press campaign."

"What the hell are you talking about, Wendell?"

"This isn't Wendell," Wendell said.

"Okay, whoever you say. Nevertheless, what're you talking about?"

"Your initial publicity foray at the restaurant last night."

"Were *you* there?"

"No, no. I just heard about it."

"Are you having me followed, Wendell?"

"This *isn't* Wendell," Wendell said again. "And the answer is a guarded *maybe*."

Okay. Now I knew that I was being followed.

"At any rate, congratulations. It's a wonderful story. It should be all over town by cocktail time. How do you dream up these things?"

"Imagination and experience," I said.

"Well, you certainly have both. And I extend my praise to the two people you hired, as well."

"I'll tell them what you said, Wendell."

"This isn't *me*, goddamn it."

"Okay—"

I could hear him take a deep breath. "But—again—congratulations."

As I hung up, I started to laugh. Jane and Susan looked concerned. "Don't worry, I'm okay."

"Harry—"

"I'm fine. Get Hal and Mabel on the phone and give them the Jessica Rumbough at La Fenice story. They can get it to all the items columns by this afternoon. And tell them I'll be calling Liz Smith myself."

"Harry—" This time Jane was even more serious. "Are you sure you know what you're doing?"

"Very sure. And both of you can stop worrying about me. Only my pride is injured. The rest of me survives."

Susan smiled. "Welcome back to the living, Mr. Baker."

The phones started to ring. The morning coffee break was over for the rest of New York as well.

■　■　■

I spent the next half hour talking with Tom Haskins about the deal I'd make with Phil Persky. We agreed on everything. We also agreed that it wouldn't be necessary for us to sign anything until I got back from Europe.

"What're you going for anyway?" Tom asked. "Any romance involved?" Since the day my wife walked out, Tom has worked on me to get married again.

"*Tom*—it's only been six months."

"Okay, okay," he chuckled, "I'll see you at the party."

Right after that, Hal Goodman called to make sure that I wanted the item about Jessica released.

Once assured, he said, "Mabel's getting a rush job on the invitations, and we'll have them all hand-delivered by tomorrow afternoon."

"You're great," I told him.

"Listen, I've owed you one for a long time."

I spent the rest of the afternoon catching up on correspondence. There was an ebullient note from Alice. She was feeling fine, and she was off to Puerto Rico for a week. At six, when Jane and Susan were ready to leave, I was still dictating.

"Take it easy, Harry," Jane said.

"Don't worry about me," I said. "I'm fine."

"I'm not worried about you, I'm worried about myself. There's eight years' worth of dictation in those cassettes."

She blew me a kiss, Susan waved, and they were gone. I worked until seven, turned on the news, made a note to call the lighting director—an old friend—about the possibility of a little less light on the set, went back to work again, and stayed at my desk until nine.

I walked over to Lello's on East Fifty-Fourth for a late supper and a chance, finally, to read *The Times*. There were still several people dining, and the conversational hum was pleasant, aided quite a bit by a particularly patrician-looking couple seated across from me.

Mario, the maître d'hôtel, left their table and came over to say hello. He lowered his voice: "I was born in Arezzo, and *they* are telling *me* how to pronounce Arezzo."

Dinner was fine, the bath was fine, and bed was even better. Then I got the call.

An accented voice said, "Be at Tenth Street and Fifth Avenue in half an hour. Walk between Tenth and Washington Square until your friend walks with you—"

I hung up.

Ten seconds later, the phone rang again. And, again, it was the accented voice: "In half an hour you should—"

"It's late," I said, and hung up.

It rang a third time. It was Wendell. "For God's sake, Harry. Don't you understand security? Now you've forced me to call as myself."

"What's wrong with that?"

"It's just not—not—secure."

"Wendell, do you think anyone in his right mind would accept the instructions of a total stranger, a stranger who has the most sinister accent ever handled by the facilities of the Bell Telephone System—especially if those instructions are that he should go walking on lower Fifth Avenue in the middle of the night?"

"It's only eleven-fifteen."

"Do you—?"

"*I* would."

"Fine, then, you go," I said.

"Look, Harry—" Wendell was angry and trying not to show it —"the whole idea was for you to *meet* me."

"Why?"

"I want to tell you something."

"Tell me now."

"I can't."

"Why not?"

Wendell's voice got higher and more nasal than usual. "Harry, I would greatly appreciate it if you would meet me on lower Fifth Avenue between Tenth Street and Washington Square within thirty minutes." He tried to lower his voice dramatically. "I don't mind playing the fool occasionally if it amuses you, Harry—but don't push me."

What the hell, I thought. I've gone this far. "I'll be there in half an hour," I said.

"Good." He hung up immediately.

It was nearly midnight by the time I got out of the cab. I had given the driver a slightly incorrect address because I had seen Humphrey Bogart do that once when he was going to a clandestine rendezvous with Ingrid Bergman. But in real life, it doesn't work very well. I had just paid the driver when a second cab pulled up behind and out stepped Wendell.

"For God's sake—" he said.

"I'm sorry." I told him why I had given the wrong address.

"As a matter of fact, I did the same thing, Harry. It's SOP—Standard Operating Procedure—in our branch."

"It shouldn't be," I said.

"Why?"

"It doesn't work."

Wendell looked annoyed. "Let's start walking toward Washington Square."

We walked for a while without speaking.

Finally, as we started to cross Ninth Street, Wendell said, "We've got the body."

"Got what—?"

Wendell swore under his breath. *"The—body."*

"When?"

"As of two hours ago."

"How'd you get it?"

"A double agent. That is—a double agent *now.* Two hours ago she was just a defector."

"She?"

"Forget that I said that."

"But why did she defect?"

"For Christ's sake," Wendell hissed. "Why? *Why?* What country do you live in, Harry?"

We walked another block in silence.

"So you can stop worrying about it," Wendell finally said.

"Who was he? The body, I mean."

"M told you the other day, didn't he? An international mercenary. Whoever killed him did the rest of the world a favor."

"Who *did* kill him?"

"We don't know." Wendell's walk became brisk. "Let's pick up the pace," he said. "It gets chilly in October."

We turned at Washington Square and started up the other side of Fifth Avenue.

"By the way," Wendell turned. "M likes you very much, I think."

"That's nice," I said, wondering if it really was.

"Can't you tell? He's already invited you to cocktails in his office, and he even had canapes."

"That was very considerate," I said.

"And now this—" Wendell whistled appreciatively.

"What?"

"M actually plans to come up to New York to see you off." Wendell whistled a second time, making it even clearer that M wasn't given to that sort of thing.

"That's very good of him," I said. I was beginning to sound like an inchoate M myself. "But won't he be afraid of being seen with me?"

"Oh, he won't be seen. You can rest assured of that. But, nevertheless, he wants to come up to send you off, personally. I think it's quite a gesture."

I stopped walking. "Wendell—"

"Yes—"

"Did you get me out here just to let me know that M is planning to see me off?"

"No, no—of course not. I just remembered that. Thought you'd like to know."

"Why, then?"

"The body. Wanted to let you know that we had it. No need to wonder about it now, and no need to worry about blackmail."

"That's all?"

"That's enough, isn't it?"

"But couldn't you have told me that over the phone?"

"Certainly *not*." Wendell's voice made it final.

We walked back up to Fourteenth Street, where Wendell suddenly hailed a cab, got in without looking at me, slammed the door shut, and sped off. I stood there for a moment or two, then tried to hail my own cab. An *hour* later, I was home in bed cursing Wendell Crittenden, M, and the whole lot of them.

Ah, yes—the things we do for our country.

CHAPTER

16

THE NEXT few days went by quickly. When you represent seventeen clients, and you're trying to get ready for a two-week vacation, you usually end up canceling it because it's too much trouble. In this case, I had no choice: I would be going to London. Uncle Sam wanted me. Again.

Jane kept reassuring me that things would run smoothly; Tom's wife volunteered to help if Susan should happen to get another acting job; and for her part, Susan offered to forego auditions while I was gone—an offer which I rejected. Out of gratitude, Susan brought in a friend, another actress, who could be her understudy as receptionist—just in case.

At her interview, the potential understudy revealed that she was an eager worker (by also revealing that she wore no bra), when she closed the door of my office and pulled off her T-shirt.

"I'll do anything to get into show business," she gasped. *"Susan—"*

Susan came running in. She glared at her topless friend. "You promised—"

The friend left. It was decided that there would be no understudy.

And suddenly it was the day of the farewell party. Both big rooms on the second floor of the Friars Club were filled. The hallway landing between them was packed. Almost all the press was there—the papers, the radio stations, and the television crews.

Of course, to get the coverage, you've got to have the bait—someone or something to write about. In the case of my party, the bait wasn't me, it was my clients. And they had cooperated without complaint, even though every one of them was puzzled by it all.

"It's certainly not like you, Harry," Dan said, "but if that's what you want—I'll be there."

So was everyone else. I suddenly loved them all even more than usual. There are rewards in this business, and this was one of them. All of these wonderful men and women, most of them not the partying kind, were attending a fatiguing press affair—no questions asked—just because I'd made the request.

"I think *everybody* is here," Jane chortled. "And the coverage is great. *Superb.*"

"Thanks—" Hal beamed.

"All the TV channels—CNN—radio. You got everybody. And Liz Smith is here, and the mayor—a senator—"

Hal laughed. "Jane, would you be *my* press agent?"

"Never. I'm loyal to the old boss here." She pecked me on the cheek. "It's going great, Harry. Is it—doing—whatever you want it to do?"

"Absolutely." I moved toward the bar. "Excuse me, Jane—there's Peter Jennings—"

It was at this point that Howard Cosell appeared. Only it wasn't Howard Cosell. And I was the only one who knew it because he came directly to me, and left immediately.

"Hello, Mr. Baker." The Cosell-Clone's clothes were rumpled. He looked exhausted. "I'm getting out before

you—but with any luck I'll see you again—in London.
Good luck—to both of us."

He disappeared.

■   ■   ■

"Where did The Coach go?" one of the ABC sports
producers asked me.

"Excuse me—?"

"Where did Howard run off to?"

"Oh—I believe he's on his way to London."

"When? We're taping a special tomorrow night."

"I must have heard wrong," I said. "Excuse me, I have
to check the bar—"

I smiled and started to *mingle*.

■   ■   ■

An hour later, it was all over, and I was thanking everyone, especially Hal and Mabel.

The party would make all the newspapers, all the television, most of the radio stations, several magazines, and
it even got a headline in *The National Enquirer* that read:
What Do TV News Men and Women Do Behind Closed Doors?

The last person had left, and I was about to relax and
enjoy a drink when my name was paged.

It was Wendell: "The St. Regis, suite fourteen twenty-
one—repeat, the St. Regis, suite fourteen twenty-one."
He hung up.

This time, I didn't question anything. I walked directly
down the block to the St. Regis Hotel.

Wendell opened the door. "Thank you for being so
prompt," he said.

I followed him into the living room of the suite. Wendell and M had been playing poker. Wendell busied himself with picking up the chips and tidying the table, while
M stood beaming over a champagne bucket. "I won't

even ask," he said, pouring with a broad flourish, "I'm simply going to pour you some champagne. And you must have at least a glass. As a sort of—celebration."

M had quite obviously been drinking. He continued on, a New Year's Eve party smile on his face: "Really—truly—congratulations on a fine job. We're very proud of you, and I wish to apologize for any doubts along the way about your ability to pull off this first phase of *Operation Morris*." He raised his glass. "To a splendid party, with first-rate press coverage—"

The three of us drank.

"You don't seem to be very talkative, Harry," Wendell said.

I suppressed a desire to point out that, because of M's ebullience, I hadn't as yet had a moment in which to speak.

"I'm overwhelmed," I said, as pleasantly as possible.

M smiled at me, and said to Wendell, rather in defense of me, "And he must be damned exhausted, Crittenden." He raised his glass a second time. "I drink again—to you, Harry Baker. Splendid job, just splendid."

M had never addressed me by my first name before. But then, I had never seen him slightly tipsy before. His James Angleton–Foster Dulles image was now in slight disarray.

Wendell must have sensed my thoughts. He said, "I'm glad the chief is relaxing. It's the first time in years that I've seen him this way."

M laughed. "True, true. Quite true." He poured more champagne. "I'm afraid that I was becoming too dull for words. That city—Washington—is a strange place. One becomes enmeshed in all of those curiously grinding gears and doesn't see that he has reduced himself to nothing but a link in the chain that winds over—" (M was beginning to sound like Frank Rich of *The Times*)—"the sprocket of bureaucratic sameness. This one evening has done me a world of good. Very refreshing."

"I'm glad for you," I said.

"Oh, but make no mistake," M said. "My motive was you. I wanted to see you off. And to wish you luck."

We drank again and he poured more wine. "Crittenden and I ordered some extra canapes. Thought you might enjoy a snack."

"No, thanks," I said. "I'm afraid that that's all I did at my party."

M chuckled again. "Of course, of course. Must be awfully difficult to keep one's weight down. . . ."

. . . And that's the way the conversation drifted for the next ten minutes or so. We talked about keeping in shape; we talked about the theater (M wanted to catch "a damned good musical before going back to Foggy Bottom"); we talked about good restaurants, vacations, and women.

". . . in front of Notre Dame at one o'clock, she told me," (M was simultaneously finishing a story of early love, and yet another bottle of champagne). "I waited for hours. But I never saw her again. To this day, I've always wondered—you know, my French wasn't that good in those days—perhaps she said *behind* Notre Dame." He sighed. "I'll never know. But she was, undoubtedly, the most beautiful woman I've ever seen."

Wendell then told his obligatory tale of early love. It, too, ended in tragedy, although I suspected that Wendell might have tailored his ending so that he wouldn't appear to be topping his chief.

My turn came. I made one up. Not half bad. I made her an Indian princess—Iroquois. My ending was also sad. I had her riding off on a Palomino (I have no idea what a Palomino looks like), alone on the western desert.

"I thought you said she was an Iroquois," Wendell said.

"She was. Iroquois."

"They're an eastern tribe. How could she ride across the desert?"

I quickly parried. "That's the worst part. She even left her own people."

"Why?"

"That's another tale for another time," I said briskly, getting up and trying to sound friendly, but businesslike. "Gentlemen, I'm supposed to fly to London tomorrow afternoon, and I still don't know what I'm supposed to do."

M smiled warmly. "Good man. Splendid. Very good indeed."

Wendell rose, rubbing his hands together, refusing to be outbrisked by the likes of me. "Tomorrow morning. Nine o'clock. Breakfast," he barked.

M stood at the door, a smile on his face. "Until tomorrow morning then. Thank you for coming up. And have a good night." Just before closing the door, he cautioned Wendell, "And don't forget, you owe me eleven dollars and forty-five cents." He winked at me—"Crittenden is a very obvious poker player."

At the elevator, Wendell was even brisker than before. "Nine A.M. Please don't be late. And get some sleep."

The elevator door closed, but not before I felt the urge to salute.

CHAPTER

17

J ANE WAS sitting in the big leather chair in my living room. She was very drunk. This seemed to be everybody's night for it.

"Hello, boss." She smiled and blushed a bit. "This is the first time I've ever used my key for anything but business."

"No need to apologize," I said.

"And I've had too much to drink."

"Not to worry—"

"And I'm in no shape to try to make it back to my apartment—and—" Jane raised a hand before I could reply—"*and* you certainly shouldn't try to take me there because you have too big a day tomorrow, *so—*"

"You'll spend the night here—"

"Hey, what a great idea." Jane grinned and poured herself an enormous Cognac.

"*Jane—*"

"Don't worry, Harry. I've had so much tonight my body will never even notice this."

I got some sheets and blankets, threw them towards the living room sofa, and put a pair of my pajamas on the bed for Jane.

"We'll be just like Clark Gable and Claudette Colbert in *It Happened One Night*," I told her. "Only we won't have to hang a blanket between us. We've got the walls of the good old Stratford Arms."

"But you shouldn't have to sleep on the sofa," she said. "It's your apartment."

"Gentlemen always sleep on the sofa."

"Whose rule is that?"

"Mine. I just made it up. Now get into my pajamas and hit the hay while you can still find the bed."

By the time I had showered, she was in bed with the blankets up to her chin. I smiled reassuringly and started for the living room.

"Harry—?"

"Yes—?"

"Harry, don't hold this against me tomorrow, but— well, I can't fall asleep because the whole room is whirling. Would you lie here with me for just a few minutes. Until I fall off?"

For a moment I thought that Jane was making overtures of lust, but that's not our relationship. "Sure." I lay down on the bed and held her hand. "I hope you don't feel tomorrow the way I think you're going to feel," I said.

Jane laughed. "Oh, Harry, you're so funny."

"It must be my timing," I said. "I didn't realize I'd said anything funny."

"You didn't. It's just you. You don't have to lie there shivering after your shower. Cover up and stop worrying about catching a cold. I'll be asleep in two minutes."

Jane knows my hypochondriasis well. I got under the blankets and held her hand again. "There. Now go to sleep."

After about a minute, Jane said. "I'm really drunk. Have you been drinking at all tonight?"

"A little."

"Good—" She suddenly rolled towards me and I realized very quickly that she hadn't bothered to put on any pajamas.

It took an entire twenty-seven seconds to decide what to do. Twenty-seven seconds is an extremely long time at a moment like that. But, even ignoring the fact that I had an early meeting which would be followed by a flight to London, the truth was that I'd always felt like a kind of brother to Jane. But you certainly don't try to explain that to a beautiful woman who has just rolled over to your side of the sack with no clothes on.

"Jane—"

"Yes?"

"Jane, I've had too much to drink."

"Oh, Harry—"

"And so have you. I wouldn't want to take advantage of you."

"Harry—"

"No—I think too much of you. I respect you too much." (It was all true, so I could say it all with the ardor of an honest man.)

"Harry—"

"I wouldn't want you to wake up tomorrow feeling that you'd been part of something tawdry. It would ruin a relationship of over a year."

"It wouldn't—"

"No. I'm sorry. Good night, Jane." I got out of bed. I stood there for a long time, waiting, but she said nothing. "Sleep well, Jane."

There was a pause and then she said, "You, too, Harry. Good night."

I went into the living room, made my bed, and decided to have a nightcap after all. My God, I thought, times certainly have changed since the days of Clark Gable and *It Happened One Night*. When he refused to give in to passion, Claudette Colbert knew for certain that he was a gentleman. But now, in this day and age, Jane is probably lying in there wondering if I'm a fag.

■ ■ ■

It was exactly eight fifty-five the next morning when I knocked on the door of M's suite at the St. Regis.

He answered himself, looking fresh and awake. "Oh, I thought it was Crittenden."

"Why—did I knock in code?" I asked breezily, just to make conversation.

"Yes—as a matter of fact—you did." M looked perturbed.

"An accident—"

"Yes, but just the same, very disturbing. Coffee?" The remains of breakfast were still on the room service table.

"Yes, please."

M poured some into a fresh cup.

"Nothing like a good cup of coffee to set one up for the day," he said. He raised a finger to his lips and then waggled it back and forth as a sign of warning. "Absolutely nothing—"

There was a knock on the door.

M scowled and glanced over at me. "The same damned knock," he said.

He opened the door, and Wendell Crittenden came in. "No one followed him," Wendell told M.

"Make a note about changing pass signs," M said.

"Before we get started with details," I said, "I'd like to—"

Again M waggled his finger in warning, as Wendell handed me a note written on hotel stationery. It read: "Although we have *no reason to be suspicious* of this suite of rooms, we are, nevertheless, going to proceed with extreme caution. Do the following: Buy jogging shorts and shoes and go jogging at precisely eleven o'clock on the Sheep Meadow track in Central Park. You will be contacted."

As I finished reading the note, M caught my eye, smiled benevolently, and wrote a postscript to Wendell's note: "I read in today's paper that they are having a sale on jogging shorts at Herman's," it said.

■   ■   ■

If I had kept a diary over the past two weeks, it would have read like the ravings of a lunatic. Something I had surely become. This, I thought, is one of the most idiotic things that I have ever done in my life—and this jogging costume is an embarrassment.

I jogged on.

And Wendell and M weren't making a whole hell of a lot of sense either, I thought.

A bicycle bell sounded behind me several times. I got to one side of the path to allow the bike to pass, but it pulled abreast of me and stayed. It was M.

"Why couldn't I have gotten a bike, too?" I puffed, sounding like a seven-year-old who'd been denied a piece of candy.

"There's a reason," M said, looking as if he weren't quite sure what it was.

He stared straight ahead as he talked. We continued to jog and to bike at a modest pace. "I'll drop something in a moment. Read it, memorize it, and burn it," he said. "It will be your method of making contact with our man in London. It's rather complicated, but it has to be. We must be sure of ourselves."

"What are we talking about—?" I was tired from jogging and getting irritable.

"You know—such as, you say, 'Nice morning for a stroll, isn't it?' and he says, 'Much too windy,' and then *you* say, 'I don't mind wind'—et cetera."

"Is that what I'm to memorize?"

"Well, something like that. Yours is quite different, actually. But that's the idea—that sort of thing."

"Can't we just stop and talk?"

"Certainly not," M answered. "Now I *assume* that you have your air tickets, traveler's checks, et cetera?"

"Jane arranged everything."

"And she booked you at Claridge's?"

"A suite. And I *assume* that you're going to repay me for all of this someday."

"Of course. Now you'll make your first contact immediately after your arrival at Claridge's. Right after you sign in and they show you your suite—" M smiled, apparently recalling a happy memory. "You'll wash up and—"

M scowled. "I hope you got your suite on the second floor."

"Yes. Jane is very thorough."

"Excellent." M nodded appreciatively. "You'll wash up or whatever, spending *exactly* twenty minutes in your rooms. By the way, this is all in the envelope which I'll drop for you. Again, study it—learn it—and burn it." M scowled again, apparently to show the importance of his statement. "After *exactly* twenty minutes you'll come out, descend the great staircase from the second floor, and your contact will be waiting for you. He'll be wearing—"

"Hold it—" I could only gasp. "I can't jog another step."

"You've got to," M said. "What other excuse do we have for being seen together?"

"How the hell do I know? My knees are weak."

"How weak?" M scoffed.

"*How* weak? Who do you think I am, Johnny Carson?"

"All right, all right," M said, with deliberate asperity. "I'll pretend that something is wrong with my cycle, and you stop to assist me."

"Great idea," I gasped.

"I haven't been in this business thirty years for nothing," M said sternly.

He allowed his bike to coast to a stop. I collapsed near a large oak and tried to catch my breath.

"Up, man, up." M commanded. "You're supposed to be helping me."

Together, we began to fiddle with the chain of his bike.

M droned on: "When I ride off, don't follow me. Go back the other way." He covertly pulled a brown envelope from inside his jacket and placed it on the ground. "All of your instructions are here. As I said before, read, memorize and destroy. Now—"

I interrupted. "I thought we weren't supposed to talk together?"

M frowned. "I've changed my mind," he said tartly. "It's your first show with us. And you may have some questions." M cleared his throat and began again. "As you descend the staircase, your contact will be waiting for you. He'll be wearing taupe trousers—" M somehow managed to make *taupe trousers* sound very mysterious— "a double-breasted blue blazer, a red, blue, and *green* regimental striped tie, and—something completely out of character for that mode of dress—a small, diamond stickpin in his tie. He'll say, 'Didn't I just see you check in?'— he'll have a Scottish accent—and you'll say, 'Yes, about *twenty minutes* ago,' and then he'll say—"

The instructions took several minutes. I seriously doubted that I would ever be able to memorize them. But in the end, I had only two questions.

"What's the first one?" M asked, obviously pleased that he had done so well with his instructions.

"The final double-check question will always be: 'Do you speak any Italian?'"

M nodded. "Yes. *Always* Italian. And the person who is asked the question will *always* say, 'Yes. A little.'"

"Then whoever asks the question will say, 'Does *Amacord* have one *m* or two *m*'s in it?'"

"Right. Use any Italian word, but," M smiled encouragingly, "*Amacord* is a very good example."

"And the one asked the question will say, 'I'm not sure, but I do know this:' and then he has to sing? '—*M* is for the many things—she gave me—'"

"Precisely."

"But for God's sake—*sing*?"

"It doesn't have to be in tune. And one can do it softly if one is self-conscious."

"Why sing?"

"Q-13—that's the Technical Services Division—came up with it as a final, fail-safe check. I think it's a very good idea. By the way," M added modestly, "the *M* was Q-13's and Code's idea, not mine."

I bellowed, "*M* is for the many things—she gave me—" M's eyes bulged. *"Not here."*

"Sorry."

"What's your other question?" He was sitting on his bike, pretending to thank me for my aid, and preparing to ride off.

"Why, within my first two hours in London, do I walk

to the chocolate shop on South Molton Street and say, 'A
large box of your assorted chocolates, please?'"

"Why?" M looked heavenward in dismay. "Why? Because they're very good, of course. You'll love them."

"Of course."

M rode off with a flourish and a last, "Good show, old
man."

"Thanks."

I started to jog again, wearing my jogging shorts
bought at a sale at Herman's, humming *"M—is for the
many things—she gave me—"* and looking forward to
London, even though I now knew for certain that I must
be absolutely mad.

CHAPTER

18

A H, TO BE in London now that—*any* month is there.

Even with the time change, and the lack of sleep, I felt absolutely ebullient as I checked in at Claridge's.

The huge bathtub was more than inviting, but being keenly aware of M's admonition about *exactly* twenty minutes, I settled for a shave and a change of shirt.

In *exactly* twenty minutes, I left my room, descended the great staircase, and there he was, waiting for me at the bottom.

I was aware of a nervous smile on my face, and a vague surging of my pulse rate; I had never had occasion to meet a real *Contact* before. It was just like a movie.

My impulsive instincts were to go down to him, shake his hand, and introduce myself. But, thinking again of M, I tried to be as professional as possible. I forced myself to stop halfway down the staircase and pretend to check my wallet while, actually, I checked out the man.

Yes. All was in order. Taupe trousers. Blue blazer.

Double-breasted. Regimental striped tie of red, blue, and green. Also, as promised, he had gray hair, blue eyes, and he was wearing horn-rimmed glasses. Perfect. I continued on down the staircase.

As I got close to him, I realized that there was no jarring diamond stickpin in his tie but thought, what the hell, even professional *Contacts* aren't perfect.

And when he said, "Didn't I just see you check in?", and I had answered, "Yes, about *twenty minutes* ago," exactly as planned, I silently saluted M and Q-13 and the Code Department, and marveled at how perfectly they made these things work.

We continued on as the orders had indicated; I was glad that I had memorized them so well. Now that I was meeting an honest-to-God professional *Contact* in International Intelligence, I wanted to be professional myself.

"Twenty minutes?" he asked. "*Exactly* twenty minutes ago?"

It was fun. "*Exactly* twenty minutes ago," I replied professionally.

"From the States?"

"Yes."

"New York?"

"Yes—the city. (God, but spy patter was fun.) I thought of Peter Lorre. I thought of all those movies with Charles Boyer.

"Ah, flights are so tiring. Would you like to slip into the lounge for a drink? It would be very relaxing."

I marveled afresh at his professionalism. And my own, too, for that matter.

"Sounds like a good idea," I said. (Should I have replied, "Sounds like a *very* good idea?" No, simply "good" was right.)

He smiled an extremely friendly smile. "We can drink and talk. What would you like to talk about?"

(Ah, here it comes.) "Words always interest me," I said. "Do you speak any Italian?"

He smiled again. "A little. Why?"

Perfect. Amazing. Remarkable. I continued: "Does the Italian word *Amacord* have one *m* or two *m*'s in it?"

He pursed his lips. "I'm afraid I don't know that word."

According to my instructions, he wasn't supposed to say that. But I realized, with appreciation for his skill, that I was dealing with an old pro. While I had learned my instructions by rote, and was going through them like a third-year piano student, he was using the basic melody and then making slight, yet fascinating variations—just to be sure.

"It was a Fellini movie," I said.

"I must have missed it."

"How about the word *minestrone*?" It was the only other *m* word I could think of, and not a good choice, since it would force him to say, "I'm not sure—" when, of course, anybody knows that there is only one *m* in *minestrone*.

"One," he said.

"Pardon?"

"There's one *m* in *minestrone*."

"Are you sure?"

"Of course," he said. "Anybody knows that there's only one *m* in *minestrone*."

"What else do you know?" I was a little frantic, but I kept my voice low as I sang, *"M—is for the many things—she gave me. . . ."*

"I beg your pardon."

I sang again. *"M—is for the many things—she gave me. . . ."*

He stepped back one step and raised his voice, just slightly, but in anger. "Look, you silly son-of-a-bitch," he hissed. "I thought you felt like a little—companionship. I can see I was wrong."

I was intrepid and tenacious to the end. *"M—is for the many things—she gave me. . . ."* I sang again.

"Idiot!" He turned on his heel—and left.

Then I saw the *other* fellow in taupe trousers, blue double-breasted blazer, red, blue, and green regimental striped necktie, gray hair, blue eyes, horn-rimmed glasses, *and* a subtly jarring diamond stickpin, with his eyes riveted on mine, imploring me to talk to him.

We went through the whole routine all over again. As for me, my performance was markedly less zestful.

When we got to the word *Amacord* again, he answered crisply, "I'm not sure, but I do know this:" and then he sang in a lilting Irish tenor voice, *"M—is for the many things—she gave me. . . ."*

Wait a minute. Irish. "You're supposed to be a Scotsman," I said.

"That I am, lad, that I am," he burred back at me.

I'd been burned once, and I was not about to let it happen a second time. "If you're working for the same outfit that I am, you shouldn't have done that," I said. "You saw what just happened. On the other hand, maybe you and I *aren't* working for the same outfit."

"You're right, lad. I shouldn't 'ave done it. I lost my head. I've had nothin' to do for a month. From now on—all business. Let's go into the lounge for that drink."

We each ordered a sherry and didn't speak until the waiter had brought the drinks. My Contact, or whatever the hell he was, spent the time busying himself with his pipe. I spent the time wondering what to do next. I had a single London phone number to call if I got into an emergency situation, but I damned well didn't want to make an emergency call just five minutes into my mission.

I could just hear M clucking his tongue and muttering, "Good God, *five minutes* and he needed help, you say?"

And Wendell Crittenden would never let me forget it.

"Your sherry, gentlemen."

"Thank you," we said, almost in unison.

My *Contact* (?) smiled at the departing waiter, puffed on his pipe, sipped some sherry, then hunched forward to talk. "Again, I'm sorry, lad. That wasn't very professional of me." He sighed with eloquent ennui, "Too many years, I suppose, too many years. . . ."

I had never tried to fix anyone with a steady, steely stare before, but it seemed to be the proper thing to do. Without any practice whatsoever, without even a glance into the mirror to check the result, I turned to him, sipped my sherry, remained silent, and fixed him with a steady, steely stare.

It worked. "All right, lad. I know what you're thinkin'. I'm the one who mucked up, so now I'm the one who's got to prove himself. All right, here goes—The last question you asked M—"

He must have seen my reaction to the name in my eyes. He smiled. "Oh sure, I know him, too. Your last question was: 'Why, within my first two hours in London, do I walk to the chocolate shop on South Molton Street and say, "A large box of your assorted chocolates, please?"'" He smiled again. "Isn't that what you said?"

"Yes," I said. "But no one—"

He laughed. "Good for you, lad, good for you. And here's the countersign. M said, 'Why? Why? Because they're very good, of course. You'll love them.'"

"Amazing."

"Not really."

"No, I meant that it's amazing that you should know any of that, when there's no need to know it."

"Ah, yes there is, lad. That's Q-13's ultimate backup, the fail-safe beyond the fail-safe."

I didn't say anything.

"Haven't I proved myself?" he asked.

"I'm not sure."

He sighed. "All right, lad, we could start all over again." He spoke in a singsong stilted manner: "Didn't I just see you check in?"

"Yes, about *twenty minutes* ago."

"Twenty minutes? *Exactly*—"

I broke in. "Okay, fine. It's just that I've never done this sort of thing before, and when one little thing is off, I mean—after that first guy."

He shook his head. "Don't apologize. *I* apologize." He stuck out his hand. "Bill Ferguson."

"Harry Baker." We shook hands.

"It's good to meet you, Mr. Baker. Actually, we've got a lot in common. My cover is the same as yours."

"Your cover?"

"My front. Same as yours. I'm a theatrical agent, too."

I had to smile at myself. Until that moment, I had never realized that I was just a bit snobbish about my clients. "Actually, I represent only news people—journalists. Correspondents, commentators, writers, producers," I said.

"Well, it's the same thing," Ferguson said. "Almost. Drop by the office while you're in London." He handed me a card and continued talking, his voice perceptibly lower. "And if you're in trouble, this is really your number to call for your safe house."

"Thanks."

The card read: *Ferguson, Freaks and Ferguson. Anything, anybody, for Pantomime, Stage, Screen, Television, and Radio.*

"There's nobody named Freaks," he said, "and there's only one Ferguson. Me. When my grandfather started the whole thing, it was *Ferguson's Freaks*. My Dad made the change."

"A wise decision." I said.

"Aye. Anyway, that's a good place for you if you need some help. Drop by this afternoon, or tomorrow. But always keep in mind that everybody in the office is legitimate, so I'm the only one you can talk to." He sat back. "Now let's enjoy our morning sherry, and then you've got to head off to South Molton Street to buy some chocolates."

"Then what do I do?"

"Well, enjoy 'em. They're damned good, lad."

"This is crazy."

"No, no, lad. When you get into the shop a week from now to buy a box, someone will come over to you and say, very pleasantly, "Well, you seem to be enjoying those chocolates a great deal."

"A week from now? I thought I'd be heading back home a week from now. How long will I be here?"

"Who knows? I'd say a month, maybe."

That would be the first thing that I would discuss with M whenever I talked to him next. His idea of a few weeks, and my idea of a few weeks were quite different.

"Okay." I tried to sound businesslike. "Who will be meeting me?"

"Don't know, lad, don't know." Ferguson shook his head. "As your own poet James Fenimore Longfellow said: 'Ours not to reason why, ours but to do and die—'"

"That was a British poet. That was—"

"No, lad. Longfellow was as American as kippers and bacon."

Ferguson stood up and raised his glass. "Cheers," he said, and finished his sherry. "Off you go now to South Molton Street. And don't forget, this afternoon or tomorrow, I expect to see you in my *wee* office." He smiled broadly for the first time, revealing two large gold-capped incisors.

Do Scotsmen really say *wee* office, I wondered as I walked to my chocolate rendezvous. I suppose they do, was my answer.

South Molton Street was delightful, the chocolate shop was delightful, and so was my bed at the hotel when I returned. All night on the plane and the glass of sherry had combined perfectly. I was just about to drift off when the phone rang. It was long distance. It was New York calling. It was M.

"Mr. Baker."

"Yes."

He wasted no time. "You're a fool. You should have called me immediately."

"Why?"

"*Why?* Because your—meeting didn't go as planned, of course."

I swung my legs around and sat on the edge of the bed. "You mean Ferguson isn't Ferguson?"

"Of course Ferguson is Ferguson."

"Well, if Ferguson is Ferguson, why are you upset?"

"I'm upset because Ferguson might *not* have been Ferguson."

I tried to keep it going: "But Ferguson *was* Ferguson, and Ferguson *is* Ferguson."

"Yes, of course, Ferguson is Ferguson, but—" M stopped talking. When he resumed, he was back in control. "The *second* man you met was the correct contact. And I'll even allow you your first mistake. After all, it was your initial escapade with us. But to have the second man slip up, and then to have you blithely accept it, is unforgivable. Even though he, luckily, *is* our man, Mr. Ferguson."

"How did you find out?"

"Ferguson, naturally. He called to confess his indiscretion and to throw himself on my mercy. His first mistake in thirty years. I was lenient."

"That was kind of you."

M's voice rose. "But *you*. One more major mistake like that, and I'll have you drummed out of the corps."

"You're forgetting something," I said. "I'd love to be drummed out of the corps."

M's voice was suddenly petulant. "But why?"

"You tricked me, for one thing."

"Never—"

"You said that you needed me for a few weeks. Now I'm told that I may be here a month."

M's mouth was filled with honey. "That's a few weeks, isn't it?" he asked innocently.

"But what am I supposed to be doing here?"

"Tut-tut now. Here we are chattering away on a long-distance transatlantic line—who knows? It's so expensive, too. Just—*enjoy your chocolates*. You're going to have a fine time in London. 'Bye now." M hung up quickly.

Now I was wide awake all over again.

As I was deciding what to do, the phone rang a second time. It was Jane.

Her voice was somber. "Did I wake you, Harry?"

"Wide awake. What's up?" I knew that she hadn't called me at three A.M., New York time, to ask how I liked London.

"Bad news, I'm afraid."

"What—?"

"It's Dan and Tom."

"Oh, my God—"

"They're alive. Both alive." She was speaking very rapidly. "They were together on the shuttle up from Washington. They shared a cab into the city. Bad accident."

"But they're okay."

"Yes. A bit mangled for the moment, but they're going to be fine."

"Thank God."

We talked for another ten minutes before hanging up. By that time, Jane had succeeded in reassuring me that things were stable.

"Sorry about this, Harry. But I just thought I ought to let you know as soon as possible."

"You were right, Jane. Thanks for that and for holding my hand afterwards."

"Anytime. Good night, Harry—"

"Good night, Jane."

■ ■ ■

I didn't even consider trying to sleep.

I ordered some lager and cheese from room service, watched some television, a documentary shot on the Isle of Man on the proper training of sheepdogs, drank four bottles of lager, ate most of the cheese, and fell asleep in front of the television.

When I opened my eyes again, it was three in the afternoon, London time.

I spent one wonderful hour in the enormous bathtub and emerged thoroughly relaxed and refreshed. There was a decided bounce to my step as I made my way down the stairway to the front desk.

I got the last copy of *The Times* and sauntered into the lounge for afternoon tea. Relaxed now, and really enjoying the many comforts of Claridge's—the pleasant service, the quiet, tea and sandwiches, reading *The Times*—I stopped feeling quite so sorry for myself.

Save some pity, I thought, for the poor fellow sitting to my left, his head heavily swathed in bandages, only small holes for his eyes and nose and mouth—who was, probably, also in pain—as he sat quietly with no tea, no sandwiches, and no newspaper.

I realized that I had been staring—which he had very

likely sensed—and I nodded before I looked away and read the remainder of the paper.

Later, with plenty of time, I decided against asking for a taxi, and I walked all the way to the Garrick Club, through Soho, across Piccadilly Circus, up to Leicester Square, and then to the Garrick for drinks and dinner.

■ ■ ■

The next morning, after a much longer than intended but extremely pleasant evening in the Garrick Grill, after a good night's sleep, after another luxurious bath in the great tub, and after a perfectly fine English breakfast, I was ready for, and looking forward to, the day.

There was a spring in my gait as I walked again to Leicester Square and Bill Ferguson's office.

Ferguson pretended to know me from correspondence, and I went along with it. He introduced me to his staff of three; two pleasant women in their forties who were very friendly and offered tea, and Henry Jones, who was not particularly friendly, and had clammy hands.

■ ■ ■

When I left, thirty minutes later, I had a ticket to a West End play and a suggestion for a good restaurant for supper afterwards. And that was exactly how I spent every day of my first week in London: bathing, dining, drinking, walking, the galleries, the museums, the theater, then supper—then a call to Jane to check on the condition of Dan and Tom.

Dan had only a broken leg. Tom was quite badly smashed up, but everyone seemed to feel that rest and some plastic surgery would make him as good as new.

The nightly phone call to Jane was my only discipline. The rest of my time was spent leading the life of the happy hedonist.

There were only two interruptions to my leisure, and even one of those was pleasurable. The other was exciting.

The exciting one occurred on the second day. There was a message for me to call a particular extension at the American Embassy.

When I did, I spoke with a Colonel Wayne. His voice was urgent and low, almost a whisper. "Do you know where the American Embassy is located in London?"

"Of course. Grosvenor Square."

"Good."

Good?

"Let's synchronize our watches. In twenty seconds it will be ten past the hour. Sixteen . . . fifteen . . . fourteen . . . two . . . one . . . *mark*." His voice grew more urgent. "Are we synchronized?"

"Yes—" What the hell, I was close enough.

"Good. In five minutes, walk to the statue of President Roosevelt and gaze at it. You're a tourist. I'll meet you there."

"How will I recognize you, Mr. Wayne?"

"*Colonel*—"

"Colonel."

"I'll recognize *you*. And I'll be in uniform. Check?"

This was more fun than meeting Ferguson. And unexpected at that. "Check. In five—no, *less* than five minutes from now, I'll walk to Grosvenor Square and gaze at the statue of Roosevelt."

"*President* Roosevelt."

"Sorry."

"Check. And—" Colonel Wayne was suddenly a comrade—"good luck."

"Thanks."

■　　■　　■

It would have been hard not to recognize Colonel Wayne. He was wearing a marine uniform, replete with even his sharpshooter's medal, and he was carrying an excessively long swagger stick.

"You're a tourist, asking some questions. I'll try to be helpful."

I played out my role as well as I could, and the Colonel,
by his gestures, pretended to be pointing out various
things of interest.

What he was saying was quite different, however. "I'm
not attached to the embassy here. I'm straight from the
MDW, but not the DOD. I'm the OIC of all CIA-
related—" he broke off—"but that doesn't really matter."
He had made his desired point. He had let me know, not
very subtly, that he was a most important man.

He stopped walking and looked into my eyes for the
first time. "You won't be seeing me again," he said. "But
we all wish you well, and we want you to know that." He
hadn't actually gestured towards the embassy, but I got
the feeling that everybody in the building was looking out
a window, wishing me well.

"Thanks." It seemed inadequate, but it was the best
that I could muster.

"And back home . . ."

I waited. "Yes—?"

"Well . . ."

I waited again.

He seemed to be struggling to control enormous emotions. "Well . . . if they knew of your mission, every pa-
triot in the country would wish you well, too."

In the virtual silence of Grosvenor Square, Colonel
Wayne had created an unseen orchestra and chorus, sing-
ing paeans of praise to me.

"Thanks again," I said. Now, my voice, too, was husky
with emotion.

"And—" he put both hands on my shoulders—"just
know that in the Oval Office itself—" He glanced toward
the embassy. "Deniability must be maintained at all times,
of course. But rest assured . . ." His emotions grew more
intense. "In that Oval Office . . . when your mission is
finished—" he pressed harder on my shoulders—"*Someone* will be grateful to you."

"Thank you, Colonel," I said, and realized that I was
standing at attention.

He stepped back. "Well—good luck. And—good hunt-
ing."

He raised his swagger stick in a smart salute.

I returned the salute.

As he strode away, back straight, swagger stick swinging, I did have one nagging thought.

What *was* my mission?

■   ■   ■

The other interruption, the pleasant one, was a call that very afternoon from my only British client, Sir Hugh Trevor-Maypole.

I was delighted to hear his voice, vibrant and vital on the phone.

"Well, well, old man, welcome to Blighty."

"Sir Hugh"—I had never referred to him in any other way—"I thought you were fishing in Scotland."

"So I was, old man, so I was. But I thought I'd pop back early and give you dinner at my club. Now which will it be to begin? Tea at the Savoy or drinks at the Savile?"

"By all means, drinks at the Savile."

"Splendid. See you at five?"

"Five it is."

"Splendid."

■   ■   ■

Sir Hugh Trevor-Maypole was English. And if, before one heard him speak, there was ever any doubt of that, the bespoke suit, the tattersall waistcoat and the Guards' tie quickly quashed it.

We were standing at the bar in the Grill Room of the Savile. Sir Hugh had introduced me to several friends, but now we were at one end, more or less by ourselves.

"Ah—at last. A chance to chat." Sir Hugh took a healthy swig of whiskey. "First of all, I'm dreadfully sorry that I couldn't be present at your party."

I had to chuckle. "I didn't really expect you to fly all the way to New York for a two-hour cocktail party."

"I would have, you know, if it hadn't been for the fishing." He smiled. "It's my one hobby and I love it. It's the most relaxing thing there is for me. I forget everything."

I looked at him appraisingly, pleased with what I saw. "Well, I must say, it does you a world of good. I noticed earlier, on the phone. Your voice is even a bit different. Younger sounding. And you look younger, too. I've never seen you more fit."

He seemed to blush. Something, until that moment, I had unconsciously assumed that Sir Hugh Trevor-Maypole would never do.

"Well . . . it's not just the fishing, you know." Now, he blushed noticeably. "Oh—but thank you—ah—for the compliments."

I was a bit thrown by his blush. "You're . . . you're very welcome," I finally managed to get out.

He drank some more whiskey, his face still pink, a funny smile on his face. "No—it's more than the fishing. Much more."

"Exercise, diet—"

"No—none of that." He paused. Suddenly, almost schoolboyishly, Sir Hugh Trevor-Maypole blurted out, "Oh, Harry, I've met the loveliest young thing. All of twenty-six. Her name is Julie. Beautiful. Intelligent, too." He chuckled happily. "Makes for a great motivation to lose a bit of weight—get a *tuck* or two here and there at the chin, the eyes, just a bit of touching up of the hair. Ah—did you notice?"

I was happy for him. "I told you. You look marvelous."

"No, the hair, I mean."

"Not at all."

"Now, now, you're being kind."

"No, I didn't notice. Really. Only that you look wonderful."

Sir Hugh was very pleased. "Thank you, thank you. Imagine. Someone as young as that—and a man my age—"

"Come on, you're a young man."

"Now, now—"

"Well, you certainly look younger than when I saw you last in New York."

"I *feel* younger. She does that for me. Julie does. D'you know how we met? Strangest bit of luck. . . ."

We went through two more rounds of drinks while I heard how Julie looked, how Julie laughed, how Julie talked, how she smiled, rode, fished, shot, and stroked his brow.

". . . and there we were, soaking wet, famished, me with a broken pole, and suddenly, she ran to me, embraced me, and said, 'Oh, Hughie'"—now his blush was crimson—"she, ah, calls me, Hughie. Rather—charming, don't you think?"

"Very—"

"She said, 'Oh, Hughie—I love you.'" Sir Hugh paused in wonder. "Imagine," he finally said. "Just—imagine. Me. Of all people."

We were silent for a while.

■ ■ ■

I had no dinner with Sir Hugh Trevor-Maypole that evening. Julie called and beckoned. He left apologetically, but rather proudly, after arranging for me to dine with two close and quite delightful friends.

Yes, I have never referred to him in any other way but Sir Hugh. However, this time, as he took his leave, I couldn't resist murmuring, "Have a pleasant evening—*Hughie.*"

His parting smile warmed the room.

■ ■ ■

The next day, I resumed my pattern of galleries, walking, theater, and suppers. It was a wonderful week, actually, but at the end of it, I was beginning to get just a bit lazy and a little lonely.

Jane laughed at me when I complained to her on the telephone. "Knowing you, boss—something—and by something I mean, of course, a woman—will turn up. They always do with you. And besides, don't call us to tell us about six great nights at the theater in London, and expect a great deal of sympathy."

I grinned. "I can see your point."

"And don't worry about the business. Everything is fine."

"Now I *am* worried."

"Why?"

"I'm not needed."

"Aw—not true. *The Dean of American Morning News* can't wait until you get back."

"That's comforting. Well, you know where to find me. I suppose I should relax and have a good time."

Jane sounded puzzled. "But isn't that why you went over in the first place?"

I caught myself. "Sure. Of course."

Jane's voice was warm. "Well, then, for heaven's sake enjoy yourself."

"You're damned right."

"Now you're talkin'," Jane said. "Have a great time, bring us a present to pay off your guilts, and everything'll be fine."

Good old Jane. "Thanks. And now I'm off to buy some chocolates."

"For whom? You *have* met a woman."

"For myself."

"You *never* eat candy."

"I've developed a fondness for it. The English do things so much better."

"Have fun," Jane said.

"Thanks."

I headed for South Molton Street and the chocolate shop. This was supposed to be the day.

The shop was empty when I entered, yet the moment after my purchase a woman's voice behind me said, "Well, you seem to be enjoying these chocolates a great deal—"

At last. Action.

I turned and, instantly, felt perspiration on my fore-head.

It was the Chinese woman. The tall one. The beautiful one. The one who had felt sorry for me when I had stood naked in front of her.

CHAPTER

19

SHE WAS smiling. She con-
tinued to smile as she said, "Would you share a few chocolates with me? Please?" Her eyes lowered slightly so that
she was looking at her right jacket pocket. The one with
her hand in it. And also, her glance was most eloquent,
the one with the gun in it, I quickly surmised.

"Please?" She smiled again.

"Take all you want." I proffered the box.

"No. Outside." Something inside that jacket pocket gestured toward the door. "Let us walk a bit."

Outside, I offered the box of chocolates again.

"No, thank you," she said. I don't really enjoy chocolate. It is too—chocolate-like."

"Yes. I quite agree."

"Let us go to your rooms."

"I beg your pardon?"

"Your rooms." Again, the gesture from inside her
jacket pocket was eloquent.

The presence of a gun, particularly in the other per-

son's hand, can make me extremely affable and agree-
able.

"Lead on, Macduff," I said.

"No, you lead."

"Very well."

"And who is Macduff?"

"Ah—he's a friend of Macbeth."

"Are you trying to be amusing at my expense?"

"No—no. I couldn't be amusing right now if I tried."

"But do try, please. I have a wonderful sense of humor.
Tell me a joke. I like to laugh."

We were crossing the street, heading toward Claridge's.

"I'm not a very good joke-teller," I said.

"No, a joke. Please."

Well, this *was* breaking up the monotony of baths,
booze, dinner, and the theater. "Okay. But stop me if
you've heard it— At age ninety-nine this wonderful theatrical producer dies, and who meets him at the Pearly
Gates but. . . ."

It was my best story; I told it well, and she laughed like
hell. Why, I thought, this can be fun. Then I remembered the gun. As a matter of fact, it was kind of hard to
forget the gun since she had pulled it out of her pocket
and had placed it carefully on the table in the center of
my drawing room.

"Don't move," she said.

"Don't worry. I'm not about to."

"Good. I owe you something, and I want to repay you.
I am Eurasian. And we Eurasians have a deep sense of
honor."

My tongue, my mouth, and my throat were suddenly,
and so quickly, dry, that I had not time to be aware of the
process.

"What in God's name did I ever do to you?" I asked.

"Nothing. It was I who did something to you. And,
therefore, I owe you your revenge."

"I don't want revenge."

"I was part of the process of your humiliation. And I
wish to make recompense."

"Recompense?"

"Did I not use the word correctly?"

"Yes, yes you did. But no recompense is necessary."

"Oh, but it is," she said. "For my own honor, I must do this." She touched the gun briefly. "Please do not talk and please do not move."

She took her hand away from the gun and unbuttoned her jacket and took it off. Then she unbuttoned her blouse, her eyes never leaving mine.

As she threw her bra to the floor, she said, "I am humiliating myself now."

"Hey, come on, it's—"

Her hand was momentarily back on the gun. "I asked you not to talk."

I nodded in agreement.

She continued to undress herself until she was completely naked. Six feet six inches tall—and naked. I know that *awesome* is an overused word nowadays, but since I had never used it before in describing a woman's body, I used it freely in my thoughts. From her perfect breasts to her lovely legs, her naked body was awesome.

She moved toward me, her face expressionless, and knelt down in front of me. "Hit me," she said. "Hard."

"No—"

"Strike me. I deserve it."

I tried to be breezy. "A gentleman never strikes a lady."

"I am no lady. I helped to humiliate you. Strike me."

"But I told you—I'm a gentleman."

"Then do whatever you want with me."

"Anything?"

"Yes, anything. . . ."

■ ■ ■

Three days later, as we were lying in bed, sharing the last piece of toast from our room service breakfast, I began to feel a bit guilty about not attending to my mission.

I called Bill Ferguson.

"Everything's fine," he told me. "Enjoy yourself. Have

ya' seen *The Second Mrs. Mauve* yet? I'll get ya' some lovely seats."

"I've seen it," I said. "Bill, what the hell am I supposed to be doing here in London?"

"Ya' got me, laddie, ya' got me. Don't *you* know?" Bill asked, sounding a bit surprised. "I mean, really don't ya' know?"

"Hell, no."

There was a pause, and then Bill Ferguson said, "Well, if *you* don't know. . . ." There was another pause. "How about *The First Mrs. Cooper,* have ya' seen that?" he asked.

"No."

"Drop by this afternoon. I'll have the tickets."

"Thanks, Bill."

"It's a pleasure, laddie, a pleasure."

As I was hanging up, I resolved to call M. And even though he wouldn't be able to see me, I showered, shaved, and put on a jacket and tie before I called him.

Anna had washed my back. She had told me that Anna wasn't her real name, but that I could call her that. She had also told me that she had quit *them.* And that *they* had let her quit. She had also told me that she would never tell me who *they* were.

Once Anna herself was safely in the shower, I placed my call to M.

When he came on the line, his first words were: "Good show, Baker, good show. Well done. Splendid. First-rate. Top Drawer. Wizard."

"For what?"

"You met your second contact and she is ours."

I didn't understand.

"Baker, are you still there?"

"Yes, I am," I said. "But what did I do?"

"There, there, no false modesty. I know you too well, Baker. You did a fine job—in fact, a perfect job of contacting Taiwan."

"Taiwan? M, what in hell are you talking about?"

M chuckled. "Ah, yes. No wonder you've sounded confused. You don't know."

"Don't know what?"

"Our code name for the Chinese is Taiwan."

"Oh—"

"Now you know."

"Yes." I hesitated. "I should tell you that I've had—pretty much—*constant* contact with her for the past seventy-two hours."

M chuckled again. "Boys will be boys."

The sound of the shower suddenly stopped. I lowered my voice. "I've got to talk fast," I said. "What am I supposed to do now?"

"Whatever she feels like doing."

"I'm serious."

"So am I," M said. "I've had you under surveillance for the past three days, and I knew that you've never left your room. But if you hadn't contacted me this morning, I would have contacted you. First, to congratulate you, and second, to tell you to keep it up. Follow her every whim for the next week. It's *very* important."

I was about to shout *"Week?"* when Anna—or Taiwan—came out of the bath, water glistening on all six-feet-six-inches of her body. She smiled. "Will you dry me?"

I used to have daydreams like that when I was a kid and reading *The Nobility of Boyhood.* I tried to look nonchalant. "Just let me get off the phone." The breathiness in my voice betrayed me.

"I take it she's right there beside you," M said.

"Yes, that's about it."

"All right then, I shan't detain you." M was developing a nasty habit of talking and chuckling at the same time. "Again—congratulations on a job well done, and your orders are simple. She's just defected to us. So follow her every whim for the next week. It's very important, and it'll pay off. You'll see. And—enjoy yourself." He hung up.

"Business?" she asked, as she handed me the towel.

"Yes," I said. "Business. With a Chinese friend of mine, actually."

"Oh—"

"Yeah. He's from Taiwan." I was drying her buttocks as I said it, and I tried to read them like a seismograph, for the slightest quiver of emotion. "Say, do you mind if I call you *Taiwan?*"

Not a quiver. "That is a funny name for somebody," she said.

"It's not any funnier than calling you Anna when Anna isn't your real name. I like it."

She smiled at me.

"Come on," I said. "What d'you say, *Taiwan?*"

"If you say it—I like it," she said.

"Good." I began working on her back, humming a simple work song. I had never tried to dry off anyone before, and I had had no idea that it could be such an enjoyable experience. There was no telling how really deep my work ethic ran.

Next came her shoulders. "Now, what would you like to do today? Because it's time for us to get out of this hotel and get some fresh air."

She turned. "You're not trying to get rid of me, are you?"

"Hell, no. The last thing on my mind. But we really do need some fresh air."

"Yes, once in a while." She smiled again.

"Right. And I'm ready to follow your every whim."

She kissed me on the ear.

CHAPTER
20

As IT TURNED out, her every whim followed a fairly predictable pattern.

We would sit in the lounge at Claridge's for a couple of hours, drinking, reading the papers, and discussing the world situation—she had the most remarkable knowledge of politics and history—and then we would return to my suite.

Or we would sit in the lounge at the Connaught and discuss the world situation for a couple of hours before returning to my rooms. Or the Chesterfield. Or the Park Lane. Or the Cumberland.

I was exhausted, but smiling.

One morning over a very late breakfast I asked, "Where to today? The Chesterfield? The Connaught?"

"I have to go," she said.

"Where?" I scratched her back.

She said it again with a very serious face. "No, I have to go away. I must leave you."

I blurted, "But it hasn't been a week yet."

"I beg your pardon?"

"I mean—why so sudden? Can't you stay for even one more day?"

"I am sorry, Harry. But we will see each other again. I am sure of it."

"Just till tomorrow morning—?"

"I am sorry . . ."

Eventually, having nimbly rebuffed half an hour of my best cajolery, she left. I felt like one of those guys in a television commercial who had everything going for him with a gorgeous woman until she suddenly spotted *unsightly dandruff* on his collar.

What had I done? I knew one thing that I had done. I had failed.

I called M. No answer. I went down to the lounge and sat for a while, trying to figure out my next move. I decided to call Bill Ferguson.

On the way to the telephone I nodded to the man with the bandaged head. He nodded back. He had seen me there so many times with Taiwan that we were now hotel friends. It seemed that, even behind all those bandages, I could sense an expression of, "Where's the young woman?"

Ferguson didn't answer; I went back to my room and tried M again. This time he picked up, and I made my confession of failure.

"Nonsense, Baker, nonsense. You kept it up one day short of a week. We thank you."

"But I didn't make the full week."

"Ah, yes, but as it turns out, it was *exactly* right." M chortled. "We finished our work this morning."

I relaxed. "Then everything's okay?"

"Everything is splendid," M said. "Again, congratulations. You know, Baker, you seem to have a natural talent for this sort of thing."

I dropped my eyes to the floor. "Thank you," I murmured modestly. "Thank you."

"Relax for the next twenty-four hours, and then you'll get your next assignment."

"Forget about the next assignment. I've had it. Being a

stud for my country for the last six days was fine. Once. But I didn't come all the way over here for this sort of thing."

"Of course you didn't. We agree."

"Well then—when do I do something important?"

"Everything that you have done has been of extreme importance, I can assure you." M's voice was very serious. "But I can understand your feelings."

"Well then?"

"The big show will begin any day now. And I can also assure you that you will be a very big part of it."

"When?"

"Tut, tut, tut," M cooed.

"No tut, tut," I said. "I've got a business to run. I'll give you another three or four days, and that's all."

"Fine," M said noncommittally. "Now relax and I'll be talking to you tomorrow."

But I couldn't relax. The thought of my business going down the drain had mobilized all of my worry cells. I felt sudden and terrible remorse for my actions of the past week. M had drawn out all of my obvious latent decadence.

And I was feeling lonely—I had a need to speak to real people.

I called my wife. Ex-wife.

"Hello—"

"It's Harry. How are you?"

"Harry—? Are you okay?"

"Fine. What're you doing?"

"Making breakfast."

"I could sure use some of your scrambled eggs."

"Yeah—you always could. What's up, Harry?"

"I'm in London. . . ." I wanted to tell her what I was doing, but to confide in anyone was against the rules. So we talked.

She told me a joke. I told her a joke. We hung up.

Then I called the children and was lucky enough to reach all four. I felt like a human being again.

To finish it all off, I called Jane at the office, and we spoke for nearly an hour. Then I called every client I had, except for the still hospitalized Tom, and spoke at length with each of them. After that, I spent another hour making related business calls to New York, Los Angeles, and Chicago. So it was getting well into early afternoon by the time I walked over to Soho for a late lunch.

I was headed for Wheeler's, with the pleasant thought of oysters and lemon sole dancing in my head; but an Italian restaurant on Old Compton Street struck my fancy and I went in.

I was sipping wine and glancing at the front page of the *Herald-Trib* when I spotted Jessica Rumbough, my warm, witty, and wonderful former client. She was alone, reading a movie magazine, and eating a huge plate of lasagna.

Two thoughts crossed my mind at the same time: one, a memory of her coup de grace as she made her exit at La Fenice, and two, something that Lauren Bacall had done to Gregory Peck in *Designing Woman,* one of my all-time favorite films.

I got up and went over to her table. "Hello, Jessica," I purred. "So nice to see you."

She seemed barely to recognize me. "Oh—hello."

"What brings you to London?" I asked, my voice oily and unctuous.

"Uh—holiday," she said.

"Ah—how nice."

She was very stiff, and her voice was rather stilted. She must have sensed that I was planning my retribution. I played a bit more with her—a very menacing cat with a very frightened mouse.

"And what a coincidence that we should happen to run into each other at a small restaurant in Soho," I said.

Her forehead creased. "Yes. Yes, it is."

"I was just remembering—fondly, of course—the last dinner we had together, at La Fenice in New York. Charming, wasn't it?" I was actually sounding just a bit like Adolph Menjou, and that pleased me greatly.

"Charming," Jessica almost whispered.

"I beg your pardon?"

"It was charming," she repeated.

"Yes, wasn't it? And the lovely way you left me. How could I ever forget that?"

With that I leaned toward her, gently pushed her plate of lasagna with my left hand, and deftly maneuvered the whole glistening mess into her lap.

Of course, when Lauren Bacall did that to Gregory Peck, it was an act fraught with much more grace and panache. But my action had at least as much effect.

Jessica's lap looked like a Neapolitan disaster area. She stared at me.

"Oh, good heavens, look what I've done," I exclaimed. "I'll get the waiter."

Jessica stared straight ahead, her eyes bulging. I think she was trying to scream, but no sound came out. One blessing, anyway. Jessica was a rare person; she had the ability to make the world a better place by simply choosing to keep her mouth closed.

A waiter arrived, accompanied by a captain and a bus boy. As they ministered to a shattered Jessica, who was still staring at me, speechless, I left a large tip on my table, waved her a cheerful good-bye, and took my leave.

All in all, it had been an extremely satisfying luncheon, even though I hadn't actually eaten anything.

So it was Wheeler's after all, and oysters, and lemon sole, and the *Herald-Trib*. And the superb house wine. It all made for a most pleasant hour.

But as I left, whistling, there was a vague, ill-defined sense of worry in the back of my mind. I tried to dismiss it as a spy's professional paranoia. M's business was getting the better of me.

■   ■   ■

All worries vanished, however, when I opened the door to my suite. Taiwan was back. I might not have recognized her had she been fully clothed, but she was her usual six-feet-six naked self.

She grabbed me around the waist, threw me on the

bed, and jumped on top of me in the manner of a professional wrestler.

"I am back," she cried.

"I realize that. I really do. But why did you think it was necessary to hurl me onto the bed like this?"

"I am just in a playful mood."

"Ah, but when one is in a playful mood, and one is six-feet-six-inches tall, while one's partner is only six—one must be careful not to break one's partner's back—which I think you've just done."

"Oh, Harry, you are so cute."

"I'm even cuter without a broken back," I said.

She laughed.

"Okay, now let me up. The fun is over."

She smiled down at me.

"Up, up, and away." I tried to roll out from under her, but her legs held me tighter.

I felt not a little bit silly and—although I didn't like to admit the feeling to myself—just a bit menaced.

"Are you going to keep me like this all afternoon?" I asked, trying to sound breezy.

She had never stopped smiling. "No, of course not." With one long and graceful move she rolled off me, off the bed, picked up her blouse and started to dress.

"Did you miss me?" she asked.

"You were only gone for eight hours."

"I know. But did you miss me? The truth."

I hesitated. "Yes—actually, I did. I didn't realize it until now."

The smile left her face, and she looked directly at me for a moment or two. "Good," she finally said. "After all, I am a woman."

"*Really?*" I said. "By golly, so you are."

She laughed. "I thought that you would never notice."

"And," I said. "I've just noticed that you have quite a stunning body."

She laughed some more. "You did not realize that before, either?"

"No, it's your mind, you see. Your mind is so amazing that it tends to cast a shadow over everything else."

"Oh, yes, I have a most amazing mind. What did you do while I was gone?"

"What did *you* do?" I countered. "Your dramatic exit left a clear impression that you were leaving for some time—weeks, months, years. You could have just said: 'I'll see you later in the day.'"

"I thought it would be for some time. But I was wrong," she said.

"But where were you?"

"A private matter. My family."

"Oh—" I didn't believe her.

"What about you?" she asked. "Where were you?" We've all had the experience of having someone ask a question quite casually, and knowing that the question isn't casual at all, and that the person asking the question has not quite succeeded in covering over the tensions that lie beneath the attempt at casualness.

"I beg your pardon?" I wanted to hear her say it again, to make sure.

She smiled. "What about you?" Hearing her ask it a second time, I knew that I had been right. This was a *very* important question to her.

It was probably the reason that she had returned, I decided.

"I'm afraid I was on the phone back to New York for several hours," I said. "Business. Nothing very exciting."

"Didn't you go out at all?" She was still standing there with bare buttocks, fiddling with a button on her blouse.

"Why do you ask?"

"I am just interested, that's all."

I decided to let out the information in dribs and drabs, just to see if she would pursue further, just to find out, if possible, what she was going for, what was important to her.

"Yes, as a matter of fact, I did go out," was all that I answered.

"Oh? Where?" That blouse button was apparently giving her an unusual amount of trouble.

"To Soho," I said.

"Why Soho?"

"Lunch."

"Did you have a good lunch?"

"Delicious."

"What did you have?"

"Belon oysters in shallot sauce, some wonderful lemon sole, and a great bottle of wine."

She turned too quickly. "Oh, but nothing Italian. . . ?" Our eyes met. I knew exactly what she was thinking. Her eyes avoided mine, and she went back to work on the button.

"Why Italian?" I asked.

"Oh—I do not know—there are so many exceptional Italian restaurants in Soho."

"Yes, there are." I waited for her to continue her questioning. But she had been daunted by her Italian gaffe. So I helped her out. "As a matter of fact, I almost did have lunch at an Italian restaurant. A nice little place just before you get to Wheeler's. It's on Old Compton Street."

She smiled. "See. I was right."

"Yes, you were."

"Why did you not?"

"Why didn't I what?"

"Have lunch there."

"I ran into a friend. No, that's not true, I ran into a former client."

"But why would that prevent you from having lunch?"

"Well, for the first time, I believe, in my adult life, I indulged in—in fact, wallowed in—total, complete childish revenge."

"What happened?"

"I—accidentally—deliberately—pushed a plate of lasagna into someone's lap. And that's not even the terrible part. The really terrible part is that I have no remorse whatsoever."

"Who was it? Anyone I might know?" Once again, extreme tensions lay just beneath the surface of that elaborate attempt to sound casual.

"No, you wouldn't—oh, yeah, you might at that. One of television's fastest rising young women—Jessica Rumbough."

"Really? Was it really Jessica Rumbough?"

"That's right."

"Really?"

"Positively, yes. Why're you so interested?"

"I am one of her greatest admirers. I think that she is wonderful."

"That's Jessica," I said. "Warm and wonderful."

"I wish I had been there with you," Taiwan said.

There was a brisk knock at the door.

When I opened it, I was, for one of the few times in my life, totally speechless.

"Hello, Harry. They told me in New York that you were staying here."

"Well, my God." I wished that I had never opened the door.

It was Alice, wearing a big smile and another diaphanous blouse.

"Alice—"

She laughed. "You always had a way with words, Harry."

"I'm surprised."

"I know." Alice gave me a long kiss.

"I wasn't expecting you at all."

"That's obvious." There was a sudden, brittle edge to her voice. She broke away from me, and went to a bikini and a pair of corduroy slacks that had been thrown on a chair.

"What is she, an Amazon?"

The door to the bath opened, and out stepped Taiwan. "What do *you* think?" she asked. Even though she was naked from the waist down, she still maintained her dignity.

"What the hell is this, Harry?" Alice's eyes blazed.

"What the hell is what, Alice?"

"A *woman. In—your—room.*" Alice of all people, sounded like something out of a very bad melodrama. I couldn't suppress my laughter.

"Go ahead and laugh at me, Harry. Ridicule me. A friend who calls on you in cold and lonely London out of friendship, only to find a half-naked Amazon—"

"Alice, you're too old to pretend jealousy."

"Jealousy! I'm talking about friendship—dignity—morality—"

Right about then Taiwan made her move. "I do not like to be referred to as a half-naked Amazon."

"How about a half-naked call-girl klutz?" Alice ad-libbed. It sounded vaguely familiar. Something from Wycherley and Congreve, I decided.

"What is a klutz?" Taiwan asked, eyes narrowing.

"An Amazon who needs a bath."

Taiwan struck. With one swift and easy move she picked up Alice and threw her onto the bed. But Alice was much more resilient than I had been; she bounced once on the bed and bounded back to the floor, landing on her feet in a boxer's stance.

"Okay," Alice said. "If that's the way you want it." She pasted Taiwan with a hard right to the ribs.

The fight that ensued was like a great stag opposing a feisty dog. Or, more accurately, an extremely attractive great stag and an extremely attractive feisty dog.

Besides being extremely attractive, they had other things in common: As the fight raged on, neither of them paid any attention to my cries to stop.

When I realized that shouting wasn't going to work, I tried to pry my way between them. It was just after Taiwan had executed a particularly difficult double-shoulder spin on Alice, throwing her onto the sofa, and Alice had retaliated with a crude but effective kick to Taiwan's right shin.

That's when I dived in.

I don't know who hit me, but it hurt, and the blow knocked me to my knees; I fell forward on my hands with a low groan. It was effective because it stopped the fight. They dropped to the floor, one on either side, and began to minister to me. Seeing the inadvertent good results of my actions, I continued to emit low groans for the next little while.

"Harry, are you okay?" Taiwan implored.

(A *great* groan.)

"Harry, speak to me." Alice stifled a sob.

(Another *pitiful* groan.)

Then the two of them simultaneously: "Oh, Harry—"

(I let out a cadenza of groans, ending on one so dramatic, and of such great intensity, that it would have pleased Lord Olivier himself.)

They gasped. And I started to laugh. In a moment we were all laughing.

Alice said, "I'm sorry, Harry. I didn't know I had such a green streak. It was just that—well, I've always told you about—other men. I never stopped to think that you— well—you know. I'm sorry."

"It's okay, Alice."

"*Oh*—This is so awful. You are *Alice*. Of course." A passionate flood of Chinese erupted from Taiwan.

Hands clasped tightly together, she fell to her knees before Alice. On her *knees,* Taiwan's face was slightly above Alice's. Her voice was husky and imploring: "Will you ever forgive me? *Please?*"

Alice recognized her finally. "Good God. *Good God,* Harry. You certainly have your quirks. Bopping around London with the head of a torture team—that must be a hell of a lot of kicks."

"Alice, please—"

"*Good God,*" Alice said again. She tried to pull back from Taiwan, but Taiwan passionately clasped Alice in her arms.

"Please, please—forgive me? *Please?*" There were tears in Taiwan's eyes and her voice was trembling.

"Let go!"

"*Please.* I was only following orders."

"*Only what?*"

"I was following orders. They made me do it. They told me that no one would *touch* you. And they lied. And I deserted and hid from them, and now I am against them, and it all began that day. That day they lied. I *hated* them. And I still do." Taiwan glanced up at me. "Ask—"

"It's true, Alice. She's on our side now."

"What do you mean by *our* side. What's *our* side?"

"I can't tell you."

Alice's eyes began to blaze anew.

"It's—ah—I'm doing something for the government temporarily. It's very small and insignificant—and unimportant. But it's a secret." I did my best to chuckle convincingly. "Look, Alice, you know me—I feel like an idiot saying, it's a secret. But it is. Later," I lied, "I'll tell you all about it."

"Please—forgive." Taiwan clasped Alice to her with even greater intensity, then released her and backed away on her knees.

"But I will never forgive myself." Taiwan's voice lowered. "Perhaps I should not ask you to, either. But will you understand? They lied. And I'm filled with shame."

They stayed that way for several long moments, their eyes meeting, Taiwan still on her knees.

Finally, Alice spoke. "You're sorry?"

"Very."

Another long moment passed, then Alice said, "And I'm sorry, too."

"For what?"

"For anything I said that insulted you." Alice tried to smile. "You're very beautiful." They touched hands.

"You are very beautiful, too," Taiwan said.

"Well, now that we're all friends, let's get dressed and go down to the lounge for a drink." I grinned. "I wish Jane could see me now. Here I am with absolutely the two most beautiful women in the world, and I say, 'Let's get dressed and have a drink.' Jane would be proud of me. Or else she would be convinced that I really do have unfortunate sexual proclivities."

"Don't you worry," Alice said.

"I'm not. Come on to the lounge."

"Yes, let us," Taiwan said. "Now that we are all friends it will be fun to drink together."

"Yes, friends," Alice said.

Alice helped Taiwan to her feet.

I smiled at Alice. And I smiled at Taiwan. And I wondered if anybody in the room was a friend of anyone else.

"I'm going to have a nice cold lager," I said.

CHAPTER

21

WE WERE sitting in the lounge at Claridge's. "What a truly wonderful place," Alice was saying. She raised her glass. "To Claridge's. Cheers."

"Cheers—Cheers," Taiwan and I echoed Alice.

"Ah—" Alice let out a long sigh and took a second sip. "Just the thing for after a fight." She smiled and touched Taiwan's arm, and they both giggled.

"You are funny," Taiwan said. "I like you."

"And you have wonderfully good taste." Alice grinned.

"Where're your friends?" I asked Alice.

"What friends, Harry?"

"Just about six minutes and thirty-three seconds ago you told us that you had flown over with two friends, and that they were going to meet you here."

"Six minutes and thirty-*four* seconds ago, Harry."

"Thirty-three," I countered.

"You don't believe me. You never do." Tears gushed from Alice's eyes.

"Oh—" Taiwan was touched and moved to comfort Alice.

"It's okay, Taiwan," I said. "The tears are ersatz. Another of her myriad talents."

The tears immediately stopped. *"Taiwan,"* Alice said. "What a perfectly lovely name."

"It's not really my name, but thank you."

"Well, it should be your name. It really should."

"Thank you again."

"My senior year," Alice said.

"I beg your pardon." Taiwan's face was questioning.

"Chemistry class."

"Chemistry—?"

"Yes," Alice smiled while remembering. "I never knew that I had this perfectly wonderful gift till then. I was taking a chemistry test—actually, it was taking me—and the questions could have been in Greek for all I could understand them, and I was completely desperate, and I thought, what can I do? If I flunk this class in chemistry, I won't be graduated from high school. And out of my *total* desperation it came. God knows from where—but it *came.*"

Taiwan, her eyes wide, was on the edge of the sofa. I was smiling. I had heard the story three or four times by now; it was always essentially the same, although the setting varied. Sometimes it was a French class, or biology class. And one time it was while being confronted by a raging bull during a postprandial stroll in Mexico. Whatever the setting, the ending was always the same.

". . . And I looked up into that algebra teacher's face—"

"Chemistry—" I prompted.

"Chemistry teacher's face—" she didn't miss a beat— "and I began to cry. Huge, beautiful, delightful tears. Like this." Alice turned on her gift again, and the tears flowed once more.

"My heavens—" Taiwan's voice was filled with wonder.

"It was a kind of coup de theatre. I cried for thirty minutes straight. All very silently." Alice giggled again. "That was the real *genius* of it. Never a sound. And then, after I'd handed in a completely blank test paper, and

Mr. Evans—that was his name—he had the cutest blue eyes—they'd be red quite a lot of the time, but they were cute—and Mr. Evans asked me to see him after school, and I did, and cried for *another* thirty minutes, and then he said, 'There, there, don't worry about a thing,' and he passed me."

Alice sat back, acting very much as if she were Madame Curie, and she had just explained her isolation of radium to the press.

"Remarkable," said Taiwan.

"Yes, isn't it? A gift."

I applauded. After she bowed, I asked, "Well, if we don't know where they are, *who* are your friends?"

"They're fascinating," Alice said, "absolutely fascinating."

"I assumed that."

"Well, first of all—in addition to flying together—they're living together."

"I won't say a word."

"No, no, you don't understand. They're married."

"You're right. I *don't* understand. The phrase *living together* has more or less come to mean that a couple—*usually* a man and a woman—has acquired every other condition of marriage—washing dishes, garbage control, and shared bathroom facilities—excepting a ceremony and a license."

"Well, they had the ceremony—very small and civil and chic, very hush-hush, and they have the license. But she doesn't like the word *marriage*—I don't think he really minds it too much—but she loathes it. She prefers the phrase *living together*."

"Whatever she likes."

"She's quite a stickler about certain things."

"Another gift," I said.

"You see, she's a leading feminist. And quite militant. But, of course," Alice quickly reassured, "in a very chic and sophisticated way."

"Of course."

"And he's a filmmaker."

"Oh? What's he produced?"

"He doesn't *produce*."

"Directed?"

"He doesn't *direct* either," Alice said primly. "He's a filmmaker, Harry. No one *directs* anymore. At least not anybody who appears in *The New Yorker*. He's a *filmmaker*."

"I stand corrected," I said.

"They're here together to make a film from her book. They have a Guggenheim Grant."

"No one ever spends Guggenheim money in, say, Pittsburgh, or West Virginia. It's always Paris or London."

"It's necessary. Her book deals with the common brutalization of British and American women."

"*Gosh*. I must get myself a copy."

"Don't be a wise guy, Harry. I'm talking about Elizabeth Sprague-Murray."

"Who?"

"My God, Harry. She wrote *Cry Womb!*"

"Never heard of her."

"Then you certainly never heard of him."

"Try me. What's he done? I mean made."

"*Several—experimental* student films at N.Y.U. He just finished his Ph.D. there. It's his second. His name is Dr. Mark Murray."

"As in Elizabeth Sprague-Murray."

"I hate you when you get like this," Alice said. "He's the brother of Dr. Scott Murray."

"Another household word?"

"Dr. Scott Murray is the famous—" her lips formed the quotation marks—"Psychiatrist to the Stars."

"He practices in Los Angeles."

"Well, at least you've heard of *him*."

"Just a wild guess."

"Sometimes I don't understand you, Harry." She turned to Taiwan. "Do you understand him?"

"I have not understood the entire conversation for the past three minutes," Taiwan said.

"Well, let me explain then. I forgot that English is your second language."

"Actually, it's my fifth," Taiwan said innocently.

Alice missed that. "Let me recapitulate," she said, in a voice that was redolent with earnestness.

The recapitulation began, but I didn't hear it. Entering the Brook Street entrance of Claridge's was The Man Who Looked Like Howard Cosell.

Actually, *entering* was the wrong word; he was *running;* and running should be modified with the word *desperately.*

As he paused in the center of the lobby to catch his breath, two men who had been sitting near us, unnoticed, moved out toward him as quickly and as stealthily as two leopards. Before his eyes had even turned up to them, they were on either side, pinning his arms, and half-carrying him out the door.

I stood. *"Hey—"*

"Shh. Harry, for heaven's sake," Alice remonstrated.

I ran toward the entrance and out to the street. A Jaguar, British racing green, was screeching away from the curb. I assumed that the two men were inside with the man who looked like Howard Cosell.

I ran after the car, but after twenty-five or thirty yards, I realized my folly and gave up the chase. I smiled to myself as I returned to the hotel. And what, I wondered, would I have done if I had caught the Jaguar?

A London taxi bore down on me and stopped at the edge of the curb. A rear door opened and an abrasive voice said: "I didn't know you were into jogging, Harry." It was Jessica Rumbough again.

I formed a smile. "Hello, Jessica."

"I'm on my way to the Savoy. That's where I'm staying. How about coming along for a drink while we bury the hatchet."

"I'd love to, I really would. But I have friends inside."

"But I just saw you running down the sidewalk in the other direction."

"I was—running—after some other—ah, friends."

Jessica reddened. "That's the last fucking time I try to bury the hatchet with you, Harry."

"Yes—good idea," I said.

"Fuck you, Harry." Jessica slammed the door, and the taxi took off.

The language of Milton. The language of Shakespeare. The language of Keats and Shelley and Siegfried Sasson. The English language. One of the best examples of the unfairness of the way of the world was to know that Jessica Rumbough also spoke it.

Back at our table, Alice was petulant. "My God, Harry, you're behaving like a German tourist. *Everybody* looked at us when you shouted."

I tried to look contrite. "I'm sorry."

"Well—all right." My show of contriteness pleased her greatly.

We were about to order a second round of drinks when Alice's two friends arrived, so we ordered for everyone.

They looked exactly like a man named Dr. Mark Murray, who has two Ph.D.'s and is an experimental *filmmaker,* and a woman named Elizabeth Sprague-Murray, who is quite a militant feminist, but in a chic and sophisticated way, and has written a book entitled *Cry Womb!*—and like two who are about to make a film of it with money from a Guggenheim Grant—*BLUES.*

And they talked that way, too.

My mind drifted . . . to Jessice Rumbough. Something had been wrong in Soho . . . Something . . . what. . . ?

". . . *isn't* it, Harry?"

"I beg your pardon?"

"I was just saying that the time is ripe for this kind of film."

"Oh, yes. Yes, it certainly is. I envy you—ah, filmmakers."

Having contributed so very much to that particular part of the conversation, my eyes again glazed, and my mind drifted back to Jessica.

Yes. . . . *Something* . . . was wrong.

Oh . . . of course. Yes . . . *of course.*

CHAPTER

22

· · · THE ITALIAN restaurant in Soho. And just now on the sidewalk in front of Claridge's. Two conversations. Two different conversations. Very different.

True, in Soho Jessica had used the English *holiday* instead of the American *vacation*. I had noticed that at the time, but had chalked it up to a bit of pretentiousness on Jessica's part. Perhaps, on someone else, I would have thought—*admiration* of the English language. But not Jessica.

No, not Jessica.

Jessica had not the slightest appreciation of the English language. Or—as Jessica might say—the fucking funny way they talk.

Ah, yes. That was it. That was it, all right.

I had dumped an entire dish of lasagna on Jessica's lap, and she hadn't uttered a single, ugly Anglo-Saxon sound.

That had been very unlike Jessica. But why?

Ah, well. I tried to put it out of my mind and to rejoin the conversation.

Elizabeth Sprague-Murray was still holding forth: ". . . and the main thing that *I* try to do when *I* write is to put down what *I* really think, *my* thoughts, what *I* believe to be the . . ."

And they call it the *me* generation.

. . . *Jessica* . . . What about her? Aw, cut it out, I told myself. So she wasn't herself for one brief moment. Accept, with gratitude, the fact that for that moment the world was a better place and then forget it.

I couldn't.

"Will you excuse me for a few moments. I'll be right back."

"Harry, that's so unlike you," Alice said.

"What is?"

"Well, you of all people—I mean, you just couldn't be deliberately rude." By that, of course, Alice meant that I was being rude. "Elizabeth was just *sharing* with us, explaining the reason for the ending of *Cry Womb!*"

"I'm just running up to get my copy of the book." I looked at Elizabeth Sprague-Murray in what I hoped she would consider an expression of bashful admiration: "Would you mind giving me an autograph?"

She didn't smile, but, for the first time, she came close to it. "Why, of course. I'd be delighted," she said.

"Then excuse me for just a moment. I'll be right back—order another round, Alice—" I more or less backed out of the lounge before running up the stairs two at a time.

My intention had been to call M and tell him about the strangeness of Jessica, and my feelings about her—accept his probable ridicule—but feel that I had, at least, dutifully passed my thoughts upward.

But the phone rang as I entered my room, and Jane was on the other end.

"How goes it, boss?"

"Not bad, not bad. How're you?"

"Fine." Jane smiled through the phone. "I'm sorry to

bother you, but something came up here in New York that I thought you'd want to know."

"It's never a bother with you, Jane. You know that. What's up?"

"Well, it's rumored that CBS wants to put a weather man on their new morning show."

"They have *another* new morning show? Since I left?"

"No—this is still the latest new morning show. It's over three weeks old now."

"How'd you hear about the weather man?"

"Cy Romberg."

"That's a good source, all right."

"And that same good source hinted that they're looking over at Paul Jonathan."

"Yeah?"

"Well, here's the good part." Jane's voice rose in volume. "Paul Jonathan has heard the same thing. His contract will be up in just over ninety days, *and* less than ten minutes ago he called this office and asked for you."

"Well?"

"*Well?* Harry, he probably wants you to represent him."

It took me all of two seconds to make up my mind. "I'm not interested," I said.

"*Not interested?* Why? He's so cute. And he's *hot* just now."

"We have the same barber," I said.

"You what?"

"We have the same barber."

"What's that have to do with not representing him? Honest to Pete, Harry."

"He's dull, he's pompous, and his idea of self-improvement is to spend seventy-five dollars a week on having his hair curled. In short, he's not for me."

Jane was hurt, and it showed in her voice. "Gee, it seemed that it was worth a call, Harry."

"It certainly was, Jane. How were you to know that you work for such an opinionated old codger? Anything else?"

"No. It's pretty quiet here. How're you doing?"

"Not bad. Oh, I ran into our friend Jessica Rumbough."

"Yeah, I read in *Variety* that she was going over for a quick vacation and an attempt at an interview with Lady Di. How is she?"

"Her usual charming self. As she left me, she cooed a soft and sentimental, 'Fuck you, Harry.'"

"God, I get a lump in my throat just hearing it all second-hand."

"Romantic, huh?"

"Romantic."

"Actually, I ran into her before," I said. "And it was like running into two different Jessica Rumboughs."

"What d'you mean?"

"I don't know, Jane, but . . ." And the obvious finally hit me. The *vaguely* obvious at least.

"Harry?"

"Yeah, I'm here. Jane, I've been brooding about Jessica all day—and it all seemed silly and probably paranoid until just now. It's just hit me. Look, I've already run into a man who looks like Howard Cosell. Why couldn't I have run into a woman who looks like Jessica Rumbough?"

"Maestro, are you okay?"

"You're damned right. I don't think that *was* Jessica in Soho. Just as I *know* that it wasn't Howard in New York."

"But what if it wasn't—Jessica, I mean?"

"I don't know. But at least it means that there's some kind of pattern. And I've now been involved twice with this same kind of thing."

"I'm not quite following, Harry."

"I know. I'm sorry, Jane—but talking to you helps me think. This is all off the top of my head."

"It's okay. Go ahead."

"I've got to call M for sure now."

"Who?"

"A phone call. I've got to make an important one right away. Is there anything else that's important from the office?"

"Nothing." A pause. "Harry?"

"Yes?"

"Are you all right? Can I do anything?"

"I'm fine. But thanks for the concern. I've got to run. G'bye, Jane, and thanks for the call."

"G'bye, Harry. Harry—?"

"Yeah?"

"Take care of yourself."

I waited for a few seconds and then placed a transatlantic call to M.

He sounded cheerful. "Hello, hello, Baker, how are things going?"

I told him.

"And you really feel that there is a *probability* that you were talking to your second physically similar, but distinctly different person?"

"Absolutely," I said.

"I'll be coming over," M snapped.

"You will?" M would never know it—and it surprised me—but I was pleased to hear that news.

"Yes. I don't like the expense—we're trying to peel down the budget, you know—but, if you're correct, then you're onto something important."

"I—think—that I might be," I said. Now that I knew that M himself was going to make a personal move because of me, I wasn't nearly so certain.

He must have heard the hint of a quaver in my voice. "Now, now, Baker. It's your duty to report what you see, and what you sense. And you've done well. Admirably. If there is some kind of pattern then we must know about it."

"Maybe—"

"No, no I should be there. Let's see—I'll catch a plane out of Dulles tonight and I'll be arriving—I'm just guessing now, depending on the airline I take—at Heathrow at approximately eight A.M. London time. I suggest that you stay within the confines of Claridge's, have an early night, and we'll meet for breakfast in the Causerie there at, say, nine A.M. tomorrow."

"Won't that be early for you? Jet lag and all?"

M chuckled. "Never seems to bother me. And I sleep like a baby on a plane. Besides, we'll have work to

do. Have a good night, and I'll see you at eight. And
Baker—"

"Yes?"

"You were right to call. Even if it all turns out to be a
wash, you did the right thing."

"Thanks, M." What startled me was that I meant it.

"See you at nine tomorrow morning." He rang off.

I went back to the lounge and listened to Elizabeth
Sprague-Murray hold forth on every subject known to
mankind.

CHAPTER
23

IT WAS only a kind of scratching sound—metal against metal—but it was enough to snap open my eyes and awaken me from a deep sleep. My left hand pushed back the blankets and my right reached for the gun, as I simultaneously slid down to the floor. At that point, my right hand and I both blushed. I had momentarily forgotten that I had no gun.

A few more moments and the scratching at the door stopped. I looked at my watch. It was twenty after one. I waited another fifteen minutes in the darkness before I allowed myself to relax.

The phone rang. It was Alice. "Harry, I've got to talk to you."

"Alice, are you drunk?"

"I've been drinking, but I'm not drunk."

"It's the middle of the night."

"Harry, it's important."

"Okay, Alice, what is it?" I had never known Alice to think that anything was unimportant.

"I've got to talk to you, Harry."

"Fine, Alice, talk," I said.

Her voice turned to a desperate whisper. *"Not—on—the—telephone, Harry."*

"Why not?"

"Harry," Alice's voice dropped even lower in volume, "someone is planning to kidnap you, and I know all about it."

"What—?"

"Meet me in the lounge."

It took me seconds to dress. I was hesitant about opening the door, but when I finally did, the hall was empty.

Alice was seated in a chair at the entrance to the lounge. She rose quickly to greet me.

"Let's go outside."

"Alice, it's almost two in the morning."

"Harry, let's go outside. Please. You never know who's going to overhear whom in this place. God knows, that's how I heard. I *over*heard."

"Overheard what?"

"That someone's planning to—you know. Let's go outside."

I followed her out. She moved to the edge of the sidewalk.

"Alice, we're practically in the street, for God's sake."

"Harry, be serious. You should be. I don't know what you're up to, but from what I overheard in there, you should be serious."

She was right. "Sorry, Alice. What did you hear?"

"Well, after you left us, that lovely Taiwan stayed for another round of drinks with the three of us. We had a marvelous time, but after about half an hour Taiwan had to leave, an errand or something, and then Dr. Mark Murray had to leave, too. Something about checking on a lens or something, but if you ask me he had a rendezvous with Taiwan planned, but thank goodness Elizabeth Sprague-Murray didn't seem to notice the coincidence of their living together—" Alice giggled—"I meant *leaving* together. Is that a Freudian slip or is that a Freudian slip, Harry?"

"Alice, please—get on with it."

"I'm just trying to give you the background, Harry."

"I appreciate that. But, so far, your story has given me no reason for alarm, and—no reason to get dressed and stand out here at this time of night."

"Well, if you're going to go on and on, ranting and raving, you're right. I never *will* finish my story. May I? Please?"

"Yes. I'm sorry."

Alice smiled benignly. "Underneath, you're a real gentleman, Harry."

"Thank you."

"You're welcome." Her story-telling voice returned. "At any rate, there we were, Elizabeth Sprague-Murray and I, so we walked over to Grosvenor Square, and who do you think we ran into—?"

She paused and waited, obliging me to say, "Who?"

"Taiwan, of all people. So she really hadn't had a tryst with Dr. Mark Murray after all. So then the three of us walked down to the Connaught, and, lucky for us, they'd had a last-minute cancellation, and we were able to have dinner. I ordered the lamb, because it's always so good there, and Elizabeth Sprague-Murray had . . ."

My teeth were literally grating together. I could hear them. And if Alice hadn't been so keenly in tune with the sound of her own voice, she would have heard them, too.

Her lusty logorrhea continued for another several minutes while I was wearing down at least half a dozen examples of Dr. Brofsky's finest dental work.

". . . and there we were, back in front of Claridge's, and I suggested that we all have a nightcap, and Elizabeth Sprague-Murray agreed, but then she changed her mind and decided to go back to her hotel, and Taiwan volunteered to walk with her, she really is a very lovely person, and they headed back for the Chesterfield Hotel which is just off Berkeley Square, which she says is just lovely. The hotel, I mean, is lovely. Well, for that matter, so is Berkeley Square, for heaven's sake. So I decided to treat myself to—"

I could bear it no longer. "Alice, for God's sake, what did you want to tell me?"

She looked at me, astonished, as if seeing me for the first time to be a madman.

"Honestly, Harry, one of these days that impatient temperament of yours is going to be your undoing."

"Yes, it very probably will."

Alice smiled. A night nurse's smile. "Well, at least you're aware of it. That's a start."

"Yes. Yes, I am."

"That's good."

I was completely, totally, absolutely, utterly defeated. "Did you have any more that you wanted to tell me?" I asked in the voice of the vanquished.

"Why, of course. You don't think I'd get you out of bed just for that, do you? Honestly, Harry." She exhaled and clucked her tongue. "I'm just getting to the point of the whole story."

"Good. I'm glad," I said. I had never been more honest in my life.

Alice pulled me out to the very edge of the sidewalk, nearly onto the curb. Her voice was lower than a stage whisper.

"I went into the lounge and was sitting alone with my nightcap. There were only a few others there. One was a man who was sitting alone like me. Only a few feet away. He was reading a paper."

"Alice—"

"This is it, Harry. Another man came in and said something to him in a very low voice. But I could hear it. The man who entered said: 'We have to take our friend Baker for a tour of the countryside tonight.' And the other man said: 'Okay.' That was all. They left and I called you."

I clasped her arm with both of my hands. "Thanks, Alice."

She smiled. "Anytime, Harry. Anytime."

Alice put a cigarette to her lips and lit it with an expensive-looking lighter.

"This is the first time that I've ever seen you smoke," I said.

"You know me, Harry. I was at Selfridge's, and I saw this cute lighter, and I couldn't resist it. So I bought it. Then to go with it, I had to buy my first pack of—"

I didn't hear any more. A car squealed quickly down Brook Street and pulled to a stop beside us. It was a Jaguar. Probably, it was British racing green. Somebody opened the rear door and reached for me, and then something hit me on the head from behind.

■   ■   ■

By now, I was very accustomed to the situation: regaining consciousness in the back seat of an automobile with my wrists handcuffed together, wearing a blindfold.

I decided that I should probably have an extremely well-tailored blindfold made up for myself on Savile Row, which I could carry in a breast pocket, while wearing suitably sporty handcuffs around my wrists—something that, in addition to making my personal life more efficient, might catch on in Beverly Hills on Rodeo Drive ("stainless steel, silver, gold, or platinum, sir?") and net me a small fortune.

I wondered if it all would be tax deductible—at least my personal set—if I could prove to the Internal Revenue Service that I seemed to use them almost weekly in my line of business.

I wondered, too, where we were going. And who we all were.

No one was talking. There was someone on either side of me, and someone, obviously, was driving. So there were at least three other people.

I sensed that one of the others, the person on my right, was Taiwan. Perhaps I smelled her scent. Perhaps I was being superpsychic. Perhaps I was bananas by now.

"Is that you, Taiwan?"

Not a sound.

I wondered how the hell I had gotten back into this silly situation. Then I remembered the Jaguar. The bang on the back of the head. Alice.

Alice. I've been told many times that I'm too trusting. That's flattering, but probably not true. But it is true that I have very little paranoia in my bones. So I didn't think I was flirting with paranoia now.

Alice had got me out of bed and downstairs. Alice had got me out to the sidewalk. Alice had edged us both out to the curb. And then—for the first time in her life—Alice had flipped a lighter in order to light a cigarette. But why?

The answer so depressed me that I tried to think of other things.

We were driving smoothly on what seemed to be an extremely wide road for Britain. Probably one of the M roads. Therefore we were traveling either—north, south, east, or west. So much for my brilliantly deductive mind.

We continued on for about an hour, moved off the main highway to a secondary road, then turned into what seemed to be a village—winding streets and very little noise.

We stopped. A revolver barrel was pressed hard into my right side. I heard the left car door open, and the person on that side pulled at my arm, urging me out of the seat.

And suddenly, there was a problem. I sensed it. Something had gone wrong. Everyone was whispering with nervous intensity. Rising above the muffled apprehension, a single voice rasped, "Back—"

I was shoved into the car a second time, and we quickly sped off. The ride—back to London, I assumed—was quite different. Once again, no one spoke, but the people were constantly moving (passing notes, I wondered?), and the drive was not calm and deliberate as before. We were speeding, perhaps indiscreetly.

In much less than a hour, one could sense London again. The increase in traffic. The night sounds. The car continued to speed.

And then it happened. Something hit us from the side with such enormous force that the Jaguar seemed to skid for several yards before turning over.

My blindfold was ripped off, there was blood running down my face, and I was in a state of semiconsciousness and semihysteria. But all of the adrenaline seemed to be pumping into that lobe of the brain that controlled animal-escape.

The car was sitting exactly on its roof with two doors thrust open on one side, the nose of a large lorry penetrating the doors of the other. I managed to get myself over an unconscious body and to pull myself out of the wreckage.

Then I put my head down and ran. And when I

couldn't run any longer, I loped, and when I couldn't do that I walked, and then I staggered.

The only lucky thing that had happened to me all night was that the crash had occurred, and that it had occurred near St. George's Arms, on Lambeth Road, so I knew where I was.

Coming up along Berkeley Square, walking now, wondering what the hell to do about the handcuffs—it seemed rather unlikely that anyone had ever before entered Claridge's while wearing handcuffs—I heard the sound of an old car. It was very loud in the early morning stillness.

Something told me, probably not instinct, probably just plain fear, to step behind one of the great trees in Berkeley Square. After a moment, an ancient Morris Minor moved past.

Inside were Taiwan and Alice.

I hid behind trees, in doorways, any place I could find as the Morris Minor circled Berkeley Square twice. Alice and Taiwan were very determined searchers.

After they had apparently given up, I made my way through the shadows of Davies Street, around the corner, and into the entrance of Claridge's, my head held high, an insouciant smile on my face, making a brave attempt to appear completely at ease, to be merely an American version of a capricious toff.

"Good evening, doorman."

"Evening, sir," I saw his eyes bulge only a bit.

"I say, my good man, is there someone who can get me out of these?" I held up my handcuffed hands.

He was completely nonplussed, but determined not to show it. "Well, sir, I could call the maintenance man."

"Yes, would you do that, please?" The role I was playing pleased me greatly and gave me some badly needed confidence.

"Excuse me, sir. You *are* a guest, aren't you sir?"

"Indeed, my good man, indeed. Mr. Baker, Suite 202."

"Thank you, sir. And excuse me for any rudeness I may have—"

"Not at all, my good man. Only doing your duty, *what?*"
That sounded so good that I added a *Quite.*

Because of my own role-playing, I wasn't sure when the
maintenance man saw my condition and said, "Cor blimey,"
if he were putting me on, or sending me up, or what.

Both he and the solicitous assistant manager were very
careful not to refer to the awkwardness of my state, and
they were extremely careful not to ask how I had got that
way—so I volunteered. Just to clear the air.

"It's the last time I go out with a blonde from Sweden," I
confided merrily. "Their idea of fun is a bit too bizarre for
me. Well, I may be a bit bloodied—but unbowed, *what?*"

That embarrassed the two of them completely. It was
obvious that my already questionable good taste had deserted me completely. To ease the situation, I amended
the story slightly. "I haven't been on a scavenger hunt for
years, and we were supposed to bring back a set of handcuffs, but she lost the key, of all things."

They looked a bit relieved and managed stilted chuckles.

Finally, the maintenance man said, "There you are, sir.
Hope I didn't hurt you."

"Not at all, not at all." I offered a five-pound note, which
he refused. I pressed it upon him, and he still refused. He
wanted only to leave as quickly as possible, and he did,
mumbling under his breath about the silliness of the rich.

The assistant manager bowed slightly, smiled slightly,
and left quickly.

During all of this I had been keenly aware of my vul-
nerability while standing in the open lobby, so I had maneuvered the three of us as far to one side of the
doorway as possible. From that angle I now saw the Morris Minor pull up on the street.

I bolted for the stairway and made for my room with
all the speed of a frightened man who had just had his
handcuffs removed, and before that had been in a hor-
rifying accident, and before that had been kidnaped.

CHAPTER

24

HALF AN HOUR later, I still sat in the large Queen Anne chair, watching the door, waiting for their next move—and for the hundredth time, wondering who in hell *they* were.

M and Wendell had really told me nothing; in the beginning, in my burst of patriotism, it had seemed to make sense, what with security and all, but by now I was frustrated and angry.

I had tried to call my so-called safe house at Ferguson, Freaks and Ferguson, but there had been no answer.

That was the point at which my frustration had burst out of the bottle. A month before I had never even heard of a safe house, and now, here I was, playing some ridiculous game whose rules I didn't know: I had just played the only card I *did* know, calling my safe house—and there had been *no goddamned answer.*

And so the next half hour went by. And I tried to figure things out.

I had only sensed Taiwan in the car. I didn't really

know if she had been there. But even if she had not, I had damned well seen her on that first Washington escapade. She had even been the chief interrogator. M was wrong. Taiwan was no defector.

So—Taiwan was with them.

And Alice was with Taiwan.

So—Alice was with them, too.

I might not know who *they* were, but I did know two people who were with them.

Great. Brilliant. Smashing.

. . . When were *they* going to come. . . ?

The phone rang. I glanced at my watch. It was 7:00 A.M. My God, what a night.

It was the most tentative Hello ever uttered into a telephone instrument.

Wendell's voice barked out like an affected first sergeant. "Rise and shine. Another day is dawning. Up and at 'em—Sorry to waken you, but we've just arrived at Heathrow.

"We?"

"Yes—we." Wendell explained as if to a child. "I've arrived—with our—*friend*."

"Ah, yes. You and our friend."

"Say, are you all right?"

"Fine, just fine."

"Good. I called even before we cleared customs so you'd have time for a bath and a shave. We got here earlier than expected—nice tail wind all the way."

"That was very thoughtful of you," I said. "Very thoughtful."

"Thank you. I thought that this way you'd have plenty of time to get ready for our breakfast meeting, which now our *friend* would like to schedule for eight-thirty instead of nine. Same place."

"Eight-thirty sounds fine." My eyes never left the door.

"That way we'll have time to freshen up a bit, too, and—"

"Don't freshen up," I interrupted him. "Call me the second you get to Claridge's. Then come right up to my suite."

"But, really, we're both a bit grimy from—"

"I'll tell you what," I said. "I'll hold off my bath, too. Just to make it even."

"What the hell are you talking about, Harry?"

"I'll explain when you get here. Call me and come straight up to my suite."

I hung up, went back to the Queen Anne chair, and resumed my vigil.

■   ■   ■

The knock finally came.

I didn't open the door.

A second knock. I waited.

"Harry? It's William Morris."

I didn't answer.

"It's—*William Morris.*"

"Just a minute, Wendell." I unbolted the door, keeping the caution chain fastened, and peered out. It was Wendell and M, but the way things had been going, I wouldn't have been surprised to see George Steinbrenner standing there. I let them in.

"You were supposed to counter with—'ten percent,'" Wendell said. "Let's not get lax—" Wendell stared at me. "Are you okay?" And then—"Oh, my God, Harry. What happened?"

M pursed his lips and murmured, "Dear, dear."

I put a finger to my lips, motioned them out to the hallway, and we went up to M's suite.

There, I gave them a detailed accounting of the entire escapade, indicting Alice and Taiwan as the only two members of *they* that I actually knew.

"Taiwan, dear, dear—of all people." M was deeply distressed.

"And who's this Alice?" Wendell asked.

"She's the one you drugged during our first meeting at the Sherry-Netherland."

"Drugged? We prefer the more clinical term, which is—"

"Shut up, Wendell—" I'd had enough. "Now I have a list of questions a mile long, and I want some answers. From the beginning, you haven't told me one bloody thing about—"

"Please, Harry." Wendell looked put upon. "I'm just doing my job. I'm your Control. But your *friendly* Control, Harry."

"Shove it, Wendell." I turned to attack M.

But M was suddenly his usual brisk self. He was on his feet, pacing, hands clasped behind, his back ramrod straight.

"Yes, yes, I see now, Baker, why you wanted to stay in your own digs. Very wise. Good show."

I couldn't help but think, despite the tensions, that M had come a long way from Greencastle, Indiana.

"Did you know a Bill Blass in Indiana?" I asked him.

"Blass—Bill—No, not at all. Why?"

"You two speak alike."

"What does that have to do with this?"

"Nothing. I just wondered."

M frowned. "Really, Baker." And then more softly, "But you've had a bad time of it, of course."

"Yes," I agreed. "I have." There was a complimentary bottle of Cockburn sherry on the coffee table. "I know it's morning, but I'm going to have a glass of sherry. Gentlemen?"

Both Wendell and M declined. I poured a generous one for myself and downed it almost at once. "It's been a long night, and I'm about to desert the corps for a few hours for some sleep." I poured a second sherry.

Suddenly, the exhaustion hit. And it must have shown in my face.

"Dear boy," M's face was filled with concern, "you're completely done in. Here—don't even bother to go back to your room. Lie down right here. You need sleep."

"But you just got in from New York."

M smiled. "I told you on the phone—I sleep like a baby on a plane. Besides, you'll be safer here."

"The chief is right," Wendell agreed, something he always did. "Stay here and get some sleep."

"Thanks—thanks, I'll do that." I lay on the bed and followed their conversation for a few seconds until it slid away into the distance, and then I could barely hear it, and then not at all, and I was asleep.

■   ■   ■

I woke up abruptly, still feeling a need for more sleep, but in much better condition. A glance at my watch explained my assessment. I had slept only a few minutes over two hours.

But I was wide awake. And smiling. And then chuckling.

"Dawn has finally broken through the dense fog," I announced cheerfully to the empty room.

". . . If there's a shine on your shoes,
There's a melody in your heart. . . ."

I picked myself up, dusted myself off, and showered and shaved in M's bedroom. I was amused, but certainly not surprised, to discover that M still used a straight razor.

It was easily the best I had felt in my life after a sound, healthy night's sleep of a solid two hours and three minutes.

Looking at my face in the mirror as I combed my hair, I announced: "You were crazy, Baker. But no more. You're not a member of the Intelligence Corps; you didn't take a sacred vow of loyalty; you've done your bit—*totally in the dark—and more*."

I finished combing my hair. "So now—you're going to get the hell out of here."

After about a twenty-two-second debate with myself— one side *valor*, arguing that I had every right to leave, and that there was no need for me to slink furtively out of the hotel—the other side *caution*, arguing, "Just get the hell out any way you can, and don't stir up trouble."

It didn't take the dean of the Harvard Law School to adjudicate. It was a landslide win for *caution*.

So I *furtively* opened the door, saw that the hallway was

empty, decided to avoid the elevator, and chose instead to *slink* down the stairs.

One floor below was my own room, with the door closed. But Wendell's voice seeped out. Then Ferguson replied.

Wendell was speaking again, and I got close enough to listen. It was difficult. His voice was low.

". . . and then he said he called his safe house. That's you. You were supposed to be in. Where the hell were you?"

"I was still tryin' to right the bloody Jaguar 'nd get it outta there, what d'ya think?"

"Does M know anything about the crash?"

"From our end?"

"Of course."

"Nothin'."

"Good," Wendell said.

My God, I thought, are they double agents?

Wendell said, "I'll wait until the situation has calmed down. Then I'll tell him."

I decided then and there to mistrust everybody.

I held my breath and walked past my door, thinking stupidly that I was about to leave behind the beautiful shaving kit that Jane had given me, and vowing to get word to somebody in authority about what was going on in the name of the U.S. government. *After* I got out.

At last I was on the broad stairway that leads to the great lobby of Claridge's. Lovely morning sunlight caused the whole enormous area to glow, and into that setting came a glowing and lovely Jane.

We saw each other simultaneously. Jane smiled. "Hello, Maestro. I was worried. So I took it upon myself to fly over. I hope you're not cross?"

"Cross, hell. If I had the time I'd kiss you. But right now we have one mission—we're getting the hell out of here."

"Where're we going?" Jane was still smiling, probably thinking that I was merely being the charming, zany, and lovable man that I always was in New York—in my own opinion, at any rate.

"To Heathrow," I said.

"Airport?"

"The same."

"But I just came from there."

"Good. It looks even better leaving than entering. Do you have any bags here?"

Jane grinned. "I'm at a slightly less expensive hotel. Money." She did her Brooklyn accent: "You see, I work for this guy in New York, and he's so cheap that—"

I had her arm and was leading her out the door to Brook Street.

She frowned as we turned the corner at Davies. "Harry, where *are* we going?"

"The Landsdowne Club. We can get a taxi there. It's safer than waiting for one here."

"You're serious about going to Heathrow?" We were walking fast now.

"Yup. I'm sorry about your bag. I'll make it up to you in New York. Do you have your passport?"

"Of course."

"With you?"

"Yes."

"Good." We were a third of the way along Berkeley Square. I looked back. So far, so good.

Henry at the Landsdowne was, as always, charmingly efficient, and, within two or three minutes after our arrival, we were driving down Curzon Street headed for Heathrow.

As the driver made his turn past the Wellington Monument onto Knightsbridge Road, skirting the edge of Hyde Park, Jane giggled.

"What—?" Her giggle made me grin.

"You've never been dull to work for, Harry. Never."

"Thanks." I kissed her cheek.

"What're we going to do at Heathrow?"

"One guess."

"Fly somewhere."

"My God. Remarkable. Probably not one person out of a hundred would have known that answer."

Jane was still smiling. "And where are we flying to?"

"New York."

She frowned. "You're not serious—"

"I am. Very."

"But why? I thought this was going to be some kind of a lark, and that maybe you were going to fly me to Paris for lunch—something like that."

"Avaricious women. They're everywhere."

Jane's mood changed perceptibly. She straightened up in the seat and faced me as best she could.

"All right, Harry. Tell me what the hell is going on. And don't deny it, because something is, and I think that it's about time I knew."

"You're right. It is." I started from the beginning; my initial meeting with Wendell Crittenden at the Sherry-Netherland, and went through the whole crazy thing. (I did edit Alice's actions a bit, and left out some details about my times with Taiwan, but that was all.)

Jane's voice was very subdued when I finished. "I knew it was something serious, Harry. Well—I *felt* that it probably was." Unthinkingly, she grasped my hand and squeezed it hard. "Oh, Harry. Oh, my God."

The driver was pulling into Heathrow. "If I might make a suggestion, mate—I'd take the next plane out, no matter where it's goin'." He pulled the cab to a stop and touched the bill of his cap. "Not to be impertinent, mind you."

"Not at all," I said. As the driver came around to open the door, I said to Jane, "I'm certainly the world's worst cloak and dagger man. I forgot all about the driver."

"So did I." Jane shook her head. "Now he's got a juicy story to tell his wife tonight." She frowned. "You don't suppose—"

"No, Jane, I don't. But it was still pretty stupid of me."

As I paid the driver his fare, leaving a goodly amount for a tip, he touched the bill of his cap again: "It was a bit nervy of me, mate, but I couldn't 'elp but over'ear."

I tried to make light of it. "Did I tell a good story?"

"That you did, Gov, that you did. Well 'ave a good flight—wherever it is you're goin'."

"Thanks." Even though I had scoffed at Jane, I was glad that he didn't know our flight destination.

■　■　■

We were very early. There was a long line. Jane said, "He had a point."

"Who?"

"The cab driver. Maybe we should just find a short line, buy a ticket, and get out."

"This line will move quickly."

"There's a short line right over there. Let's fly to Edinborough."

"Jane—"

"Harry, if you're in danger in London, then—"

"Hey," I gave her a hug. "You've just heard the story, and you're all revved up. Relax."

"Okay, boss." She tried to smile. "Are you going to splurge and go first-class?"

"Of course. How many first-class tickets have you bought for our clients over the years?"

"Yes, and how many have I bought for you?"

"Okay, but today we go first class."

"I'm going to buy something to read on the plane," Jane said. "Anything for you?"

"An American *Variety,* if they have it."

She was gone for about twenty minutes, and when she returned I had moved up from twentieth to fourteenth in line. It took another forty minutes to get our tickets, during which time I composed several imaginary letters to the president of the airline. The first ones were short, witty epistles; but after another fifteen minutes they segued into stern rebukes; then to righteous indignation, to vitriolic wrath to—but I never had to stoop that low; we were finally at the head of the line.

There was still an hour to go before the flight. We passed through customs and headed for the first-class lounge.

I had barely spotted the entrance to the lounge when I saw them. They were on the opposite side of the terminal, and they hadn't seen me. My voice was urgent. "Don't look around, Jane. Just follow me."

She obeyed, and we doubled back on our route and slowly picked up our pace.

After a few seconds she said, sotto voce, "What is it?"

"Who."

"What?"

"*Who*'s on first? *What* plays second."

"It's not funny, Harry."

"No, it's not. I have a strange streak in me of making jokes and acting silly when there are problems."

"Please, Harry," we were walking still faster, "this is no time for deep, personal analysis. What did you see?"

"My two buddies, Wendell Crittenden and Fergie Ferguson."

"Oh, my God."

"My God is right. And—well, what d'ya know—there's my good old friend Alice and her newfound buddy Taiwan. If we wanted to, we could have a convention."

"Are you sure?"

"I'm positive. You were right, Jane. We should've bought tickets to anywhere—and flown the hell out of here."

There was a cloud across Jane's face. "We have over an hour before our flight. They're going to find us, Harry."

"Maybe not—"

"What're we going to do?"

"I'll think of something," I said. I liked the defiant quality of my voice, much like a Paul Newman in an equally hopeless situation. But besides lacking the talent and the good looks of Paul Newman, I lacked something even greater. I lacked a script to look at to see what kind of *something* the writer had concocted for me to think of.

"But what?"

"I'll think of something." I was a stuck record. "Don't worry," I added with my personal brand of panache.

Jane's voice was shaky. "I keep looking around for

them—then I remember that I don't know what they look like."

"They're in the terminal. So if you see anyone moving toward us with undue speed, let me know. And—" I saw it. There it was—what could possibly be the next page of the script, a page worthy of a Paul Newman. "Follow me, Jane—and run."

There it had been high up in the air terminal: the electronic board that displayed information on incoming and outgoing flights; and there was an Aer Lingus flight leaving for Dublin in twelve—now, eleven—minutes.

We ran to the Aer Lingus counter. I definitely didn't want to affect a burlesque brogue and—justly—incur everyone's wrath, but I did my best to sound like a Boston Irishman, whose father's name was Baker, but whose mother was a Kennealy from County Clare—and, "My mother is waitin' for us in Dublin right now, her first time there, and her first time out of Boston even. She'll be scared to death, poor thing."

A purser standing behind the ticket seller listened sympathetically. "We'll get ya on, don't worry." He picked up a red phone while I bought the tickets.

"Any baggage?"

"None. Stolen."

"My God, you've had your troubles all right." He went back to the phone.

We finished negotiating the tickets.

The purser hung up. "Follow me," he said. "They won't have to hold, even for a second, if we hurry."

Just before we went through the gate, I thought I saw Alice out of the corner of my eye. I wasn't sure.

A pleasant-looking blue-eyed flight attendant was at the aircraft door. "We're all set for you," she said with a smile.

"Thanks so much." I turned to the purser. "I don't know how to—"

"Aw, go on now. No need." He grinned. "Now for God's sake get in so we can leave on time."

We fastened our seat belts and the plane began to move.

"Congratulations, boss," Jane said. "You did it again."

"I hope so."

"What do you mean?"

I told her about Alice.

"But you're not sure?"

"No. No, I'm not."

Jane tried to sound reassuring. "Then it probably wasn't Alice. You know her too well. If it had been Alice, you'd be positive."

"Yeah, I suppose you're right."

I sat back in my seat as the plane left the ground. I certainly hope you're right, I thought.

CHAPTER
25

IT WAS A very pleasant
flight. It would take about an hour to get to Dublin, the
blue-eyed flight attendant had told me as she passed out
tea.

Jane was reading a magazine.

I hadn't thought of Rudyard Kipling in years: "For it's
boots, boots, boots, boots, marching up and down again;
there's no discharge in the war."

I sighed: "For it's Alice, Alice, Alice, Alice, appearing
again, again, again; 'Tis pity she's a whore."

I didn't want to believe it. I liked her too much. But big
doubts about Alice were building up in my mind.

. . . Why in hell should she be at the airport? Or anywhere, for that matter? Alice was always appearing. In
London. Without a real explanation. Now, I couldn't accept the story that Elizabeth Sprague-Murray had needed
moral support to begin the filming of her book. But there
was Alice at the hotel . . .

. . . And the night of the last kidnaping. I had to smile.

Life is pretty harrowing when a man can think about his *last* kidnaping. But it was Alice who had called me in the middle of the night. And Alice who had walked—or was *lured* a more apt word?—me out to the sidewalk, in fact, to the very curb . . .

. . . And it was Alice—Alice who never smoked—who had pulled out a cigarette, and flicked a newly purchased lighter—and moments later the green Jaguar had appeared.

And of course—I'm crazy, I thought—Taiwan had been tangled up with them from the beginning, and right now, at best, is probably working both sides of the street; and Alice is working with her.

I sighed again. Even now, I still didn't completely believe it. Alice was too blithe, too whacko, and—yes—too decent for any of this. There was an explanation. And, knowing Alice, it would undoubtedly be a funny one.

■ ■ ■

"More tea?" It was the blue-eyed attendant again. She smiled. "Is your friend finished?"

Jane had fallen asleep.

"Yes," I said. "Nerves of steel."

"I beg your pardon?"

"Just a joke between us."

"Oh—" She moved on.

"D'you play any golf?"

The man across the aisle from me had a rosy face and a great reddish mustache.

"It depends on how you define your terms. I'm a real duffer."

"Oh, come now—"

"I have a thirty-six handicap."

He couldn't hide his expression of pity.

But we talked golf for a while and exchanged anecdotes. He was part of a golf team that was flying to Ireland for a three-day tournament in the southwest. They would be staying at the Great Southern Hotel. He

had never been there before, and was greatly reassured
as I described the hotel and the Killarney Golf and Fishing Club with its two courses, Killeen and Mahoney's
Point, both on the edge of Lake Killarney.

"Are they difficult, then?" he asked me.

I had to laugh. "I wouldn't know," I said. "They're all
difficult for me. Thirty-six handicap, you know."

"Ah, yes." He sighed. "Pity—" He tried very hard to
smile.

"Yes, it's certainly—a pity."

He introduced me to a few of his teammates, and we
continued to talk about golf. I almost forgot my reason
for flying to Dublin.

As the plane glided lower, and we were coming into
Dublin, my aisle companion asked, "Flying over for a bit
of golf yourself, are you?"

"No, not this time, I'm afraid."

"Ah, fishing then is it?"

"Yes, fishing." Fishing indeed, I thought.

"Good, good. Well, good fishing."

"Thanks. Good golfing."

"Thank you. I'll think of you when I'm in the rough."

He busied himself with his seat belt as the No Smoking
sign went on, and I awakened Jane for the landing.

■   ■   ■

It was absolutely delightful to be in an air terminal
without Wendell and Fergie and Taiwan and Alice. I suppose I must have whistled all the way through customs—
the only minor problem was: "No baggage at all, sir, not
even carry-on?"—but the stamp on the passport was
quickly forthcoming and moments later we were in a taxi,
with a good-natured driver, on our way to the
Shelbourne Hotel.

We booked separate rooms and went to freshen up,
agreeing to meet in the lobby in fifteen minutes.

At our late breakfast in the ornate, high-ceilinged dining room, we actually had a pleasant, rambling conversa-

tion about nothing in particular, as if we were a couple of tourists.

Jane was exultant: "There's nothing quite so good as an Irish breakfast." We each had a rasher of bacon, sausage, eggs, marmalade, soda bread, pots of breakfast tea—the works.

Jane poured more tea. "After breakfast, I'm going to go out to pick up some clothes and some kind of inexpensive bag."

"Make it expensive," I said. "And keep the receipts. I'll reimburse you."

Jane wrinkled her nose and sounded like a stentorian senator: "And there are those who would say that Harry Baker is another name for Scrooge—"

"Thank you. You have my vote. I'm going to walk over to the bank, and then take a stroll in St. Stephen's Green across the way. Would you like me to wait for you?"

"No, thanks," Jane said. "Enjoy your walk."

"I'll do that. It's great to feel that the pressure is off, isn't it?"

"Wonderful, but," Jane's face was suddenly thoughtful, "Harry, I don't think we should relax so completely. It wasn't very long ago—you know—Heathrow."

"Okay," I agreed. "You were right before, and I didn't listen. What do you have in mind?"

"I'm not so sure I *was* right," Jane said. "But up in my room just now, I was thinking that, first of all, I've never been chased by anyone in my life—but I've read a lot of books and seen a lot of movies where people are on the run. And they never take a direct route. It makes it too easy for them to be followed."

"What do you think we should do then?"

"Let's fly out of here tomorrow."

"Exactly what I had in mind."

"Yes, Harry, but let's fly to Edinborough, not New York." Jane's brow wrinkled in thought. "Now I'm just making up the itinerary as I talk, but—say, fly to Edinborough, train from Edinborough to Glasgow—just to get in another mode of transportation—then fly straight to New York from there. It'll take a bit longer, but I really think it'll be *safer,* Harry. I guess what I'm saying is we can scramble up our itinerary back to New York any way you want—but let's not fly straight from Dublin."

We discussed it for only a few minutes. Jane was right. The trail would be much more difficult if we partially doubled back. And what were a few extra days if it meant safety?

On the way out, I asked the Hall Porter to get two first-class tickets to Edinborough. I was about to ask for a connecting train to Glasgow, but Jane stopped me in early sentence: "We can decide where to go from Edinborough when we get there, darling." I understood and agreed.

Going down the front steps of the Shelbourne, Jane said, "Good for you."

"Good for *you.* Semper Fidelis must be tattooed on your bottom."

"Now, now—" She grinned.

"I'll see you in a little while. Good shopping."

"Thanks."

Jane went off toward Grafton Street, and I spotted my bank just a block away, as I had remembered it.

The bank transaction took only a few minutes, after which I strolled through lovely St. Stephen's Green, thinking of Yeats, Synge, Joyce, Dillon, Lady Gregory, and Sean O'Casey. The overwrought author of my college catalogue had written of the campus: "It is an oasis of tranquility amid the city's myriad, mechanized sand dunes—indeed the loveliest of spots."

I had seen no mechanized sand dunes, but St. Stephen's Green is definitely one of the most tranquil and lovely spots in the world. Flowers, greenest of grass, pools, shrubbery, trees, and more flowers.

An artist was painting. She was good. I stood far behind her so that I wouldn't disturb, but so I could share, vicariously, her pleasure at being able to paint so pretty a scene so well.

I stayed in the park for over an hour, and when I got back to the Shelboure, there was a note at the desk. It was from Jane.

Dear Maestro,

   I'm exhausted. It must be the jet lag. So I'm going to try
to sleep until seven.
   You should try some sleep yourself.
   Ring my room at seven, and I'll ring yours, and we can
have some dinner.
   Don't forget to pick up the tickets.

Love and Kisses,
Jane

   I smiled. Jane was the perfect colleague in an office. I
did as I was told and checked on the tickets a second
time.
   Then a bath, bed, and deep sleep until nearly five-
thirty in the afternoon.

■   ■   ■

   I felt like a million dollars—rather, pounds, Irish. A
slow luxurious shave and some hot towels, followed by
witch hazel—the real stuff—provided by the hotel, raised
my worth yet another million.
   Down in the lobby, I bought an *Irish Times* and went
into the great lounge for tea, enjoying my aloneness, silently grateful that Jane would not be awake until seven.
   The lounge was nearly filled, but I was fortunate in
finding a small table for two down at the far end, situated
so that I could view the whole great room.
   There seemed to be a lot of political talk in the air, and
the first page of the *Times* explained it: The *Dail,* the Irish
Parliament, was in session just around the corner from
The Shelbourne.
   I ordered a pot of tea, declined the sweets, and settled
for plain biscuits instead. Reading the paper, sipping the
tea, and occasionally pausing to enjoy a particularly salty
bit of overheard conversation, provided me with the first
real relaxation in one hell of a long time.
   It was a delightful half hour. One, I decided, which

should be followed by yet another stroll through St. Stephen's Green.

Normally, there would still have been daylight, even in late October, but a thick foggy mist had developed while I had slept, so that now there was that particular kind of early evening light which the Irish are fond of calling *soft:* "Ah, such a *soft* evening, it is . . ." and which described perfectly the peculiar beauty that is St. Stephen's Green on a misty October evening.

Many of the paths meet at a large oval pond in the center of the green, with a wide paved area surrounding it. I was coming out onto the paved part when I saw two figures in the mist on the other side, not forty yards away, and all of my inner tranquility vanished.

It was Wendell, I was sure of it. I could hear the high, disagreeable voice. The man who seemed to be Ferguson lit a pipe. So. It *was* Ferguson. Wendell Crittenden and good old William Ferguson—what a surprise to see you here.

The pipe glowed through the mist.

From yet another path a third foggy figure emerged—homburg hat, well-tailored overcoat, walking ramrod straight.

M was here, too.

I became uncontrollably angry. Rashly, without thinking, I was striding across the paved oval.

My own voice sounded strange to me, rough and phlegmatic. "Okay, my dear three musketeers, I've had enough. I'm sick to death of being hoodwinked and lied to—and of being blindfolded and thrown into the backs of cars."

From their body language, through the fog, it was obvious that I had startled them.

"I repeat—I've had enough." I was shouting. "Now I want some *answers.*"

It was M who spoke first: "My dear fellow, I don't know what you're talking about—"

I was spent and suddenly speechless.

"However, my friends and I would be most graciously pleased if you would accompany us to the nearby

Shelbourne Hotel for a drink. It might steady your nerves." He had a full, rich voice—impeccable English with a lilting patina of the Irish.

Of course, it wasn't M.

"Yes," said the man who wasn't Ferguson, "a fine idea. And d'you smoke a pipe, by chance?" The man who wasn't Ferguson was Irish as well and was quite obviously trying to ingratiate himself with the hope of calming me, this maniac who had appeared out of the fog.

The third man looked to be too frightened to speak. The third man was a woman in slacks.

I tried very hard not to sound like the madman I'm sure they thought I was. "I'm feeling rather foolish. Please excuse me, gentlemen—madam. I thought—I mistook you for someone else. Excuse me, please."

"My dear fellow, are you sure you wouldn't like to have a drink with us?" A gentleman, I thought, to the very end.

"No—no, thank you. Very kind of you, though. I was just taking a stroll before dinner, and . . . I thought that you were someone else."

"Well—enjoy your stroll then." He doffed his homburg. "Good evening."

"Good evening," I said.

They went off very quietly toward the Shelbourne, not speaking at all until they were a goodly distance away, and then I could hear a babble of voices through the mist as, apparently, all three began to speak at once.

■   ■   ■

I wished that I did smoke a pipe. It would have been very consoling to pull out a pouch of tobacco, dip into it, tamp it down, and light up.

For the first time since it had all begun, I felt completely unhinged.

Was I going mad? (No.) A nervous breakdown? (Perhaps.) Was someone drugging my food? (Oh, come on.) Well, why not? Everything else had happened, hadn't it?

(And I was the one who had told myself smugly that I lacked even a trace of paranoia.)

Now I was seeing people who weren't there.

I stood in the fog for several minutes before I took a few deep breaths and headed, as briskly as I could, back to the hotel.

■   ■   ■

The great lounge was half empty now, so I had no trouble finding a table. The three whom I had encountered in the Green were there, and they, and I, pretended not to notice each other.

"Another pot of tea, sir?"

"No, thank you. A stout, I think. Guinness, please."

"Of course, sir."

I had only to drink about a third of it before my mind was made up. I stood up and headed for the Hall Porter. "Coming back in a minute," I told my waiter in passing.

"Yes, sir."

The Hall Porter smiled as I approached. "I have your tickets right here, Mr. Baker. I tried to get your attention when ya came in just now, but ya seemed to have your head in the clouds."

"That's about where it was, Mr. Cassidy. And I owe you an apology—" I canceled the tickets to Edinborough and asked for two first class on Aer Lingus from Dublin to New York.

"Of course. No trouble a'tall, sir."

I gave him a big tip. "I'm very sorry."

"Don't worry, Mr. Baker. Are you plannin' to leave tomorrow mornin'?"

"Yes, I am."

"If you're dining here this evenin', I'll probably have them for ya by the end of the meal."

"Perfect. Would you make a reservation for, say, seven forty-five for two?"

"Yes, sir."

"Thank you. And, again, I'm sorry about the sudden change." I gave him another tip to assuage my guilt.

"Thank you, Mr. Baker. I'm off at nine—so if ya don't have your tickets by then, Charlie McBride will be here at the desk."

"Thanks. And someone will be asking for me. A lovely woman. I'll be in the lounge."

The Hall Porter grinned. "I'll tell her, Mr. Baker."

I went back into the lounge and finished my Guinness. Jane appeared at about seven-thirty.

"Say, you forgot to call me."

I stood. "Damn. Slipped my mind, Jane. Sorry."

"No harm done. I left a wake-up call. And I needed that sleep." Jane sat down. "I'm feeling like a completely different person from the one who dragged in here this morning."

"You look wonderful. Let's go in to dinner."

She rubbed her hands together. "Now you're talkin'."

We headed for the dining room and were met by a smiling maître d'hôtel. He raised his eyebrows quizzically.

"Baker. Two for seven forty-five."

"Ah, yes, Mr. Baker. Right this way, please."

He glidingly took us to one of the tables that were on an elevated dais by the tall front windows. "I hope you like it, Mr. Baker."

"It's perfect," I said.

"Very good." He made a slight bow and left.

The captain arrived a moment later. "Madame, sir, an aperitif before dinner?" We ordered. Another Guinness for me; gin and tonic for Jane.

"Isn't Ireland wonderful?" Jane said. "He didn't rattle off a limitless list of specials for the evening."

The waiter arrived with the drinks, and, with him, the captain again with menus. "The salmon is very fresh," was all that he said.

I decided not to mention my recent aberration to Jane. It was too embarrassing. And I wanted to enjoy dinner. We sipped our drinks and talked a bit about the business back in New York. There were, of course, things that needed immediate attention when I got back, but there was nothing that was out of control. I relaxed.

"And the usual maintenance calls," Jane was saying. And maybe one mandatory lunch."

I smiled. "By that you mean, Paul Blanfield, *The Dean of American Morning News?*"

"My, my," Jane was suddenly southern. How in heaven's name did you ever guess that, Mr. Baker?"

I never could do a good Clark Gable, but I tried. "I don't know, baby. It's just something I was lucky enough to be born with, I guess."

Jane grinned. She knew what I'd been trying for. "Pretty bad, Harry."

"I know. I'll just have to keep working at it. "How's Paul's love life? Still stable?"

"By his standards, yes."

"Well, that's something."

We ordered. I asked for the sommelier and picked out the wine. We talked about the business for a while and then got onto baseball. Jane and I have often spent an entire cocktail hour talking baseball.

The waiter, a rosy-faced young man who looked like a leprechaun—"And I'd have thought that even if we were in Spain," Jane said—brought our first course.

"And please note," said an extremely pleased Jane, "that the waiter didn't say, 'Hello, my name is Patrick, and I'll be your waiter for the evening.'"

I chuckled.

"Now *that's* civilization." We toasted. "Mmmm, that's a wonderful wine."

We settled in to good conversation and a good meal.

■   ■   ■

The Hall Porter appeared. "Excuse me, Mr. Baker, for interrupting your dinner, but your tickets've arrived, and I thought I'd bring them in myself."

"Well, thank you, Mr. Cassidy, that's awfully good of you."

"Not a'tall, sir."

I glanced at my watch. It was just nine-thirty. "You've stayed a half hour late."

"No trouble, sir. I knew the tickets were comin' so I waited a few minutes."

"Well, that was awfully good of you. Will you be at the desk tomorrow?"

"That I shall, sir."

"Good. I'll see you then. And thanks again, Mr. Cassidy."

"Good evenin', Mr. Baker."

"Good evening."

He left the restaurant with the air of someone who felt fit about himself for having done a proper job.

"Well, fine," Jane said. "Now we have everything."

I looked hard at the tickets and then at Jane. "We've a slight change of plans, Jane." I quickly filled her in about the bogus incident in the Green, and, thus, my decision.

When I finished, Jane said, "The change of plans is fine, but stop worrying about going off the deep end, Harry. It's foggy tonight, that's all."

"I don't know—"

"No—" She was definite. "It's foggy. And as for changing tickets, you have to do what you think is best, Harry. Besides, it's probably just as well." She grinned, "I read too many spy novels anyway. Now, come on, let's have some of this great wine."

She raised her glass. "To a good flight to New York."

"To a good flight to New York."

I sincerely hoped so.

CHAPTER
26

AT BREAKFAST the next morning we made our good-byes to Mr. Cassidy.

As he led us down the hotel steps, he smiled cheerily, "It's been grand knowin' ya, Mr. Baker."

"And I say the same. Thanks for everything."

"Not a'tall, not a'tall. Oh—" He lowered his voice, "and I got a fine driver for ya. Sean Dillon. He'll treat ya right."

"Thanks." We shook hands again. I got in after Jane, and we were on our way to the airport.

■　■　■

Sean Dillon was, indeed, a fine driver. And a man with the gift of the gab. He was also something of a historian. He described, in historical terms, nearly everything we passed on the way to the airport. It was all very charming. Jane and I exchanged smiles.

But the topic of his main lecture was the Battle of the Boyne. ". . . Ah yes, the mornin' of July 12, 1690, was dark and rainy . . ." I hadn't the heart to tell Mr. Dillon that I knew all about the famous battle because I was enjoying so much his eloquent, lyrical description of the events—to be sure, occasionally bending the facts of history, just slightly, to favor his dramatic narrative.

As we approached the gates of Dublin Airport, Mr. Dillon's lecture came to a stirring, dramatic crescendo and finale—with a surprise ending: It seemed—according to Mr. Dillon—that the Irish under King James I, and not William of Orange, won the Battle of the Boyne.

I paid him and thanked him for his lecture.

"Would ya like to hear a bit about the airport, now?"

"We'd love to, but there's no time, I'm afraid. But next flight."

"Just ask Michael Cassidy for me—Dillon the historian. Good flight, now."

"Thank you."

■　　■　　■

We had checked through customs and were enjoying a pint of Guinness in the large waiting room beside the duty-free shop. "D'you want to buy anything?" I asked.

"No, thanks," Jane said. "Do you?"

I shook my head. "I never do. Years ago, when I landed in my first duty-free port, I bought all the bottles of liquor I was allowed. Then I dragged the package around the Caribbean for a week. I felt less like a tourist and more like a gun-bearer. When the second bottle broke, I gave the rest away, vowed never again, and enjoyed the rest of my vacation."

Jane laughed.

"What—?"

"I was just remembering Mr. Dillon. That was easily the best cab ride I've ever had."

We had a second pint of Guinness while we discussed

Mr. Dillon and Ireland in general, and then *Boarding* appeared next to our flight number.

"Let's get on right away," Jane said.

"Why?"

"I don't know." Jane gave a half-smile. "I'd just feel better—that's all. It's silly—"

"No—it's a good idea. Let's go."

■ ■ ■

We sat in the first row of the 747's first-class section. Jane had picked the seats. "I always feel better about it," Jane said apologetically. "You know—right below the pilot and all—"

"It's great." I thanked the stewardess for the glass of champagne. Jane and I automatically toasted. "I'm glad you're here, Jane."

"So am I, Maestro."

We drank champagne and ate canapes and talked of New York. By the time Aer Lingus, flight number 197, took off, at least two of its passengers were in fine spirits.

■ ■ ■

A half hour after a smooth takeoff, Jane asked, "What's the matter?"

"I've got a cramp in my leg. Let me try to walk it off right now, before it gets bad." I got up and made my way back to the first-class galley.

"Anything wrong, sir?" My God, when Irish women are beautiful, they are beautiful. She had a wide, friendly smile and short red hair.

"Just a cramp in my leg. Thought I'd walk it off. Am I in your way?"

"Not a bit." She smiled, turned away for a moment, and when she turned back she proffered a glass of champagne. "Doctor's orders."

"Sounds like an extremely intelligent specialist."

"Oh, I am." That smile again. I was glad about the cramp in my leg.

■   ■   ■

I stood at the bottom of the stairs that lead up to the passenger area on the second level, sipping champagne, flexing my leg, and generally enjoying the flight and the feeling of well-being.

A voice behind me, on the stairs, said, "I say, I'm sorry to disturb you, but would you excuse me, please?"

The voice was a bit of *déjà entendu*.

I didn't want to turn.

The voice again: "I say, old man, deeply sorry about this, but . . . mmm . . . nature *does* call, you know."

It was he, no doubt.

"Well, well." I turned to face him. "Hello, *old man*."

"Well, well, *well*." M clasped his hands together. "How are you, dear boy?"

"I thought I was fine, until now."

M frowned. "Now, now. I don't like the sound of that. Are you in trouble?"

I started to tell him.

Quickly, M put his finger to his lips. "Dear boy, please," he admonished me.

"Just tell me what's going on."

M's voice got even lower. "Can't do it, I'm afraid. All top secret, very hush-hush and all that."

"Are Wendell and Ferguson with you?"

"Yes, of course."

"Then I'm in trouble."

M looked sharply at me. "I really *don't* like—whatever it is that you're implying."

"How did you know that I'd be on this plane?"

M brightened. "Bit of all right, what? Just dumb luck, I'm afraid. But I can't tell you how pleased I am." M made an expression of pain. "Now would you excuse me for a moment. Almost forgot." He smiled. "The lavatory—ah—are you waiting?"

"No, no. Cramp in my leg. Go right ahead."

"Try walking. Usually helps." M gave me his warmest smile. "I'll be right back."

Actually, M's advice was good. I made my way through Business Class and into Tourist Class, walked the entire way to the tail of the plane, and started up the other side.

The leg felt much better.

But halfway up the aisle, *I* didn't.

I knew the back of that head like the back of my hand.

It was Alice. And the very tall person sitting next to her had to be Taiwan. They were reading magazines.

I walked down the aisle until I was next to them. "Good morning, everybody. Nice flight, isn't it?"

Alice looked startled for a moment, but she recovered quickly. "Harry, as I live and breathe. We finally caught up with you."

"Yes, you did," I said. Taiwan smiled.

Alice asked. "Are you in first class, Harry?"

"Yes."

"I thought you would be. We tried, but it was booked. Did you ever know me to ride tourist, Harry?"

"Not you—never, Alice."

"We were going to have lunch and then bribe a flight attendant or something to look for you."

"Well, you don't have to now. Here I am."

Alice motioned with a finger. "Lean closer, Harry. I want to whisper something in your ear."

I leaned down to her.

"Look, Harry," Alice's voice was a comforting purr, "I know you're in trouble. I'm pretty slow, but I know that now." She pushed me slightly away and looked intently at me. Unfortunately her eyes betrayed her. "And if you're in trouble, just know that I'm here to help—any way I can."

"Thanks, Alice." It didn't sound like the old Alice. It wasn't.

Taiwan stood up, moved past Alice, and towered over

me in the aisle. She put her hands on my shoulders and pressed, as if to remind me of her strength. She, too, bent down and whispered into my ear. "You remember how strong I am. Well, if you are in trouble, all my strength is on your side."

I managed to smile at the two of them. At least it was my fervent hope that what I was doing in some way resembled a smile.

"Thank you. Both of you," I said, with as much dignity as I could muster. "I'll be counting on both of you."

They pretended to smile back, as I turned and headed for the front of the plane.

M was just coming out of the lavatory. "How're the leg cramps? Any better?"

"Oh, much. Thanks."

M dramatically beetled his brow. I had seen him do it before under similar circumstances. I was sure that he had practiced the affected expression many times in front of a mirror before displaying it publicly.

"Baker—?"

M kept his brows beetled, but added a slight smile to his visage. "I don't like your negative implications—or, at least that's what I inferred—about Crittenden and Ferguson. Sounds to me as if you're in some kind of trouble, and I'd like to help. I'll be down in a while—after luncheon. We'll share a brandy. I'd like to talk."

"That's fine with me."

"Good, good." He gave me a thumbs-up sign as he started up the stairs. "And I'm glad to hear the good news about those leg cramps."

Back at my seat, Jane said, "Oh, good, they're just getting ready to serve lunch. How's the leg? Better?"

"Much, thank you."

Jane scowled. "My God, Maestro, what's wrong? Your face is as gray as my sweater." She touched my arm. "I'm not surprised, after what you've been through." She smiled, "Just remember, Harry—when you're in trouble, you can count on me."

I started to laugh.

"Harry—?"

I laughed some more.

"Harry, are you okay?"

"Okay? I'm fine. I don't have a worry in the world. Nearly everybody on this bloody plane is here to help me if troubled times should arrive."

I quickly explained to Jane—about M, about Alice, and about Taiwan—all ready to spring to my side in case of trouble—and all very threatening, at the same time.

"And you had to change the tickets," Jane snapped. "We could have been on our way to Edinborough. Safely."

"Hey, don't get angry. I need—"

Jane spoke soothingly, "Oh, boss, I'm not angry. I'm upset for you." She tentatively held my hand.

"I know, Jane, I know."

"—And here we are. Piping hot from the galley." It was the flight attendant with the short red hair. She had the beginnings of our meal. We dined in silence, but with occasional glances and little smiles at each other.

■   ■   ■

I ate and thought of Alice. Once again, she had turned up. By happenstance or by design? By design, of course, and it was about time that I admitted it to myself. And all the other times, too. I couldn't overlook it anymore. It was all by design.

But the torture. Her screams. Oh, come on, Harry. She and Taiwan are together in the back of the plane right now. And it was Taiwan, the interrogator, who had seated you with your back to Alice because "the imagination and the ear can torture even more than the eye." Ha, ha, ha. Alice hadn't been tortured; she had screamed dramatically (which she could always do very well) for my benefit. And I had believed it.

And that first incident at the Sherry-Netherland. What a coincidence that Alice had accidentally appeared at my first appointment with Wendell Crittenden.

And she was probably never drugged. Leave out the

probably—she was never drugged—period. She and Wendell had played out that charade so that Alice would appear to be totally innocent of what was going on, and thus above suspicion by the damned fool of the western world, Mr. Harry Baker.

If I could have smiled grimly, I would have, but there wasn't a smile left in me.

And thus began my secret government mission, I thought. I had called upon my patriotism, and I should have called upon the police. And even later—no, by then I was just stupid.

I had been duped, duped, and double-duped.

For what? Who the hell knows? But it was still going on, and they were all in on it: Wendell Crittenden, and Fergie Ferguson, and Taiwan—and Alice. And M—

I made my plans for the arrival at JFK.

CHAPTER
27

A REASON? *A reason for it all.*
What is the reason? I don't know.
All right then. What DO I know?
What has happened to me since that day when I first met with Wendell Crittenden—?

. . . I had met Wendell and had been convinced, after a show of force, to go to Washington, where I was again convinced by Wendell's flag-waving—and good cheer on M's part—to take part in a secret mission for my government. It was so secret, in fact, that everything about it was a secret. To me, at any rate.

. . . And they had known all about the incident at The Plaza with the man who had looked like Howard Cosell, and the murdered man as well. So, somehow, that was tied together. Probably.

. . . Then a kidnaping or two.

. . . And the big party and all the show of leaving the country—There was a reason for that.

. . . Then London. With nothing to do. Why? No answer.

. . . Oh, yes. And Jessica Rumbough. Jessica Real. And Jessica Ersatz.

. . . And another kidnaping—and now this. *This*. I had been encouraged to go from New York to London. *But* now I was heading back to New York—and just maybe that was *not* part of the plan.

So, therefore—maybe—possibly—perhaps—they would try to keep me from ever getting off the plane, and out of the airport, and into Manhattan.

I had to be ready.

"—Why don't you have one with me? They have Hennessey, Remy Martin, whatever you'd like."

M was standing comfortably by my seat, a brandy in his hand.

I thought of the possibilities that might occur upon landing and declined. "I'll join you, but with a Perrier, I think." The redhead quickly produced a glass.

"Whatever—" M smiled. His volume lowered as I stood up, and he spoke very quickly. "Introduce me."

"Oh, yes. Sorry." While I was doing it, I was amused at Jane. I knew her too well not to realize that, for all her apparent pleasure at meeting M, she didn't like him. M, for his part, was dazzled by her.

"Yes, it's an old school nickname," he was saying. "Ever since—ah, Choate."

After only a few moments of stilted conversation, Jane casually let it be known that she would prefer to return to the magazine she was reading.

M led me back to the commodious serving table and poured himself another splash of brandy. "Quite obviously, this is no place to talk, but I do want to reassure you that whatever you are thinking of a negative nature about our two colleagues—you're wrong. An unfortunate misunderstanding."

He smiled and raised his glass. "We can discuss it all at length once we have landed. Cheers."

"Cheers."

We talked together for a while, a forced conversation

which centered around jazz, of all things. I was surprised that M knew anything at all about jazz, or was even interested, for that matter. His favorite instrument was trumpet, and his favorite trumpet men were Joe Wilder and Bix Beiderbecke.

"*In A Mist* . . . *In A Mist*," M murmured, a trace of sadness in his voice. "Ah, yes, *In A Mist.* Beiderbecke at his best."

That seemed to have spent him emotionally. He stared into space for a moment, then said, abruptly, "Well, I'll go back up now. See you when we land." And he was gone.

I got a magazine before I went back to my seat and pretended to read. So far my plan upon landing was very simple—because I had no plan.

■　■　■

I had decided to leave Jane out of it. It would be faster, and would have a better chance of succeeding, if I were alone. And I didn't want Jane to be hurt if my wispy plan of escape didn't work.

The landing had been smooth, but we had been forced to sit on the tarmac for nearly twenty minutes before the pilot had been allowed to taxi into the temporary Aer Lingus ramp. That delay abetted the story that I had told the redheaded flight attendant: a colleague who absolutely had to be contacted at JFK airport before he flew off to Buffalo, New York with incorrect information about our company's saline capacity.

"But there are no domestic flights from JFK," she said.

"Of course. He's—planning to take a helicopter to La Guardia. I've got to catch him before he does."

She had agreed to let me stand next to her, after the plane had stopped at the ramp, so that I could be the first one out when the hatch was opened.

"Thanks." She had light, lovely freckles over the bridge of her nose. I kissed her hand. I always did have a great weakness for blue eyes, red hair, and freckles.

The hatch swung open.

I ran down the corridors, never looking back: a left, a right, bear left again, down the stairs, follow the arrows to the right—*Damn.* I had forgotten about customs.

I glanced back. No one in sight. I quickly studied the customs inspectors and deliberately picked a pleasant-looking man who was old enough to be close to retirement, and one who would probably want simply to get through the day without annoying problems.

I had been right. "No baggage at all?"

"None. Stolen." I tried to look sad.

"Tough break. Nothing to declare—jewelry, liquor, that sort of thing?"

"No, nothing."

"Well, okay. Tough break," he said again and was about to pass me through customs that quickly.

I congratulated myself on my perspicacity in picking a man who wanted to make no waves.

But—he liked to talk.

"My wife and I had that happen to us once." He still had my passport in his hands. "Only we were in upstate New York. Up near Rochester. Well, right between Rochester and Syracuse, actually. . . ."

Ferguson and, then immediately, Wendell came into the customs hall.

I reached gingerly toward my passport. "Would you mind—"

He droned on: ". . . my wife's got relatives up there. Little town called Conestoga, or Callistoga. Anyway, something like that."

They did not even bother to pretend to wait for their luggage at the carousel; Wendell had obviously decided to abandon it in the interest of speed. Each, with only a briefcase, got into a different line. Our eyes never met.

". . . and that's when we had our bags stolen. At a bus station. Can ya believe it? So I know just how you feel." He started to hand back the passport.

M came into the hall and, pretending like the others not to see me, quickly got into yet another of the customs lines.

"Hey, let's move it up there." The line was languishing behind me.

My customs friend ignored them. "Take care now. And you'll get over it," he told me.

I had the passport and the customs slip that would let me out of the hall. I got through the crowd of porters very quickly, found the official who would accept the white slip, and—

"You have no bags at all?" he asked.

(Damn.) "None. Stolen."

"Tough break. Okay—"

I was out.

Nearly the entire lobby, from the exit of the customs hall to the sidewalk, was filled with people. Hundreds of them. Friends, drivers, relatives all ready to wave, shout, or throw kisses to returning travelers. And dozens of men, many with chauffeur's uniforms, stood about holding signs that read: *Acme Limousine,* or *Komfort Kars,* while others held signs with proper names: *Johnson, Bernstein, Kanaski Family,* or *Connelly.*

I got to the street door and glanced back. There was no sign of Wendell or Ferguson. But M emerged quickly and began to make his way through the crowd. He had beaten the others through customs.

I pushed through the door and was outside under the huge porte cochere, trying to spot an empty taxi. It was useless. People were queued up in a hopelessly long line at the cab stand.

I could have risked standing in the line, but my instincts told me that once M was joined by good old Fergie and Wendell, their actions would become far more physical.

Then I saw my savior. One of New York's finest, and also one of the prettiest police officers I had ever seen. She was headed in my direction. I dashed toward her.

"I've never been happier to see a police officer in my life," I said.

She didn't return my smile. "Is your name Harry Baker?"

She wasn't a New York City police officer—she was a private guard.

"That's the man," I heard M shout from a considerable distance behind me.

She was small and slight, but she knocked me down with two quick blows.

As soon as I hit the sidewalk, I scrambled back up and ran for the only refuge I could find at the moment—JFK Terminal again.

The thought was to get deeply lost in the crowds. It worked. Until, after twenty furtive minutes, the realization dawned that getting lost was one thing, but getting out of JFK was another.

I risked approaching the taxi-limousine area for a second time and was rewarded by the comforting scene of M, Fergie, and Wendell standing beside a red Mercedes, searching the crowd for sight of me. They already knew what I had just figured out for myself, that, without any transportation of my own, I would have to return to their area.

And, way at the other end of the porte cochere, were Taiwan and Alice, still without a taxi.

Ah, it was wonderful to have so many friends who were all so deeply concerned with my well-being.

Once again I was a man without a plan.

There is always a third way, a wise person once said. And with that thought bucking me up, I found the third way. Okay, I had to get out of JFK somehow, so I would *fly* the hell out of JFK.

I headed for the Air Canada area.

That was when The Royal Canadian Mounted Police galloped to my rescue.

"Hello, Harry. You're back." It was Susan.

"Susan." I wrapped my arms around her, and we embraced. "You're a good sight in a sad world. What're you doing here?"

"I came in from L.A. this morning on the Red-Eye, and my sister and her husband were flying to Ireland, so we planned to meet and have lunch at the airport."

"What were you doing in L.A.? Work, I hope."

Susan shrugged. "Another pilot. Who knows?"

"You'll hit one yet. Maybe this is the one."

"But don't worry about your business, Harry—"

My business was the last thing in the world that I was worried about.

Susan was apologetic. "Jane called me and told me that she had to be out of the office, but we were right in the middle of shooting. I just *couldn't* leave."

"Of course you couldn't."

"But I did call a few people."

"Not the stripteaser, I hope."

"Stripteaser?"

"The braless wonder who took off her T-shirt ten seconds into her interview."

"Oh, you mean Wildflower."

"Is she an Indian?"

"No, she's just into nature. And, believe me, I wouldn't call her again. Besides, she's in an Off-Broadway show."

"With or without her clothes on?"

"I don't know. It's called *Naked Nights*," Susan said. "It's in blank verse."

I had been easing her into a protected corner. "Susan, I'm in just a bit of trouble, and I need your help."

Her hand went to her face, and her eyes were questioning.

"No, I've done nothing wrong—but it's serious. Now here's the kind of help I need."

The directions and the plan were made up as I talked to her. She was to stand in the taxi queue and get a taxi; she was to direct it to the very end of the building and have it park; she was to open the door toward the building and stand beside it with the door still open.

When she saw me running out of the terminal toward the cab, she was to walk, not run, from the car and blend into the crowd inside the terminal.

"Okay, Harry. But if you've done nothing wrong, why don't you just go to the police?"

"In an intemperate moment I did just that, and it didn't work. Besides, there's a murder involved—"

Susan's face always reflects her emotions very accurately.

I caught her hands and held them. "Keep the faith, Susan."

She squeezed back. "I will, Harry. I do."

"Good. Now take your time in the taxi line. No one watching me has ever met you."

"Okay. Good luck, Harry."

"Thanks."

She took two or three steps before turning back. "I wish I just knew that you were going to be all—"

"I will be. Don't worry. Do your job right, and I'll take you to dinner tomorrow night." I blew her a kiss.

She tried to smile as she blew one back.

CHAPTER

28

THE TAXI pulled up quickly, came to a stop, and Susan emerged. I sighed. That much had worked. I had spent so long pretending to be having difficulty with a luggage storage lock that I had almost inadvertently picked it.

Susan was standing with the cab door open, trying to appear casual as she peered into the terminal.

I eased toward the doors, all poised to make my dash.

"Harry—" It was Jane, behind me.

I turned and ran for the cab.

I could hear Jane's heels on the terminal floor. "Harry—wait."

The moment the door slammed shut, the cab started forward. "Hang on, buddy, here we go."

Through the rear window I saw M gesticulating like a combination of Lords Raglan and Cardigan urging the Charge of the Light Brigade. The Thrilling Threesome had still not managed to get into the Mercedes by the time we were out of sight.

First things first: I pulled a hundred dollar bill out of my breast pocket envelope and handed it up to the driver.

He glanced into the rearview mirror, a sturdy man in his sixties with a good face. "Hey, thanks, buddy, I'll take it. But ya oughta know—the young lady did pretty well by me."

"Susan did?"

"Is that her name? Yeah, she did pretty well. Nice young lady."

Susan had done very well indeed. She had thought to tip the driver well; she had secured a good driver and a cooperative one: Bill Hacker, brother of Sergeant Edward Hacker, NYPD, didn't like bums. And he had decided that two, at least, of the Thrilling Threesome were bums.

"Something about 'em, ya know. Makes 'em stink." He was driving expertly and very fast down the Van Wyck Expressway. "What're they doin', givin' ya the rush? We'll take you right to a precinct house to file charges. That's probably what my brother Eddie would do if he was here."

"Well, actually, they're business people I know. Business rivals, actually. And they're—trying to . . . (What?) . . . keep me from signing a contract on time."

"Bums," Bill Hacker grunted.

"Yeah, that's about it."

"Bums. That's what my brother Eddie always calls the scum and the lowlife. He never calls 'em scum or lowlife—he always calls 'em bums." There followed twenty solid minutes of talking about his brother's prowess as a police officer, as he displayed his own prowess as a driver. Emerson Fittipaldi wouldn't have driven better.

We were in a line for a toll booth at the Brooklyn entrance to the Manhattan Bridge when a cab four lanes over began a rhythmic honking of its horn.

The cab's back window lowered and Alice's face, distorted and violent, pushed out as she shouted at me.

"Who the hell's that?" Bill Hacker asked.

"She's with the bums."

"Dames, too," Hacker said with disgust, and pulled out quickly from the toll booth.

Traffic was heavy for a Sunday afternoon. Hacker had trouble cutting through it on the bridge.

"Indian Summer always brings 'em out on the weekends," he grunted. "Let the sun shine in early November and everybody goes nuts." He was whistling nervously, almost to himself, as he cut around a menacing sixteen-wheeler. "Ya wanna lose 'em, right?"

"That's it."

"Where d'ya wanna end up?"

I hadn't thought of that. "Gracie Mansion."

"Where—?"

"Gracie Mansion," I repeated. "He'll know what to do."

"Okay—I could go up the East Side Drive—but it's down to two lanes in the Sixties. My best bet is to cut down into the Wall Street area and lose 'em in the streets down there. No traffic on the weekend. We make our way across to the West Side—and get uptown fast."

"You're the driver—whatever you think."

"Okay, pal, here we go—" Bill Hacker seemed to throw his whole body into the act of driving as the cab squealed down the ramp from the bridge.

Hacker was good. And so was his plan. As we skidded around a corner at Broad and Wall in front of the Stock Exchange, I said, "Congratulations. I think you've done it. And you're right about its being empty here on a Sunday—I still haven't seen another car."

"I'm gonna hit Broadway, go up to Fulton, make it over past the twin towers, and then hit the West Side—and hold on—"

He had seen the red Mercedes coming down Nassau Street on our right just as I had spotted it, too. In the front seat, M's face was unmistakable.

"Lucky guess, you bastards," Hacker grumbled. He picked up speed on Wall, made a skidding hard right onto Broadway, and started uptown. There was light traffic now. At the Merrill-Lynch Building, Hacker cut left and headed for the West Side Highway.

"*Hold on—*" He slammed on the brakes hard and made

another sharp left as another cab approached from the opposite direction. "It's the bums' girl," Hacker grunted.

"How do you know?"

"Forty years of looking out from behind this wheel, observin'. Same make of car, same fleet, same number—"

He stopped talking to concentrate on maneuvering the cab even more evasively through the narrow streets. I kept quiet, my only contribution to our efforts. It was up to Hacker.

We might have made it—even with the two cars after us—if M and his driver hadn't apparently turned suicidal.

At Park and Twentieth—with Alice's cab several blocks behind us—the red Mercedes suddenly turned the corner at Twenty-second and came right at us down the wrong side of the street.

Hacker turned right on Twentieth and tried to slip through Gramercy Park in order to hit Third Avenue as his uptown route. The light was with us at the corner of Gramercy Park South and Irving Place, but good luck wasn't. A panel truck tried to run the red light, and we ran it and ourselves a good forty feet along the road before stopping. It was a very messy crash.

"You okay?" were Hacker's first words.

"Fine. You?"

"Naw. My ankles." Hacker swore for a straight twenty seconds and then stopped abruptly. "The Police Academy is about two blocks away. Over there." He pointed in the direction. "Tell 'em you're with Eddie Hacker's brother."

M and Wendell were climbing out of the Mercedes, Ferguson was already running toward us, and, from Irving Place, I saw Taiwan loping with great long strides in our direction.

"You're sure you're okay?"

"I'm fine," Hacker grunted. "Now get goin'—" He pointed again. "Up one and over one—"

I headed for the northern side of Gramercy Park.

"Baker—wait" It was M.

"Wait—" Taiwan's voice.

I ran faster.

■   ■   ■

A black Triumph, the top down, pulled up in front of me at Twenty-first and Gramercy. Jane was driving. Good old Jane.

I gave a jubilant shout. "The cavalry has arrived."

Jane wasn't smiling. "Just stop, Harry," was all she said.

"Jane, what the hell is this?"

"This—" she moved her right hand slightly—"is a gun. I don't want to use it, so stop."

At that moment the cab crashed into the rear of the Triumph. Jane lurched forward onto the wheel as Alice scrambled from the cab and attacked—*Jane*.

I was completely confused. For a stunned moment I did nothing but watch the two of them grapple; but then I had a fight of my own as Ferguson approached, his brow low over squinting eyes.

I had the advantage of attacking first. I hit him with a right to the jaw, two lefts, and a right again to the midsection, followed by a particularly vicious two-handed karate chop.

He picked me up and threw me at the Triumph.

Taiwan arrived to attack me next. But she belted Ferguson on the side of the head instead. I needed a scorecard to know who was on what side.

The primary battle continued: Jane's blouse was torn half off, and Alice's teeth had left a bad gash on her arm, but the fight was still a pretty even one.

Taiwan pasted Ferguson with another shot to the head. He fell at my feet. Taiwan waded in to help Alice with Jane.

Wendell and M approached at a trot. I turned on them. Wendell's eyes opened in terror and he ran. I caught him cowering in a doorway and led him back. M had pulled out a white handkerchief and was waving it in my direction. "Surrender, please. Surrender." He held the handkerchief higher. "Dear boy, d'you suppose we might discuss terms for a surrender pact?" He smiled tentatively.

A thud. Jane had fallen back into the Triumph, nearly unconscious. Much of her clothing had been ripped off, which, I knew instinctively, was the work of Alice.

Ferguson was up again and running.

Alice guarded the vanquished Jane and the cowering and completely cooperative Wendell and M with Jane's captured pistol, while Taiwan and I gave chase to Ferguson.

He was headed for the Mercedes.

He never made it.

Taiwan made a leap worthy of a gold-medaled Olympian and tackled him around the waist, pulling him and herself to the sidewalk.

Ferguson scrambled to his feet and limped on, a wounded stag. I performed my own, more modest, tackle, and Taiwan arrived for the coup de grace.

We ended up in the doorway of The Players club, rumpled, frayed, out of breath and, in Ferguson's case, unconscious.

An extremely pleasant gentleman stepped out, distinguished in appearance, wearing what was obviously a bespoke suit purchased on Savile Row, gray mustache and hair, with a nicely clipped mid-Atlantic voice.

He smiled cordially. "Well, well—how delightful of you to drop by. Perfectly delightful. Do come in, won't you?"

He held the door open and smiled warmly. "Ah—introduce yourselves, will you?"

CHAPTER

29

THE POLICE arrived promptly, and we were all taken away for questioning. Two hours later—thanks to the efforts of my attorney, confessor, and friend, Mort Lewis—Alice and I were free again. We insisted on having an immediate drink at the bar of the Gramercy Park Hotel.

"You were much, much better this time," Alice said to Mort.

Mort's face went blank. "Excuse me—?"

Alice touched Mort's arm and smiled. "Even without a course in it at Harvard, you looked much more professional when you arrived at the police station."

"Oh . . . thanks . . ." Mort looked to me for help.

I explained. "The last time you bailed us out of the clutches of the NYPD, you looked a little unsure of yourself, and Alice was surprised when it came out that you had apparently never been trained in that procedure at Harvard Law School."

Alice shook her head. "I still say, Harvard of all

places." She smiled at Mort again, "But *this* time, why—you almost looked as if you knew what you were doing."

"Yeah . . . well . . ." Mort was more than nonplussed.

Alice's smile brightened. "And I'm sure that no one but the three of us knew that you didn't—quite. Congratulations."

Mort left shortly after that, mumbling something about a need to read a few law journals. But at the door he motioned for me. His face was serious.

I excused myself from Alice and followed him to the lobby. "Thanks again, Mort. I'll try not to make this a habit."

Mort was frowning. "Harry—what the hell is this all about? I've got to know. And you've got to tell me. For your own good."

I was serious, too. "Give me half an hour to make amends to Alice. I'll grab a cab, drop her off—and come over and tell you everything I know."

The lines of worry around Mort's eyes deepened. "Good. Because at the rate you're going—well—it's trouble."

"I agree. Give me half an hour—"

"Okay."

We shook hands and Mort left.

■   ■   ■

Back at our table, I raised my glass and touched Alice's. "Here's to the sweetest person in the world—I don't know how I could ever have doubted your friendship. I'm sorry—and I apologize—and that's still insufficient."

Alice was reveling in the moment. "I was so hurt, Harry—but I forgive you." Tears flowed down her cheeks. "Yes—I forgive you." Her mouth broke into a devilish smile as she pointed to her tears. "You deserved that, you bastard."

I grinned. "I deserve anything you feel like dealing me."

Her smile broadened. "Aw, to hell with it, Harry. It's all water over the dam."

"—or down the cheek."

She laughed. "But to think that when Taiwan and I were driving all over Mayfair, you thought we were trying to harm you—Hell, we were trying to help."

I shook my head. "I thought you were in collusion with the enemy."

"That's almost funny. Anyway—we followed them—thank God. They had no idea they were being followed, so it was really easy. From Claridge's to Heathrow, to Dublin, to New York"—Alice clapped a hand to her cheek—"Oh, I see. We were all on the plane together, and you thought we were with *them*—"

I nodded. "Anyway—forgive me, Alice. I stand before you, a man filled with self-scorn."

"You're sitting, Harry."

"I'm standing." I stood. "Excuse me for a minute. I'm going to wash my hands."

"That's like saying—I'm going to go to the little boys' room."

"Not quite."

"Almost."

"Anyway—excuse me, Alice." I turned.

"—While you go to the Little Boys' Room to wash your hands."

I turned back. Alice was smiling broadly: She stuck out her tongue and tears cascaded down her face.

■ ■ ■

I was at the point of washing my hands when the Ugly Chinese walked in. I hadn't seen her since Washington, but it took only a moment for me to remember.

"I'm afraid that this is the men's room," I said to her, trying to keep my voice steady.

She said nothing. She only produced a gun and trained it carefully on my chest.

Wendell appeared, a slight smile on his face. He saw the state of my clothes and clucked his tongue. "Aw, Harry, see—I tried to play the fool, the coward, and avoid all this. But, no, you were spoiling for a fight with someone—and you just *had* to throw that flying tackle on poor old Ferguson. It's a pity. I'd say that your suit is ruined."

"What do you want?" I asked.

"Well—things got out of hand before in the park. Besides, we were all too much in the open. But now—it's time for us to have a good talk, Harry."

I heard the men's room door open and close. "Yes, I'm afraid that things will have to get just a bit more serious now"—M rounded the corner—"Dear boy."

"How did you get here?"

"I don't believe I quite understand just what you mean," M said to me.

"The police—"

M looked amused. "Dear boy, do you really think a judge or the police would hold legitimate members of a Special Branch of the United States Intelligence Service?" He smiled. "And over nothing, at that. Because that's what happened—nothing. A little squabble. A misunderstanding. Incidentally, I thought you'd be pleased that we pressed no charges against you."

"I'm most grateful," I said.

M nodded. "I thought you'd be."

Wendell moved closer. "Let's get that jacket off, Harry. And roll up your left sleeve." He trained his own gun on my chest. The Ugly Chinese put hers away and produced a hypodermic syringe and a small vial while I obeyed Wendell's orders.

"Do you faint when you get an injection, Harry?"

"Fuck you, Wendell."

Wendell looked dismayed.

I knew that the Ugly Chinese enjoyed hurting me and I was about to tell her when I began to sweat. My tongue felt thick and my knees started to buckle. It was that fast.

M and Wendell each pulled one of my arms over their

shoulders, and they got me through the lobby as best they could.

M kept up a constant banter of apparent encouragement to me. It was strange to be so lacking in control of my body and yet still be able to hear him, sounding as if he were speaking from a great distance through a huge barrel.

"That's it—very good—try to walk as best you can—now, now, no remorse; we all drink too much from time to time—some sleep is what you need now—here we go . . ."

Wendell only grunted. He was carrying most of my weight.

The Ugly Chinese had gone ahead and, with the aid of the doorman, secured a cab.

I heard M say to the doorman, "Martinis—to some people they might as well be drinking poison. Here you go, my good man—and thank you."

The last thing I remembered was that M, with a grand flourish, had presented the doorman with a quarter.

CHAPTER
30

WHEN MY brain finally defogged and I came back to consciousness again, I was greeted by the sight of M, sitting in a huge leather club chair in front of a crackling fire, sipping an enormous snifter of brandy. Wendell was standing beside him, drinking what I assumed was his usual glass of mineral water.

I was sitting in a similar club chair on the opposite side of the fireplace.

I rubbed at my face and said, "Where am I?" immediately regretting my unimaginative choice of words.

M's eyes crinkled at the edges as he smiled. "By Jove, that's good. His first words—'where am I?' *Hah.* That's good."

Wendell said, "We're at a safe house in Brooklyn Heights. Our most opulent safe house. Feel honored, Harry."

I looked around. Bookcases lined the walls, thick oriental rugs were on the floor—it could have been the library of some exclusive club.

M was solicitous. "How do you feel? Headache? Nausea?"

I took a moment to check myself out, remembering as I did what had happened. "I'm fine," I said.

M looked pleased. "Marvelous," he said, slapping his knee with pleasure. "Absolutely marvelous."

"How long was I out?"

Looking very pleased, M said, "That's the beauty of it—the sheer beauty. You were unconscious, Mr. Baker, for just about one hour." He turned to Wendell. "They've really got something here."

Wendell nodded, looking very pleased that his mentor was very pleased.

M spoke to me again, looking over the edge of his brandy snifter. "This stuff is the latest thing. It works in a matter of seconds. It doesn't completely knock out the subject at first, so he remains maneuverable in public; and he wakes up clearheaded—after *one hour.* Remarkable. It's the latest stuff," he said again.

"It's pretty nifty," Wendell said. "Don't you think so, Harry?"

"Oh, it's *nifty,* all right. It's just as *nifty* as it can be. Just what the hell is this all about, Wendell?"

Wendell held up a cautioning hand, and his voice was very soft. "Let's have no more raising of your voice to me, okay, Harry? Try to be just a bit more friendly sounding."

M guffawed. "Yes, Mr. Baker. Crittenden is giving you very sound advice, indeed. I suggest, as a matter of fact, that you be *very* friendly to him." M's eyes twinkled. "Because if it weren't for Mr. Crittenden, you would probably be quite dead by now."

Wendell nodded. "That's right, Harry. You see, I don't forget things. *Ever.* Good or bad. I didn't have any buddies in the army. But you were always . . . nice to me. I don't forget that."

M waved his hand impatiently. "Good God, Crittenden,

is that why you've got me—*considering* letting him live? Some drivel about niceness in the army?" He swallowed the remainder of his brandy in one gulp and poured himself another, glowering all the while at Wendell.

Wendell shook his head. "Of course not. But there is the human element in everything."

"Not in this business," M snapped.

Wendell bridled. "In the *business* part, I always felt— from the beginning—as you damn well know—that if push came to shove, Harry would go along with us."

"Yes, yes, yes, yes—" M murmured by way of apology. "So you did, so you did."

The *you would probably be quite dead* part of M's speech of a moment earlier did not go unheeded in my brain. I tried to be very friendly, but not unctuous, with Wendell.

"You mean that, in the beginning, you were considering telling me everything, Wendell?"

Wendell shook his head. "No, not at all. I just felt that if, at some point, we had to let you in on things, you would agree with us politically."

"It might have been better if I'd known everything," I said.

"No—why take chances when we don't have to? And it almost worked that way—the safe way. Besides, Harry, we *always* had the option of filling you in on the big picture."

I pretended to accept that. "I suppose you're right, Wendell."

Wendell smiled. "Believe me, Harry. I am."

"And, right now, Mr. Baker," M said, his voice getting slightly thick from the brandy, "we have a kind of insurance policy on you. The insurance policy says that if you don't like the political part of *Operation Morris*"—he pronounced the words as if he were reading from a bronze tablet—"we have several options. And one of those options, which, frankly, I find very appealing, is that we can—eliminate you."

He chuckled at what he, apparently, considered his wit and took another generous swallow of brandy.

"Now, let's see—" M began to pace back and forth in

front of the fireplace—"where to begin?—where to begin? Ah, yes—" he smiled broadly—"why not begin at the
beginning."

He chuckled to himself a second time. M was obviously
in the merriest of moods.

I hunched forward in my chair, determined to adore
the big picture when I heard it, and even more determined to agree with every phase of *Operation Morris*.

M turned to me. "Well, to begin with—now don't feel
hurt or let down—*Operation Morris* is only one small part,
one piece, if you will, of a much larger and greater show.
But I'll say this for it"—M's voice was avuncular in tone,
as if to mollify any hurt feelings that I might harbor—
"*Operation Morris* is one of the very important opening
guns of the big picture."

He sipped at his brandy. "You see, Mr. Baker, it's
1983—one year until the next election. The president is
certain to be re-elected—so we'll easily have the five years
necessary to implement *Plan Big Picture*."

He paused for my reaction. "You've lost me," I finally
said.

M pursed his lips. "A president can only hold office—
at least under the present laws—for two terms."

"Yes—?"

"Well, then—the president will be re-elected in 1984—
but by 1988—five years from now—the president and his
administration will, in all probability, be out."

"Yes—"

"So that gives us five years."

"But—five years for what?"

"Ah—" M's face brightened—"a good question. Right
to the mark."

"Thank you."

"As you know,"—M frowned—"or perhaps you don't
know—we deal with someone who has a direct conduit to
the Oval Office. So even though no memo, no phone call,
no cocktail conversations even, have taken place with—
ah—that office—we know precisely what is wanted."

M smiled. "*Now* do you understand?"

I wanted to say yes. But I said, "Frankly, no. What does

all of this have to do with me? At the risk of sounding egocentric, what does this have to do with why I'm now sitting in a safe house in Brooklyn Heights?"

"Our most opulent safe house, Harry—"

"Yes, Wendell—your most opulent."

Wendell turned to M. "Maybe if you started with the beginning of Harry's involvement and led up to *Plan Big Picture,* he would—"

M cut him short with, "Just what I was about to do, *Mister* Crittenden. Just what I was about to do." He smiled at me benignly as he regained his composure. "I was unfair to you. Let me explain from the *very* beginning."

"Yes—beginning with that first day in the Oak Room Bar at The Plaza Hotel."

M looked at me sadly. "Oh, you poor chap. You really *don't* understand these operations, do you? No—I'm afraid that the first day of *Operation Morris*—and again don't be forlorn that it's only one of many operations in *Plan Big Picture*—but—where was I?—ah, yes—the first day of *Operation Morris* was approximately one *year* before that day at The Plaza Hotel."

"A year? I don't understand."

"We had to—" M looked distressed—"Dear me, I know this is going to upset you, Mr. Baker—" He gestured to Wendell.

Wendell said, "We had to insert Jane into your office, Harry. I thought you'd figured that out by now."

"Jane?—oh, yeah." I had actually forgotten about Jane and the gun. Probably I had wanted to forget. "So—for a year—Jane was working with me, just pretending. . . ."

M was genuinely sympathetic. "Now, now, Baker—it's all part of the job. I'm sure she liked you very much."

"—Yes, I did, Harry. Very much." It was Jane from behind me. She moved to where I could see her.

I looked at her. "Have you been standing there all this time to say that?"

"Frankly, yes." Jane's voice was hushed. "I wanted to tell you myself, to explain. It was a job. And I took it on.

But then—well—I really liked working for you, Harry. I did."

I felt the same as I had the day my wife—my ex-wife—walked out with that golf pro with all the teeth.

"I liked working with you, too, Jane," I said.

M glared at her. "Have you quite finished?"

"Yes—"

"Well, then—"

"Yes—excuse me." Jane turned to leave, pausing only at the door to say, "I did, Harry. Really."

There was a long silence after her exit. Wendell broke it with, "For what it's worth, she used to tell me that all the time."

"Thanks, Wendell." Wendell looked embarrassed. "But what did—inserting Jane have to do with everything? And why *insert* her into *my* office?"

"A couple of reasons, Harry." Wendell continued on because M was pouring himself more brandy. "For what we wanted to accomplish with the operation, we had come to the conclusion that we needed to get ourselves involved with someone like you. At first we had tried to go it alone, but that hadn't worked at all. We needed an agency that handled important television and radio news people. There are really only three important ones in that field. The William Morris Agency itself and ICM—International Creative—"

I cut him short. "I know, Wendell."

"Oh, of course you do. Well—those two—and you, Harry. You're as important as they are in this one particular field. They're big and involve a lot of people. You're small—a one-man band."

"And you knew me in the army."

"Yeah, but that was just a little frosting on the cake. The other two reasons were the main ones."

"Main ones for what, Wendell? First Jane was—inserted. Then what? Peace and quiet for a year. Then I see a man who looks *somewhat* like Howard Cosell, a Frenchman is killed, I'm kidnaped—"

"DuBois had to be killed. We had no choice."

"Who?"

"The Frenchman."

"Roger Ro-*jeh*?"

"His name was DuBois. We had to kill him. He got hooked on drugs. He needed money. All of a sudden, he wanted to cross over. There was no choice but to do it and do it fast."

"Cross over from *what*, Wendell? *What* are we talking about?"

"Harry, if you would just—"

"He's quite right, of course, Crittenden." M's speech was quite thick by now and his face was flushed. He said to me, "Let me give you, as briefly as I can, an overview of just how *Operation Morris* fits into *Plan Big Picture*, and then the details will fall into place. It's really quite simple."

I nodded appreciatively.

M grew expansive. "It's a great country we're living in, Mr. Baker. Great. I know you agree. It's had its bad moments, of course, but right now we're standing tall again. Our military might is greater than ever. We can repel any enemy from without. *But*—we have two enemies from *within* who must be defeated. Those two relentless enemies of this great republic are—*one*, our soft judicial system—and two, the Media. *Particularly* the Media."

"Do you want to do away—" I remembered M's threat of a few moments before and caught myself. I finished lamely with—"to change that?"

"Yes. By all means, yes. The *Media*. They cause most of the problems in this country and then they smugly savor and relish their exacerbation of those problems. *The New York Times, The Washington Post,* the networks—"

M suddenly stopped short and smiled. "When I say the Moral Majority, you know who I'm talking about, of course."

"Of course."

M's smile grew wider. "The leader of the Moral Majority—what's his name—is actually planning to take over CBS. He says he wants to be Dan Rather's boss." M chuckled appreciatively. "Imagine—Dan Rather's boss."

"Yes—imagine."

"So you see, we'll have a great deal of help in our cause. There are many newspaper columnists and editors who believe as we do—but that is another operation, not *Morris*. We also have as an unconscious ally, the religious right, as well—and we've had strong financial aid from the Daughters of Young America and the League for the Republic. . . ."

M wasn't babbling or raving, but his speech grew faster and faster as his excitement rose. Minutes went by and he hadn't stopped talking.

". . . Bill Donovan—old 'Wild Bill' back in the OAS days—always called me his favorite rogue—God, there was a man—and the nickname stuck. To this day, Bill Casey calls me *Rogue*. In fact, when he set us up, about ten years ago, the then CIA Director—who was it now?— God, one drink and I . . . doesn't matter—the Director said to me, 'Get a few good rogues like yourself, get off on your own away from the rest of us—and *get this job done*.' Well, we did. So successfully that we're *still* off by ourselves. With an official code designation of *Rogue One*." M smiled proudly.

"So this is strictly our show with, of course, our own direct and covert liaison to the top. Within five years, we'll have complete, total, and absolute control of the media. And then this republic will be safe to be a great republic again."

M leaned back and sighed. "And we can say to ourselves—*Rogue One*—well done for your country."

Wendell said nothing. M sipped on his brandy and I could see his mind working. "The pity is—in your case, I mean—that there's really no way of explaining things to you without revealing too much, leaving us no alternative but your . . . ah . . . elimination."

"You asked too damned many questions, Harry," said a grim Wendell.

"Still, I suppose, at this point, the least I can do is to explain to you your important role in this massive plan. And then—" M sighed—"we'll do what is, unfortunately, necessary."

"Yes, I . . ." I had run out of jokes.

"Well, to begin with"—M had the air of someone lecturing to a class in law school—"as I think I have already indicated, *Operation Morris*—and other operations—are only the beginning of a long-term takeover of the media—we're not attempting some sudden coup, which would be doomed to certain defeat. And, believe me, when we started *Morris,* we came damn close to defeating ourselves. We made some enormous mistakes." M turned to Wendell, "Actually, Crittenden did. You'll explain?"

A chastened Wendell stood as if to make a class report. "We wanted to see if it would be possible with the aid of makeup—you know, Harry, nose putty, cotton, hair pieces—to make someone we picked look like a major television personality. It couldn't be some run-of-the-mill newsreader nobody really paid attention to. To work, it had to be good— We chose Howard Cosell. We failed— obviously. And on top of that, we were pretty silly. We overlooked—entirely—family, friends—people close to him—"

"It wasn't silly at all," M snapped. "All right, we had forgotten about reckoning with a family, et cetera. But we learned from our mistakes. We would try other means."

M turned to me. "The mistake"—he gave Wendell a withering glance—"was in the recruitment of that fool Silvestri."

"Silvestri—?"

M nodded. "Precisely. You agree with me, then."

I shook my head. "I'm not following again."

"Oh. Well, Silvestri is the name of that pompous and empty-headed jackanapes recruited by Crittenden"—M paused to allow more time for Wendell to squirm—"who *attempted* to play the role of Howard Cosell. But he was totally lacking in intelligence, and he didn't really look enough like Mr. Cosell. Fine. Stop and start over. But, no, Silvestri was a blithering idiot. A *year* later—he suddenly decided to play the role again—because he enjoyed being asked for autographs. My *God. Autographs.*"

M's scowl deepened. "He and three others were supposed to have DuBois—the Frenchman—under surveillance. Obviously in mufti. And obviously without that blasted imitation of Mr. Cosell. *Crittenden*—assigned him. *Hah*."

Wendell sighed.

"That idiot," M snarled. "Then you spotted Silvestri pretending to be Mr. Cosell—how could you miss him— DuBois contacted you, to our complete surprise, and our whole scheme was in danger of unraveling. It was one *year* after we'd planted our mole in your office, and in one hour that imbecile Silvestri was about to destroy everything."

"It was close," Wendell agreed with another sigh. "DuBois' death was a foregone conclusion. It was our bad luck that we weren't aware that he knew your—ah— friend Alice."

"We *should* have known," M snapped. "And you should have been aware that Silvestri was capable of deciding to do his Cosell act again." Wendell started to protest. "I know—I know—'after thirteen months of perfect behavior'—please don't say it again." M addressed me. "We've been trying to eliminate him ever since."

"But what was the whole plan? I mean, my part in it?" I felt like someone in a fairy tale by the Brothers Grimm, someone who genuinely wanted to know the ending of a story, but one who also knew that when the ending arrived, he would be killed.

M's eyes lit up, relishing the story once more. "Well, we had targeted you and just three of your clients to begin our operation. *And* we had learned a great deal from our various mistakes with Silvestri. We would now take into consideration the problem of family and friends who might easily recognize our—ah—duplicates."

M stood and poured himself still more brandy. "Would you like a glass? I'm afraid I've been quite rude."

I thought, well, yes, telling someone that you were going to kill him *was* rather rude. "No, thank you," I said, but M paid no attention to my answer.

"Now, somewhat wiser"—M sipped his brandy—"we had the good sense to go to our British cousins for help. For years, we've had a most favorable working relationship with a small group there, a sort of rogue group much like ourselves. It's a subgroup of MI6, Britain's ultrasecret intelligence service."

M smiled broadly. "And that, my dear fellow, was yet another reason to get you involved. There's a man there who has been with MI6 for thirty years and has worked with our Special Branch for a good twenty." M began to sound like a quizmaster. "He's a well-known BBC commentator, and he's very well known for his PBS appearances in America as well. He's a client of yours and—"

"Not Hugh," I blurted out.

"—his name is Sir Hugh Trevor-Maypole."

"Hugh—my God. He's been my client for years. I never dreamed—"

"Exactly. And, as you'll see in a minute, this will turn out to be one of the most subtle parts of our entire operation."

I was dumbfounded.

"First of all, Trevor-Maypole put us in touch with Sir John Tremaine, one of Britain's best and, for a very good reason, least known, plastic surgeons. He's worked for MI6 and for Trevor-Maypole's subgroup for years. Politically, he's affiliated with the neo-Cliveden set."

Wendell interjected, "The original Cliveden set were members of the British aristocracy who favored the Nazis and Hitler at the beginning of the Second World War and—"

"I know that, Wendell."

"Well, a lot of people *don't*," Wendell said defensively.

"Does that mean that this Sir John Tremaine is a profascist?" I asked.

"No, no, of course not. The *Neo*-Clivedens are, simply speaking, extremely conservative."

"And how was Tremaine going to help this subgroup of MI6?"

M rubbed his hands in delight. "You have a most inquiring mind, Mr. Baker—most inquiring. Good question. And thereby hangs a most intriguing tale."

He sipped more brandy. "During the war—the Second War—the British began operations of this sort in the same way that we did just now. They would substitute a good look-alike for the real person. Then, aided with makeup—a mustache, et cetera—and, most important, aided by distance and unfamiliarity—they would get away with it. They did it with Churchill, with Field Marshal Montgomery—it worked splendidly. In the Second World War.

"But the world has grown so much more sophisticated now. However, the British—unlike us, I'm sad to say— have kept up with technology in this field and can still mount these operations. Even though now they have to have nearly complete and absolute verisimilitude."

M's eyes were wide with wonder. "That's what the hands of that skilled surgeon, Sir John Tremaine, can achieve—a nearly perfect likeness of a person. And with the new laser technology, the voice can be duplicated in almost the same way. Imagine—MI6 can do all that— while we . . . we were trying to mount an operation using a method the British abandoned back in the early fifties. My God."

M stood at the fire for a moment. "It's just a damn good thing that The Media"—he seemed to spit out the loathsome term—"didn't get hold of that. We'd be the laughingstock of the world intelligence community. And we'd have every congressman who's running for re-election on our back."

M continued to stare into the fire, no doubt thinking evil thoughts about the hated media.

Wendell smiled at me. "Any questions, Harry? I'll be glad to answer them. No reason not to—now."

I had been checking myself for physical strength and balance as best I could, without drawing attention to what I was doing: standing, sitting again, moving my arms and my legs. I felt fine. No effects whatsoever from the *nifty* stuff I'd been injected with.

An objective observer, very generous in time, might give me ten minutes, at the most, unless I did something right about now. I regarded M, swaying slightly in front of the fire. Wendell was the obvious one to go for first. I counted three and made my move.

"*Stop*—or I shoot."

I stopped immediately. And when I turned, it was the Ugly Chinese who was pointing her gun at me. She smiled at me for the first time. "Thank you," she said.

Wendell, too, had a slight smile on his face. "As I said before, Harry, any questions?"

I sighed and sat down again. I had no choice but to ask questions. That would, at least, keep me alive. For a while.

"Why all the stuff about the body? You knew where it was all the time. And tying up Alice and ransacking my apartment? And the bomb? For God's sake, Wendell, you actually sent me a bomb."

Wendell smiled. "A little one, Harry. We didn't want to hurt anyone. Especially you. We needed you. That was the whole idea. It's simple, isn't it? Something inexplicable and sinister suddenly happens in your life, and along comes Uncle Sam to say, 'We need you, boy—and we're on your side.' And the body is obvious. Blackmail. We had something to hold over your head. Whether we supposedly had it, or the *they* whom we created had it. The same thing with the kidnaping in Washington and the phony torture." Wendell chuckled. "My God, but she's a hysterical young lady. We didn't harm her at all. A few pricks with the end of a clothes hanger, a little blood, and"—Wendell chuckled again—"and her hot coals were ice cubes"—he laughed—"*ice cubes.*"

"Wendell—she was naked, she was tied to a wall—she was frightened to death. *Why?*"

"Why? Why, the same thing, Harry. It was all just a variation of the old good cop—bad cop routine. We must've looked pretty friendly to you after that, didn't we?"

"Yes, I daresay we did." M was back with us once more. "From then on, we were one, big cooperative family, all hands pulling together, every oar deep in the water. From then on, right through your good-bye party, to your stay in England, everything worked splendidly."

"And why the big, splashy party?"

"Ah, yes—and this is good, this is very, very good." M

could barely contain his pride. He burbled out his explanation. "This part was fantastic in its concept. You see, dear boy, we wanted to kidnap you, in effect, and spirit you away for a period of time while we and Sir John Tremaine finished our work in the States and in England. Now we couldn't exactly do that. How d'you explain it when Harry Baker disappears? And what does Harry Baker say when he returns—because he would have to return to complete our operation. So what did we do? We simply"—M slapped his hands together several times— "we simply—kidnaped—Harry Baker—in *public*."

"Brilliant," Wendell said.

M nodded. "Yes. Quite right, Crittenden. Brilliant." He addressed me. "We have Harry Baker hold a huge party, make sure that the world, and the broadcasting industry in particular, knows that he is heading for London and a vacation. A *vacation*. No one will question that. Harry Baker needs a vacation. London's just the spot. He even has a client there, Sir Hugh Trevor-Maypole. And *off Harry Baker goes—kidnaped*. It's the most ingenious kidnaping of the century."

M laughed gleefully all the while he was pouring himself another brandy. Eventually, he turned back, still sniggering slightly. "And what about Harry Baker himself in our little public kidnaping? Why, we baptize him into intelligence, tell him that his cover will be to let the world believe that he is going on a vacation, and then send him off on a highly secret bogus mission to London"—M chortled some more—"where all of our cousins at MI6 can keep a watchful eye on him." M nearly doubled over with laughter.

Wendell joined in the laughter. "And don't forget about Sir Hugh Trevor-Maypole."

"Ah, yes, yes, yes—quite right." M said to me, "Remember when I told you that he would represent one of the most subtle parts of our operation? Well, here it is. I think you'll agree that I was hardly exaggerating."

M sat and regrouped himself after his wild paroxysm of laughter. He spoke slowly now, savoring his words, "Quite simply, the Trevor-Maypole you met in London was the result of Sir John Tremaine's first effort on our behalf."

It took a moment for what M had just said to sink in.

"My God," I said, "I can't believe it. I've known that man for years. He looked different, yes. Quite different, in fact, younger and so forth. But I'd have sworn that that was he."

M chuckled. "He looked considerably different, but you would not have really questioned that that man was your client, Sir Hugh Trevor-Maypole?"

"No—"

M allowed himself a rumble of a chuckle. "I told you that this was subtle." He was back up on his feet again, pacing. "You see, Mr. Baker, you are hearing now about the work of an *intelligence* unit, and a damn good one, by God."

He stopped pacing and stood directly in front of my chair. "You see, that's *exactly* what we wanted you to think. We wanted you to think, 'Dear, dear, what's happened to old Sir Hugh? He looks quite a bit different.' Then his almost schoolboyish explanation of having met this lovely young thing, of his being quite smitten by her; thus, the motivation to diet, a bit of touching up of the hair, and a tuck here, and a tuck there at the chin, the eyes, and so forth—it's really quite believable, isn't it?"

"Obviously. I believed it."

"It's an acceptable story."

"Yes, of course."

"And you accepted the man for what he said he was?"

"Yes—"

M grinned. "Of course, it didn't hurt that the—ah—slightly different-looking Sir Hugh Trevor-Maypole was actually—Sir Hugh Trevor-Maypole."

I looked hard at M. "Now I'm really confused."

M smiled. "It's all right, dear boy. It's all right. And quite understandable. I told you that this was subtle. And important. In fact, it's almost the linchpin of our whole operation. It's the main reason that we had to"—M smiled—"publicly kidnap you and get you to London. All the others are secondary. Very important—but secondary to this."

M sat again. "We wanted you to meet your client, Trevor-Maypole, looking rather different because of alterations by plastic surgery, but completely acceptable as being the man he claimed to be. Therefore, we used the real man—we had the surgery performed on Trevor-Maypole himself—so that, whatever changes were wrought by Sir John Tremaine, in the end, there would be no doubt that he would pass muster."

"My God, but why?"

"I thought you'd surely have guessed by now. Eventually, you will go through the same—" M stopped himself and smiled sadly. "I should amend that to—you *were* to have gone through the same sort of situation with Tom Haskins and Jessica Rumbough and Dan—"

I interrupted, "But I fouled up everything by seeing the spurious version of Jessica and the real Jessica in the same day."

"Precisely. All brought about by that damned fool woman's uncontrollable yearnings for Italian food. My God," M implored his maker, "how can we rid ourselves of the *human* element?"

"And that's why you and Wendell came to London—"

"Yes."

"And Jane—?"

"—Came with us."

"But why did she pretend to have just arrived that morning?"

"That was her mission. To stay in the shadows and to show herself only if it appeared that, for some reason or other, you were about to bolt."

"Ah—and then she was to stick with me."

"Precisely."

"And any time I made a travel decision, she would be on the phone to you."

"Exactly."

"And I thought she had a bladder condition."

M smiled. "It's rather timeworn tradecraft for a fall-back position to track a subject, but it still works."

I said, "Actually, everything did work perfectly for you. Because of my episode with Sir Hugh, when I met that fake Jessica in Soho, my only thoughts were that Jessica wasn't acting like herself and looked a little strange, but I accepted it. And, I would have all the way if I hadn't run into the real monster later in the day."

"Thank you, dear boy." M bowed his head modestly.

"And I would probably have done the same thing with Tom and Dan."

"Alas, only Haskins," M said.

I was *half*-relieved. "Why only Tom?"

"The car crash in which they were involved—"

"I've already figured that out. They're hurt. Plastically altered substitutes replace them, and I return to see them looking somewhat different, but I accept it. Ergo, if their own agent accepts them with no questions asked, why should the rest of the world have any questions. And anyway, no one expects them to look exactly the same. They've just come through a horrible accident."

"Precisely. But, as I said, only Haskins. He was terribly smashed up, you see. We made the switch when he first left the hospital and went to a sanatorium for a rest. I'm afraid, dear boy, that we had to eliminate your friend."

Poor, good, decent Tom, I thought. Well, Tom, maybe I'll be seeing you soon, because they sure as hell plan to eliminate me as well.

"And Dan?" I asked.

"He was a considerable disappointment. He came out of our arranged car crash with merely a broken leg."

"And it's a little difficult to explain any differences in the face of a man who has only suffered a broken leg."

"Exactly."

"Now what are you going to do"—I had almost run out of questions—"without me to accept your stand-ins for Tom and Jessica? I thought that I was such a linchpin in the operation."

It was Wendell who spoke. "You've got to stay malleable in this business, Harry. No operation ever goes exactly as planned. In fact, leave out the exactly. They never go as planned."

"Quite right," said M. "I believe we'll muddle through. We're going to have our first outing tomorrow on 'This Is Your Press.' I feel very confident."

"Why the London kidnaping?" What the hell, it was a question.

"Simple stupidity on Ferguson's part. And panic."

M drummed his fingers for a moment. "Well, I suppose that it's about time to. . . ."

I desperately grabbed for any kind of question I could think of. "What's . . . what's the next operation in Plan Big Picture?"

"Hmmm—" M smiled. "You know something, Baker? You have a most refreshingly curious mind. It's really a pity that you didn't pursue intelligence work. Well—" he grew expansive—"now that we're under way—barely—but under way with *Operation Morris*, we *are* ready to begin another phase of *Plan Big Picture*." He paused and became, for him, deeply philosophical. "As the Chinese say, 'The longest journey begins with one small step.' Now that we've had our first small step with Morris"—he had tied it all together with remarkable clarity—"our next step will be—*Operation Associated*."

"And the countersign is *Press*," I said.

M's mouth was open. "Remarkable. Truly remarkable," he said.

"But there's no need to tell Harry anything more about that," Wendell said.

"Of course not. And I wasn't about to," M snapped. He looked at me and smiled wistfully. "Well, Mr. Baker, it's been most stimulating to know you. I only wish—"

I grasped for one more question. "And Taiwan. How did she fit in?"

M smiled. "You two grew quite genuinely fond of each other, didn't you?"

"Yes—actually, we did."

"A fine young woman—lovely." M was, all at once, a paterfamilias bestowing his blessing.

"Yes, she is," I agreed.

"Well, it's quite simple, really. We needed someone to keep you—ah—occupied whilst in London, and she seemed to be the perfect one to do it. So we told you that she had defected to us, while in reality she, and everyone else in that phony group, which we had created for your benefit, was a member of our tight little band at *Rogue One.*"

"They were very convincing. And so was her defection."

"Oh, you thought so, did you? Good. What we didn't bargain on was that Taiwan's *association* with you"—M made sure that I knew that he was using a euphemism—"would affect her so deeply that she really would defect from us."

One more question. Anything. "How do you get someone like that to work for you? I mean—"

"I know what you mean," M said. "How do you recruit someone who is so young, beautiful, and intelligent to work for a band of cutthroats who spend their days and nights performing dirty tricks." M smiled. "I forgive you. In her case, it was quite simple. She actually is from Taiwan, by the way. Her father is a general there. In intelligence. So when she arrived at Stanford for schooling, it seemed only natural for us to recruit her. Her senior year. She wasn't even surprised."

I had another question ready, but Wendell said, "Don't you think it's time to call Sebastian?"

"Yes," M said, "it is."

"We should've called ten minutes ago."

"Well, we didn't, did we? Call now."

By the time Wendell got off the phone, M's attitude towards me had changed completely. I was no longer present in the room, so far as he was concerned.

M chuckled and slapped Wendell on the back. "You know, I always play a little game with myself whenever we have to call in Sebastian and his group. I bet myself a drink as to how they're actually going to do it. With their last job—that unfortunate private plane crash near Baltimore—I lost. So I owed myself a drink." He chuckled again. "If I'd won—I'd also have owed myself a drink."

The door to what was probably a hallway opened quickly and Taiwan appeared. In the split second in which I first saw her, I knew that I had been betrayed again and that Taiwan had always been on their side.

In the next split second, I saw her raise her pistol, heard a short, high cough, and heard the Ugly Chinese behind me gasp and fall to the floor.

Wendell was reaching inside his jacket. Taiwan wheeled in his direction. "Drop it on the floor when you get it," she said. "The other hand—over your head. High."

Without a word, Wendell did as he had been directed.

"You, too," she said to M.

"Really. In thirty-seven years in this—"

"You, too," she said again.

M dropped his gun.

Taiwan didn't look at me. She kept her eyes on the two men. "Get their guns and get over here."

I did as I was told.

"I can't kill you," she said to Wendell and M. "You were comrades I worked with and liked. And you, M, have been a good friend to my father for many years—"

"Yes, exactly—so why don't you just—"

"*But*—I shall be outside this house for ten minutes, and I shall be forced to shoot *anyone* who tries to follow this man. Anyone."

We backed out the door. Taiwan slammed it shut and quickly led me down a stairway two steps at a time.

At the bottom, she paused, aimed, and fired a round back up at the door to the room we had just left. I heard the cough of the silencer and the sound of splintering wood.

"Time—" she muttered.

A door opened. It was Jane. "Get back, Jane, you'll be killed." Even as I was saying it, I was aware of the strangeness of my knee-jerk loyalty.

Out on the tree-lined street, it had been raining. Taiwan and I ran across to a corner where we could see the front and back doors to the safe house.

"Down to the next corner, turn right, a black Toyota

halfway down the block. Alice is in it." Her eyes never left the house.

"What about you?"

"Get going."

"With you—"

"Go—*now*."

"Not without you."

She sighed. "All right. Wait until someone tries to come out. That will give us another five minutes."

Less than a minute later, the back door opened, tentatively, then was thrust quickly open all the way, and a figure, probably Wendell, scampered out and headed toward the adjacent garage.

Taiwan fired. The figure fell immediately.

We turned and ran. The Toyota's headlights were on, the motor running, and Alice was behind the wheel, her eyes very large, but relieved at the sight of us.

Without a word, we leapt into the car, and Alice took off at breakneck speed.

"I didn't know you could drive," I said.

We screeched around a corner and headed for the Brooklyn Bridge.

"I can't," Alice said.

CHAPTER

31

Aᶠᵗᵉʳ A short debate, our only conversation in the car, we decided on a motel on Tenth Avenue, almost in the Hudson.

"We'll go in one at a time and register separately. I'll go first. No matter what floor my room is on, I'll go to the third floor and wait for you. Then we'll go to my room. And space it apart. Alice, five minutes after me. Taiwan, ten." I remembered who the professional was. "Okay, Taiwan?"

She smiled. "Fine."

Twenty minutes later, we closed the door to my room. The first thing I did was to throw my arms around Taiwan and give her a huge hug. "Thanks isn't much—but thanks."

She smiled and nodded her head.

"And how the hell did you know where to look for me?"

"That was easy. That was the first place I thought of

when Alice came back to the apartment without you. We all know about that safe house. And it's M's favorite."

Alice was looking proudly at Taiwan. "And you were right not to have that drink with us, Taiwan. Otherwise, they'd have captured you, too. And then—oh, my God—both of you."

Taiwan nodded. "Yes. Exactly. I know them. I warned you both that they would be out in nine shakes of a lamb's tail."

I let that one go.

Taiwan sat on the bed and was quickly all business again. "The question is—what do we do now? We are not safe. Just remember that."

I called Mort Lewis. No answer.

"Call the FBI," Alice said.

"And say what?" I asked.

"Why . . . say that a branch of our intelligence service has gone mad."

"And they'll say—so what else is new?"

"No, no, I'm serious, Harry. Tell them everything. Tell about your secret mission to London, the kidnapings—all of it."

"Can you hear the questions? And can you prove any of this, Mr. Baker?"

"Well—of course you can."

"How?"

"Well—I'll tell them you're telling the truth."

I made no comment.

"You are right, of course," Taiwan said. "We cannot call the FBI—we cannot call even the New York City Police. And least of all can we call the CIA."

"In short, we are in a pickle." I tried Mort again. No answer.

When I hung up, Taiwan said, "At least M is in the same ship."

"Pardon—?"

"He cannot call the CIA either. He is in the—"

"—in the same *boat*."

"Thank you."

"I'm sorry," I said. "I'm irritable."

"So what *do* we do?" Alice looked distraught. "Just sit here all night, and all day tomorrow, and—"

"I'll eventually get Mort," I said.

Alice sighed.

"We are not safe here like this, all together in one room," Taiwan said.

"Would it be better if we separated?" I asked. A sudden sound made me jump.

"Sorry, Harry." Alice had turned on the television.

"No," Taiwan said. "But perhaps it would be better if we were to drive around until you contact your friend."

"And drive right into them?"

"Well—sit in the car. This—it bothers me."

"Look, Harry," Alice exclaimed. "There's Tom Haskins."

I looked. It *was* Tom.

It was a promo for "This Is Your Press," the one mentioned by M, the dominant news show on Sunday mornings. There were pictures of other people who would appear on the program: two senators, a congressman, two newspaper reporters, and several television correspondents.

Tom's face came on the screen again.

"Okay, Taiwan," I said. "Let's go with your instincts. Let's get out of here."

"What're we going to do?" Alice asked.

"Leave this room," Taiwan said. "We shall spend the night in the car."

"And then what?"

"I'll tell you what," I said. I couldn't keep the rising excitement out of my voice. "Tomorrow morning I'm going to take in a live television show."

Alice looked perplexed. "What show? Why?"

I motioned toward the television set. "'This Is Your Press'—I'll explain." I turned to Taiwan, "Let's get out of here."

We started out.

"Hot dog," I said.

CHAPTER

32

I HAD bought a disposable razor and had managed a shave in the men's room of the St. Regis, cursing Mort all the while for staying out all night.

I cut myself twice. I was excited and the adrenaline was surging.

Taiwan and Alice met me outside the men's room, both of them looking haggard and wan. None of us had slept.

Alice had a worried expression on her face. "Harry—?"

"Yeah—"

She looked around to make sure the three of us were alone. "Why are you doing this, Harry? You're an agent in the broadcasting business. Not a superspy."

I smiled at her genuine concern. "I know."

"Well, then—why?"

"Because—I just have to."

"Some answer."

"Well—Wendell asked me once if I cared for my country. Yeah, I do. So—I have to, Alice."

"Have to?"

"Yes. Have to."

■   ■   ■

They were ice-skating in Rockefeller Center. Alice paused to watch. "Isn't it beautiful, Harry? It's always so—festive."

"Yes, beautiful. Festive."

"That's not what I was saying."

"Then what *were* you saying?"

"You know damn well what I was saying, Harry Baker. I was saying that I still think this is all crazy, your going up to that studio. You've got no plan—"

"I've got a plan."

"What plan? You're just going to go up there and"—Alice suddenly embraced me—"Oh, Harry, don't get yourself killed."

"I've got a plan," I said again doggedly.

We turned from the skating rink, crossed the street, and entered the art deco magnificence of the RCA Building. Enormously high ceilings, 1930s *art deco* murals of dirigibles and old biplanes and sinewy men toiling to erect ancient buildings, and the dark marble floor—I had always loved it.

At the bank of elevators which led up to floors one through ten, there was the usual security guard standing behind his high desk as, indeed, there were guards at every bank of elevators. NBC was, out of necessity, extremely strict with regard to security.

"Hello, Billy, how are you?" I said to the young security man.

"Well, Hello, Mr. Baker. Heard you were in London. Have a nice time?"

"Wonderful, Billy. A real vacation."

I had counted on my familiarity with NBC security personnel to be able to maneuver with a fair amount of ease.

"I'm going up to 'This Is Your Press,' Billy." I glanced at my watch. "By the looks of it, I'll just about make it."

"Aw, don't worry, Mr. Baker. You've got a good ten minutes. Pass—?"

I was prepared for his routine question. I tried to appear surprised and frustrated. "Oh, my God, I've been away too long, Billy. Forgot all about a pass. Still, Jane should've—hell, I can't blame her—she makes about one mistake a year."

The guard was troubled. "Gee, Mr. Baker, you know the rules around here—"

"Of course. Of course, Billy. I'm just trying to figure out what to do. I've got four clients on the show."

Billy frowned. He understood the business. "Four—?"

A few minutes of sympathetic conversation followed, and Billy let me sign in Taiwan and Alice on a form that said that they were being allowed in on my valid pass. I promised Billy to have that valid pass to him by the next day.

"Don't worry, I'll come through for you, Billy."

Billy smiled. "I'm not worried, Mr. Baker." His smile broadened. "Besides, I don't really think you're the sort to try to get back out of here with a typewriter tucked under your coat."

■   ■   ■

We got off on the eighth floor and headed for the famous Studio 8-H, still redolent with the sounds of Toscanini and the NBC Symphony, "Saturday Night Live," and a lot of other wonderful things.

I tried to look very busy and harried as I nodded to another two of the pages and scurried in, followed by Alice and Taiwan.

A third page tiptoed quickly over to me: "No time to make the clients' booth, Mr. Baker. Too close to air time. You'll just have to stay here. Would you tell your guests, please, behind the cameras and—quiet."

"Right. Thanks." It was just what I had wanted.

Studio 8-H is enormous, as was the program's set, which stood at one end. It was made up of huge abstractly designed flats depicting the workings of the press, typewriters, microphones, television towers, printing presses, and the like.

In front of all that were several chairs set in a semicircle on a raised dais, and considerably above the dais, center stage, there stood a very modern, Scandinavian-looking desk, where the host of the program sat.

The last of the press people took her place on the dais as the stage manager, standing, for the moment, in front of the cameras, with earphones over his head and a microphone attached, much like an airline pilot, announced in a loud, firm voice: "One minute to air, please."

The stage manager cupped his microphone and spoke into it very briefly; he then pressed an earphone tighter to his ear, finally announcing, "Thirty seconds, please . . . fifteen seconds . . . ten . . ." He silently counted the remainder, from ten down to one, with his fingers clearly visible for all to see, particularly for the staff announcer who stood to one side, out of range of the cameras. After six, the stage manager silently counted with his right hand, and held up his other, palm toward the announcer as a signal of "steady—be ready"—and after "one" he gave a sweeping movement with both hands toward the staff announcer, who immediately began to speak—

—"Welcome to another Sunday morning edition of [Music under] 'This Is Your Press.' With us today, the distinguished ABC News correspondent, Mr. Sam Donaldson; also from ABC, correspondent Tom Haskins . . . from CBS, Dan . . . and from . . . and Sir Hugh Trevor-Maypole of the BBC and. . . . Joining us also will be today's important guests: the distinguished Speaker of the House, Mr. . . . Senator . . . Mayor Alvin . . . and our moderator, Paul Blanfield, the *Dean of American Morning News.*"

A very urbane and professional-looking Paul Blanfield gave a very urbane and professional look into a camera and began to speak, permitting a slight, insouciant smile to appear on his face: "Good morning, ladies and gentlemen. Welcome to 'This Is Your Press.' I should mention immediately that 'The Rector Report,' which usually follows this program, will not be seen today, but will return to its regularly scheduled time one week from today."

Paul Blanfield's visage now took on a deep and serious expression. "Because of the importance of this week's news, our program will be twice its usual length, with twice as many reporters and correspondents, who will, undoubtedly"—*The Dean* allowed a slight smile, a trademark, to appear again on his face—"ask twice as many questions."

A ripple of laughter flowed through the group on the dais.

The program began.

I now had time to look around. There were at least six men, maybe more, wearing dark suits, white shirts, and nondescript ties. They were watching the studio and not the program. I assumed that they were Secret Service men. Probably they were there for the senators and the congressman.

M and Wendell were visible up in the clients' booth, Wendell with his left arm in a sling, the result, I assumed, of Taiwan's marksmanship.

Everything else in Studio 8-H seemed to be normal for a television program.

I could act at any moment.

But, I didn't.

I took a good five minutes to re-examine my plan. Would it work? Was there an alternative? If so, what?

In short—I had an extremely serious case of cold feet.

I glanced at my watch. The five minutes had now dragged into ten minutes. If I didn't act soon, the program, and my opportunity, would be over.

I glanced up at the clients' booth for the dozenth time and saw that M and Wendell had finally spotted me and were talking to each other, their eyes staring in my direction.

I took several deep breaths, counted to three, and moved a few paces up to a page, and whispered, "The program is still live, isn't it?—not on tape?"

He nodded affirmatively and put a warning finger to his lips.

It was time.

I moved as slowly and stealthily as possible until I was nearly beside one of the cameramen.

I glanced up at the booth again. Wendell and M were no longer there.

I edged closer to the cameraman.

The stage manager had seen me. He waved me away and started to tiptoe in my direction.

Time to go.

I raced out into the middle of the set and started hollering: "Tom Haskins is a fraud—Jessica Rumbough is a fraud. They're not the people they pretend to be—Check their fingerprints—"

I ran to a camera where the red tally light was on, indicating that its picture was going out on the air at that moment.

"Check their fingerprints—*check their fingerprints*—they're frauds. Check their fingerprints. *Jessica Rumbough—Tom Haskins*. Those two are phonies—impostors—check their *fingerprints*—I know—check their—"

The whole thing took a few seconds, but that was how quickly a reporter like Sam Donaldson works.

I felt an arm grasp me tightly around the shoulders. With his other hand he was holding the small lavaliere microphone which had been attached to his tie.

"You are *the* Harry Baker—the agent?"

"That's right—check their—"

"And you say these two—Tom Haskins and Jessica Rumbough, are *posing* as your clients?"

"Check their fingerprints. Check them."

Donaldson wheeled closer to the camera, still holding me tightly. "Ladies and gentlemen, this is not some scheduled prank to enliven the proceedings on—"

There was a sudden tremendous crash as some equipment was knocked over.

And with a whining roar of rage M dashed towards me—"Stop—stop—You bloody Goddamned fool—you're ruining everything—you leftist liberal bastard—you're ruining everything—"

M was babbling incoherently as he tackled me from the side, knocking me down to the stage floor. He stood quickly, pulled a pistol from inside his jacket, and fired.

From one knee, the microphone still in his hand, Donaldson struck upward at M's wrist. The shot hit a scoop light in the grid above and debris fell to the floor.

Some of it fell on me as I scampered for safety behind a portable lighting board.

M fired in my direction a second time, hitting another lighting fixture. "—You leftist, liberal son of a bitch—" —He turned wildly and fired at one of the Secret Service men running towards him.

"Get him—not me. We're the patriots. Not these villains and scoundrels of the—*Media*." He waved his gun at the reporters on the dais as everyone ducked behind his desk.

"We'll control them—you'll see—We'll control them—and then this country will—"

Two quick shots rang out. High, barking shots from another weapon. M fell, blood gushing from his abdomen.

Wendell had done it.

Two Secret Service men started toward him. But they stopped.

Wendell had shot himself, as well.

■   ■   ■

A doctor quickly appeared and ministered to M. His head was placed on a rolled up blanket and another blanket was thrown on his body.

His face was white.

The doctor whispered to me, "He's only got a few minutes. He asked to speak to you."

Surprised, I went to him and bent down on one knee.

His whisper was very hard to hear. "Well, it's been exciting for you, I hope."

"Very—"

"They won't tell me, but I've got just a few ticks left—"

"Well—"

"Oh, no. I know," M smiled. "Come just a bit closer, would you?"

I obliged.

"Just wanted to finally express my true feelings to you . . . dear boy."

I leaned still closer.

"Ta-ta . . . *dear . . . boy.* . . ."

M spit in my face.

His eyes closed and he was dead.

■　■　■

I was still on one knee, almost catatonic, looking at him, as Sam Donaldson's voice, firm and authoritative, rang out.

He was standing now, looking into one of the cameras, still holding the small lavaliere microphone in his hand.

"No one, of course, knows quite what all of this means. Only this: Two men are dead, one murdered, one a suicide. And one man, who claims to be the well-known broadcasting agent, Harry Baker, has accused two people on this television set behind me of being other than who they appear to be."

He paused for only a second and went on. "Tune in to your *ABC* stations for up-to-the-minute bulletins as news of this bizarre happening develops."

There was another slight pause and just the barest of smiles appeared on Donaldson's lips:

"This is Sam Donaldson, reporting for *ABC* News from—*NBC.*"

CHAPTER

33

THE NEXT day was Monday, and what better place to spend a Monday afternoon than the grill of the Sherry-Netherland Hotel.

We were on our fourth bottle of Dom Perignon. I emptied it and the three of us silently touched glasses and drank.

Taiwan leaned back against the banquette. "I know you said that you did not want to talk about it. But you were very brave yesterday."

"Thanks, Taiwan. And you're right—I don't want to talk about it." I smiled to let her know that I was serious, but still friendly.

"What was it like this morning, Harry?" Alice had always been slow to take a hint.

"A lot of questions. A lot of testimony."

Alice sighed. "And it'll go on for weeks, won't it?"

"Probably. But Mort will take care of me. Taiwan, too."

Alice smiled. "But you won, Harry. You did it."

I chuckled. "Somehow . . . we all did it."

Alice frowned. "Was it rough this morning?"

"No. Taiwan will tell you. She'll tell you—later."

Alice paused, thinking. "Does that mean that you don't want to talk about it, Harry?"

"Yes, Alice, it does."

Alice smiled her lovely smile. "Then—not another word, Harry. That is—if you'll spring for another bottle of the bubbly."

"Only if you promise never to use that expression again."

Alice grinned. "I knew I could get a rise out of you, Harry."

I ordered more champagne and poured the first round. "Cheers—"

"Cheers—cheers."

"Um, what good bubbly."

"*Alice*—"

She giggled.

It was Taiwan's turn to be serious. "I'm so glad I did it," she said.

I could hear in her voice, and in Alice's, and they probably heard it in mine, that the three of us were starting to get pretty well sloshed.

"Did what?" I asked.

"Left them." Taiwan was looking right into my eyes. "And do you know what really did it, Harry?"—she had never called me Harry before—"It was you. You did it."

Alice knows *something amiss* when she hears *something amiss* better than anyone else in the world. She tried to be light: "Well—what's *this* all about?"

Taiwan's eyes were still on me. "Harry, himself, won me over to his side."

I hoped that I wasn't blushing.

"How?" By now, Alice was vitally interested.

Taiwan turned to her. "Why—by treating me with respect. As an equal. Is there anything more decent?"

And now Alice *did* blush. "Why, no," she said, "nothing."

"Was that *really* it?" I asked. "That week of—conversations—that changed your mind?"

"Yes—of course," Taiwan said, a slight twinkle in her eyes.

Alice hiccuped. "Excuse me—" She raised a glass. "Anyway—I'm glad that Taiwan and I formed our *London Alliance*—in London." Alice hiccuped again and tears flowed from her eyes.

Taiwan laughed and so did Alice.

After a moment or two Alice sighed and said, "Gee, this is nice, isn't it?"

All three of us smiled and nodded. We were quiet for quite a while.

"You know something, Harry," Alice's arm was around me, and her face was very close. "You're a peach. A real peach." She paused and then chortled to herself.

"What was that?"

"Peaches. Have you ever had peaches and cold salmon?"

"Sounds good."

"Good. It's maddeningly magnificent."

"What made you think of that?"

"I said the word *peaches*."

"And—?"

"I was remembering eating peaches and cold salmon for the first time. With Olaf."

"Olaf?"

"Olaf. He was that fly-fishing instructor in Iceland three years ago. Six-three, blond—"

I pulled away from her.

She peered at me, her eyes strange and, somehow, knowing. "Harry—?"

"I'm sorry," I said.

"*I'm* sorry, Harry. I really am."

"It was—the last straw, I suppose."

We were silent. Meanwhile, Taiwan was massaging the inside of my left thigh, her eyes slightly glazed.

"I'm sorry," Alice said again.

"I know."

She touched my face with her cupped hands and gently forced me to face her. "Harry—?"

"Yeah—?"

"Do you—well, maybe just a little—care quite a bit for me?"

I started to say no. "I'm not sure," I said. Then, "Yeah, I guess I do."

Alice put both her hands to my cheeks. "Kiss me, Harry."

We had never kissed like that before. Usually, we joked with each other.

"Oh, Harry. I care quite a bit for you, too."

We kissed again and, when we pulled apart, there were tears running down her cheeks.

"Harry," her voice had a kind of somber lilt to it, "these are real, Harry. For the first time in my life—*real* tears."

There we were. The three of us. Alice with her arms around me—Taiwan with one hand tickling my ear and the other briskly massaging my thigh.

I felt like some kind of Southern California cult leader.

CHAPTER

34

I CALLED for a limousine a while after that. Taiwan and Alice couldn't be trusted to wend their way home to Alice's apartment, and anyway, it seemed the gentlemanly thing to do.

Besides such noble reasons, I wanted to be by myself for a while—while I was still *somewhat* sober.

At the cloakroom they got cute.

"We were just talking in the ladies' room," Alice said, "and we're not going to leave until you answer just two—teeny little questions."

Anything to get them into the limousine.

"Okay," I said. "Seems fair."

"How did you know when you ran out onto that television set that they wouldn't just stop the show?"

"If they'd been taping, the director would've stopped it in a second."

"But even live—the way it was?"

"I know television. By the time the director realized what was happening, got to Master Control, got permission to get off, and got off the air—my point would've been made."

"Oh—" Alice thought for a moment—"But he never *did* go off the air."

I smiled. "If you were directing a live news program and some apparent lunatic ran out onto the set, followed by someone else who shoots at him—would you go off the air?"

Alice smiled. "I don't suppose I would, Harry."

"But they could've killed you, Harry." Taiwan's eyes were wide with admiration and wine.

I grinned sheepishly. "To be honest—I didn't think about that until later. And then I was scared to death."

"Oh, Harry—"

■ ■ ■

Several hugs and kisses, words of endearment, and vows of eternal friendship later, and the two of them were off in the limousine.

I returned their waves of good-bye until they were out of sight.

I crossed Fifth Avenue and walked to the stone wall that girds Central Park and stood beside the book stalls, watching a man feed pigeons until he ran out of bread-crumbs.

He noticed me. "Good evening."

"Good evening."

"Well, that's it for tonight." He smiled. I watched him as he limped away.

I stood there alone for a while, looking in at the park, enjoying the last blue hour of evening. The soft silence was suddenly broken as a resonant voice boomed out behind me.

"Ah me, to think that the tattered touch of the tatter-demalion has twice trimmed my own torn tunic."

It was the voice of The Man Who Looked Like Howard Cosell.

I turned to find him, indeed, tattered and torn, his suit ripped and sullied. But there was a smile on his face.

He touched his torn suit and winked an eye. "The results of following the philosophy of my noble precursor, Sir John Falstaff: 'He who fights and runs away, lives to fight . . .' et cetera."

"Very wise," I said.

He shook his head and smiled sheepishly. "Quite a time, huh?"

"Yes, quite a time. I'm glad they've cleared you."

His smile broadened. "Well, I did agree to testify." He guffawed. "In fact, I volunteered. They've granted me full immunity from prosecution. And"—he nearly burst with happiness—"they've also agreed not to prosecute me for impersonation of another person."

"Good. I'm glad to hear it."

"And *He*"—his tone was reverential—"*He* said—he couldn't care less. He wouldn't even *consider* pressing charges. Wasn't that generous of him?"

"Sounds like Howard," I said.

"Yeah." He grinned shyly. "You've probably guessed— I've always sort of idolized him, you know."

"Well—he's quite a man."

He pushed his hands deep into his pockets and stood nervously on one leg like a little boy. "Would you . . . do me a favor?"

"If I can—sure. What is it?"

"Well . . . maybe . . . sometime . . . if it's not too inconvenient for him—and you, too, of course—maybe . . . would you introduce me to him?"

"Sure." I looked at him. "Sure I will."

He smiled and sighed. "Thanks. Thanks a lot."

We stood silently for a moment.

Finally, I shook hands with The Man Who Looked Like Howard Cosell and headed for the Oak Room Bar.